Praise for

MARANATHA ROAD

———

"*Maranatha Road* is an ode to beauty and suffering, grief and hope in a small mountain town. Within its pages, Heather Bell Adams brings to vivid life two strong, Southern women, at odds yet bound by love's saving grace. I'll be thinking of Sadie and Tinley for a long time to come, and waiting eagerly for more to read from this gifted new writer.

—Amy Greene, author of *Bloodroot, Long Man,*
and *The Nature of Fire*

"Moving and deeply satisfying."

—Gregg Cusick, author of *My Father Moves
through Time like a Dirigible*

"Rare is the book that has the power to change our way of thinking, and ever rarer is the writer who can blow the dust off our hearts and remind us what it means to feel, to love, and to rediscover the pathways to our own humanity. You are well advised to follow what will undoubtedly be the rapid rise of this stunning new voice in the literary arena."

—Wil Mara, author of *Frame 232* and *The Nevada Testament*

"Filled with the poetry of shattered lives, *Maranatha Road* is the novel of the desperado. A haunting debut."

—Harriet Levin Millan, author of *How Fast Can You Run*

"The prose in Heather Adams's exquisite novel sparkles with honesty and vitality—both poetic and musical in the way of the best southern writing. Her characters crackle with humanity and their alternating voices tell a sweeping story of love, compassion, and the timeless bonds of family."

—Mary Akers, author of *Bones of an Inland Sea*

MARANATHA ROAD

ℝ A NOVEL ℞

———

HEATHER BELL ADAMS

———

VANDALIA PRESS

MORGANTOWN 2017

First edition published 2017 by Vandalia Press,

an imprint of West Virginia University Press

ISBN:

PB: 978-1-943665-75-4

EPUB: 978-1-943665-76-1

PDF: 978-1-943665-77-8

Library of Congress Cataloging-in-Publication Data

is available from the Library of Congress

Book and cover design by Than Saffel

Excerpts from this novel have been published
as short stories in print and online journals as follows:
"When We Could See But Did Not Know," *Pembroke Magazine*, Vol. 47, 2015
"Out at Poplar Springs," *Southern Writers Magazine*, Summer 2014
"Blue Eyes," *Hermeneutic Chaos*, July 2014
"Green River Gorge," *The Bluestone Review*, 2014

This book is dedicated to my father, Doley Bell.

ACKNOWLEDGMENTS

———

My heartfelt thanks to Abby Freeland and West Virginia University Press, Derek Krissoff, Than Saffel, Jason Gosnell, Sharon Thompsonowak, Melissa Hill, Melody and Doley Bell, Louise Bell, Michelle Bell, Elese Adams, Susie and William Adams, Lucille and Kenneth Cook, Kristin Caid, Julie Artz, Patricia Gibson, Pam Van Dyk, Pamela Reitman, Parul Kapur Hinzen, Jenny Lynn, Andrea Short, Pamela Jeffrey, Keri Prince, Kevin Morgan Watson, Robert Morgan, Kimberly Brock, Kim Church, Wil Mara, Gregg Cusick, Amy Greene, the Appalachian Writing Project, my son, Davis Adams, and my husband, Geoff Adams.

PART ONE

Tinley Greene

APRIL 1998

CHAPTER 1

If Mr. Haughtry comes crawling down the driveway in his big gold Buick, it will mean they haven't found Mama and Daddy. It's dark in the old chicken shed and nobody knows where I am. When I bend down, I can see through a hole in the wood—the fig tree, the gravel driveway, the road with fields on both sides, green and slippery in the rain.

If I see my mother's little hatchback, then it's easy. Some of the roads could have been washed out and they took a while to get back. Daddy will shake his head and say, "I'm awfully sorry everybody was worried." They were supposed to be back before supper yesterday and now it's almost suppertime a day later. But they're not back yet and, as far as I know, nobody has seen them. I should've gone with them. That way, whatever happened, we would be together.

If no cars come down the driveway, then maybe they're still looking—some of the neighbors and Mr. Haughtry, the man my father works for and who lets us stay in a trailer on his land. Maybe they'll keep looking after it gets dark, even though it's Sunday and they would usually head back to church after supper, everybody but Mr. Haughtry who says he wouldn't darken the church doorstep if somebody paid him.

I keep watch, but nothing comes down the driveway except the rain.

Earlier today, Mrs. Haughtry offered to let me wait up at the house with her.

"But I guess you're sixteen and can go where you please," she said, letting out a sigh. "Just have sense enough to stay out of the rain."

This afternoon, to keep my mind off worrying, I started some laundry in the Haughtrys' basement. The clean scent of the detergent cut through the underground mushroom smell, and I took a deep breath, telling myself everything would be all right. My parents would come back with their shopping bags and we would shake our heads at how awful the weather was. While I waited on the laundry, I straightened up the canning jars—most of them full of half-runner beans. When I thought of how my mother would've wiped off the dusty lids with her apron, I bit my lip so hard I tasted blood. If they didn't come back, I wouldn't have any family. No aunts or uncles or cousins. Nobody.

Tugging the basement door shut behind me, I stumbled through the rain to look for a new place to wait. If I went back inside, Mrs. Haughtry would keep telling me to settle down, turning me away from the living room window so I'd stop staring out at the driveway. She had noticed the way I looked down the hill where my father's light blue truck was parked. My parents never took his truck when they went shopping in town. I reminded myself over and over again that they'd taken Mama's car. But when I spotted the truck something fluttered in my chest and I thought—only for a second—they were finally back. I pressed my hand against my chest, imagining a tiny bird trapped there. Didn't Emily Dickinson say hope is the thing with feathers?

Now I keep watch from the chicken shed where it's quiet and I can be by myself. I can still smell corn or seeds, something the chickens used to eat, and there's no telling what might be watching me in the dark— mice scratching in the dust or bats hanging upside down from the wooden beams. Even though there haven't been chickens here in a long time, everybody still calls it the chicken shed. Now there's only a dirt floor and rough wooden walls. Sometimes after Daddy washes Mr. Haughtry's Buick with the hose, he parks it here to keep the birds off. But whenever Mr. Haughtry drives it, he parks outside by the house and it gets dirty again before long.

I step back and measure out three, four boards with my arms, imagining I see the irregular shape of North Carolina in the wood's lines. Choosing a board on the left—the western part of the state—I trace the bumps in the wood, pretending they're places my parents have gone. The largest bump is Garnet, the county seat of Wynette County, and the only place I've ever lived. Lots of farmland and nice farmhouses set back from the road. Tin roof barns, herds of cows, and rows of green beans and tomatoes and corn. Solid Rock Baptist Church with its pointy white steeple. Apple orchards and summer camps with long shaded driveways. I imagine Mama and Daddy hunched against the rain as they hurry past the shops on Main Street and the clock tower shaped like a black bear on its hind legs, the numbered face in its belly. Or right this minute they could be on the highway—not where it dips down into South Carolina or arches up over the gorge, but maybe where it loops around town near the new mall and car dealerships.

I shake my head. They were going to the grocery store and the hardware store. Even though I don't think they mentioned going anywhere else, I sift through everything I remember in case I missed something, a sort of clue.

At breakfast, Mrs. Haughtry had glanced at the wall calendar from the gas company and mentioned something to Mama about a blackberry winter. Mr. Haughtry told Daddy that once it stopped raining he needed to see about fixing the tiller. At the Haughtrys' stove, my mother laid a paper towel over a pile of bacon, the smoky smell of it hovering over the kitchen. Her hair was pulled back tight like she always wore it, ever since the time Mr. Haughtry held up a long hair at the breakfast table, asking if it was hers and laying it on the side of his plate in a straight line.

Back at the trailer, Daddy shook out the worst of the rain from his jacket and slipped it on again, saying something about running to the grocery store and hardware store. Mama found her see-through rain bonnet—the kind they give out for free at the beauty parlor Mrs. Haughtry goes to—and tied it under her chin.

"We'll be back before supper," she said. I'm sure they hugged me before they left, but I don't remember what it felt like or how hard I squeezed in return.

"See you in a bit," Daddy must have said. Maybe he called me doll, the way he sometimes did. I can't remember that either even though it was only yesterday. Yesterday is already a far-off, shadowy place.

I press my finger into the bumps and lines on the wood—hundreds, thousands of splinters waiting to come apart. Through the rain, which refuses to let up, wheels crunch on the gravel driveway. I lean closer to the hole in the wall, my eyelashes brushing the wood. There's a flash of white and in the curve a long car appears.

The back door of the house sticks and somebody kicks it open. Mrs. Haughtry comes out, wearing her brown raincoat, and looks toward the driveway.

As the white car draws closer, I make out Mr. Stepp with both hands on the steering wheel. Mrs. Haughtry's brother. Not Mr. Haughtry. Not my parents. I dig my fingernails into my arms, not understanding why Mr. Stepp has come or what it means. He pulls around to the side yard where the grass is worn down, parks, and swings his long legs out of the car.

"You shouldn't be out here in this mess," he calls out to Mrs. Haughtry.

"What's going on, A.B.? Did you find 'em? Any sign one way or another?"

"Where's Tinley?"

"Went outside a little bit ago. Left her jacket so Lord knows she's cold and probably wet too."

I inch one of the shed doors open so I can hear them better.

Mr. Stepp comes up to the porch. "Want me to go look for her?"

"What'd you find out?"

He shakes his head. "I'd rather tell you both. No use in saying it twice. She's old enough to hear it."

"Just come on inside. She'll be here in a minute." She looks right at the shed.

"Better off waiting for the sheriff to get here anyway," Mr. Stepp says and he disappears inside the house.

When the sheriff's car rolls down the driveway a few seconds later, Mrs. Haughtry calls for me, stretching out my name. The same way she calls her cat, Calico, if he hasn't shown up for breakfast. I push the door open, scraping the mud underneath, until there's enough room to squeeze through.

CHAPTER 2

———

As I trudge up the hill to the Haughtrys' house, my stomach clenches in a knot and I weigh whether I could sneak down to the trailer instead. Maybe I could crawl into my bed and hide like a little kid. Even though it doesn't make sense, a half-formed idea flickers—that my mother and father are at home waiting for me.

I pause, letting the rain trickle down my back and remembering the way our trailer wobbles, especially if you close a door hard, like the whole thing might tip over. And cooking smells sink into everything—the carpet, the couch, the bedspreads. Up ahead, the Haughtrys' house stands solid, made of brick. There you can barely tell if anybody is walking around because nothing rattles to give them away.

Mrs. Haughtry calls for me again, reminding me that I won't be able to hide forever. Sooner or later I have to hear what they've found, so I drag myself up to the house.

Sheriff Wilkins stands up when I come into the kitchen. His hat rests on the table and his eyes look tired. He's always pale, which my father says is the sign of a man who spends too much time inside, and today he's white all over except for the pink tip of his nose.

"Tinley, you come on in," he says, "and take a seat so we can visit for a minute." Mr. Stepp and Mrs. Haughtry are already sitting at the table, not meeting my eyes. Mrs. Haughtry bunches up her apron between her fingers. Mr. Stepp turns a coffee cup around in a circle. Rain tumbles down outside the window and behind me the raincoats drip on the porch.

Wondering when the sheriff will say something, I ease into a chair and start rubbing my fingers over the oilcloth, slick in some places and sticky in others. He frowns and I move my hand under the cloth, feeling for the cottony felt underneath. When I pick at it, the felt comes off in tiny pieces and I let them fall to the floor.

The sheriff's radio buzzes and he gets up from the table, holding his finger in the air like he's saying just a minute. Mrs. Haughtry shows him where the phone is and I wait for him to get back, willing my father to burst through the door and fix everything.

The thing about Daddy is that he can fix whatever is broken, whether it's a water pipe or farm machinery or most anything else. He's always walking around with his box of tools and whistling as he puts it down. If something looks hard at first, he rubs his hands together. "Now I'll need to study on that one for a minute," he says. When Mr. Haughtry is in a good mood, he tells Daddy he would've made a good engineer. He works for the Haughtrys every day but Sunday. Most everybody in Garnet is up at Solid Rock on Sundays. But Mama likes to sleep late and go through the paper for the coupons and Daddy believes God is waiting for us outside too. So we stay home. During the week some people in town act like they don't see me at school or Mama at the store because they don't know us from church. We might as well be strangers.

Some Sunday afternoons if the wind is right and the weather is warm, Daddy puts our kites in the back of the truck with a rock on top so they won't fly away, and we go up to Poplar Springs. Up on a high hill, we find the flat, carved-out spot where you can run after your kite without worrying about falling. The ground ahead is the same as what's behind and all you have to do is hold onto the kite and go wherever it goes.

"All you have to do is hold on," Daddy says, laughing as we watch the kite take flight.

When I think about my mother, she's sitting at the sewing machine.

Her leg shakes when she presses the pedal. Or she's at the kitchen counter, scooping batter out of a thick bowl and dropping it in the skillet sizzling with butter.

Sheriff Wilkins sits down again, muttering something about how Mr. Haughtry won't be back until later because he's helping at the scene. I don't ask what scene. Already my breathing is ragged, nervous sweat beading on my neck.

The sheriff clears his throat and Mrs. Haughtry tells him to go ahead. He nods and says, "We've found your mother's car, Tinley. The roads are awful slippery with all this rain." He leans forward. "And with all that water, the banks in some parts have clear washed away."

I can picture them going around those curves, Mama with her hand on the dashboard and Daddy squinting through the window, trying to make his way through the rain. The sheriff keeps talking and I imagine the rest too, the way the car must have slid down the mud. The bumping and twisting toward the water below, higher than it is most days and the rain still coming. Mama screaming and Daddy's mouth closed hard. The sky where the ground should be and the ground where the sky should be and the hungry mouth of the river opening wider and wider until it swallows them up.

The sheriff says the bodies have been identified and I dig my fingernail into my leg. Part of me wants to scream, but I don't. Instead I close my eyes. And I'm not in the Haughtrys' kitchen anymore. I'm out at Poplar Springs. Mama leans back against the side of the truck and Daddy looks up at the sky with his whole face open and spread out like a blanket getting warm in the sun.

PART TWO

— Sadie Caswell —

OCTOBER 1998

CHAPTER 3

———

The last time our son, Mark, and his fiancé, Maddie, came up to the house for Sunday dinner was in October, a couple months before they were supposed to get married. Maddie was the kind of girl everything is easy for, the way breathing is for the rest of us. When Mark met her, there wasn't any way of knowing how it would all turn out. But no matter what he did, he loved her. That was something he tried to tell me the last time I saw him.

Mark had gotten a good job out of high school working with the logging company. He and a boy from work moved into one of the rental houses we owned, but he still stayed with us a couple times a week. When my husband, Clive, and I saw Mark coming down the driveway, we never knew how he'd be once he walked in the door. Sometimes he laughed at any little thing that happened, the kind of laugh somebody across the room would notice. And other days, he moved slowly, like he was underwater. The way I see it, people will do just about anything they can for their children, but when Mark got like that, there was nothing Clive or I could do to pull him up. He would look way off in the distance, like he could see where it was all going, only there was no way to go someplace different because he was stuck.

It all started because he was up at the house the Saturday the Spencers—Maddie's family—first came by. They were new in town and already asking for money for some church committee. Maybe things would've turned out another way if he had been somewhere else, out fishing with his cap on backwards the way he liked it or washing off his new truck, the rag dripping water and the air smelling like soap. But he'd been cleaning out the barn and was inside getting something to drink when the Spencers drove up in that black Cadillac of theirs. We all sat in the den that day, Dr. Spencer with his golf shirt and his wife squeezed into a too-small poplin skirt. And their daughter Maddie, maybe twenty years old—a year or two younger than Mark. Pretty in that perfect way like you can't imagine her getting dirty or waking up in the morning looking any different than she did at three o'clock in the afternoon.

I remember thinking Mark would go back outside, but he sat down across from Maddie and watched her take a sip of iced tea. When she rested her glass on her lap, he kept his eyes on her like he couldn't wait to see what she would do next. He leaned back in his chair, smiling in a way I hadn't seen in a long time, and when she looked back at him, something settled over him like a soft quilt. That was the start of it.

Once they were seeing each other, we had a few weeks—or maybe months—when Mark and Maddie came up to the house after church to eat with me and Clive. On that last Sunday, shortly before they were getting married, church let out around noon or a little after. At dinner, Clive sat at the head of the table like he always did. He was tall and lean with tan arms from working outside and a full head of hair that seemed like it had jumped from black to white overnight. After he blessed the food, Mark passed him the bowl of snap beans.

"Appreciate it," Clive said, spooning some on his plate and passing it on to me.

As soon as we started eating, Mark shoveled food like he had somewhere to be fast. Maddie asked if he was okay, but he just nodded, stuffing chicken and potatoes in his mouth and gulping down a long sip of water before he had a chance to swallow anything.

Once he and Maddie had started seeing each other, I thought he was going to be all right. As long as she was around, it was like Mark fit in his own skin better than he did other times. Something would come up—somebody being late or something burnt or too much rain—and he'd wave his hand in the air like it was easy to fix. He was back to how he'd been when he was younger, not moving too fast or too slow. Every Sunday afternoon he sat with Maddie looking like he didn't need another thing in the world beyond that.

But that day his leg bounced under the table and, when he wasn't eating or drinking, he was running his fingers through his thick, dark hair. I thought he would settle down when I brought up the wedding, so I asked what kind of music they were going to have even though I'd already heard something about a harp. Maddie dabbed her mouth with her napkin, but before she got the chance to answer, Mark asked if we had to talk about the wedding all the time.

"Can't we have a minute of quiet?" he asked, even as he scraped his fork across his plate.

Maddie put her napkin in her lap and straightened the belt on her pink dress, watching Mark and blinking.

"I just mean Maddie's got it all worked out. She knows what she wants, Mama." Mark looked down at the gravy hanging on his fork and then he scooted his chair back and started stacking up the plates and serving bowls.

After we cleaned off the table, Clive went outside still wearing his church clothes and I washed the dishes. Mark and Maddie stayed in the den and she was talking about the chairs for the reception. When they had told me and Clive they were getting married, I thought it was the best thing for Mark, even if it had happened quickly. Clive and I never talked about it, but he must've thought the same thing.

Just when I turned down the radio to hear better, Maddie asked Mark if he wanted the metal folding chairs in the fellowship hall or if they could bring in something different.

"They don't all need to match, but what if we had some wooden chairs? At least for the wedding party, I mean. Didn't your mama say there were some in the attic we could use?"

"I think so, yeah. Probably."

"Can you ask her sometime? They'd look so much better, don't you think? They would be really pretty. Hey, where are you going?"

"I'll go ask her right now, I guess," Mark said, and the next thing I knew he appeared in the kitchen. His blue dress shirt was still pressed smooth, the way it had been when we'd left for church that morning. But he was breathing hard and his eyes started to water. I set a glass upside down on a towel to dry and asked if he wanted anything to drink. He shook his head, flicking the cabinet doors open and shut. Ever since he'd met Maddie, I reminded myself, he'd been doing better. All he needed was to calm down.

"What is it, Mark? You need something?" I tried to sound like there was nothing to worry about.

He slammed a drawer closed and sighed. "I don't need anything. It's just a mess, all of it. And I'm not talking about the chairs."

"What do you mean? I'm sure whatever it is—" My words trailed off as I let the drain plug out and started rinsing out the sink. "Look, I don't know what kind of nonsense you're talking about, but everything will turn out all right."

He didn't answer me, just banged his fist down on the counter. I tried to reach for his arm, but he pulled back from me and bumped a glass behind him. We both watched it swaying on the counter. It didn't make a bit of sense, but I thought if the glass righted itself and didn't fall, then Mark would right himself too. He crossed his arms in front of his chest, still breathing hard. The glass settled until it was still, but Mark picked it up and smashed it against the counter, and he stared at the blood bursting on his hand like he'd been waiting for it.

CHAPTER 4

———

When Maddie flew into the kitchen asking about the noise, Mark asked if his daddy could take her home. He wouldn't even look at her. He kept moving his eyes anywhere but where she was standing while I yelled out the back door for Clive.

Blood dripped off Mark's hand and he let me wrap the dishcloth around it. I asked him what in the world was the matter, if something had happened at church or at dinner. He shook his head and wouldn't say anything. When I got out the broom, Maddie offered to help, but I told her I'd take care of it and she stood off to the side, looking out the window where the sun was shining on the field out back. The floor in the kitchen was wood like the rest of the house, beat-down from years of people walking on it, and I had to pry up some of the smallest glass pieces with my fingernail from where they'd fallen in the cracks.

Before long Clive came up the back steps, stomping the mud off his shoes.

"Don't worry about that for now," I said. "You go on and take Maddie home."

Clive didn't say anything—just dug around in his pocket for his keys. I held the back door open for Maddie, but she acted like she didn't want to leave.

"I'll stay," she said, looking back and forth between me and Mark. "Let me help. Mark can take me home later."

"He's not in any kind of shape to be driving."

"He's going to be okay, right? I don't know—I've never seen him acting like this."

"He'll be fine." Mark sat in one of the kitchen chairs holding the dishcloth to his hand and shaking his head every so often. "I think he must be coming down with something. Maybe you'd better head on."

"You'll call me, right?" Maddie touched Mark's arm and he nodded, staring at his hand.

Once they were gone, I sat down with Mark, trying not to look at him, keeping my eyes on the tablecloth instead—light green, the color of Granny Smith apples, and made out of polyester that ironed easy. On top I kept a stack of paper napkins stamped with sunflowers and the brown dish of butter getting soft. Mark sniffed and the clock in the den ticked. I wanted to ask if he was tired, if his stomach hurt, if he needed a drink of water—even though part of me knew it wasn't anything like that. He'd been fine for months, but something had happened to pull him under again.

After a while Mark unwound the dishcloth from his hand. He handed it to me and I scrubbed the bloodstain at the sink to where it didn't look like anything but tomato juice. His hand didn't look bad—probably didn't even need a bandage. "Do you think you're feeling a little better?"

He shrugged and I wished he'd say something, anything really. When Clive's truck came down the driveway, he sighed.

"Mama, I'm going upstairs to bed."

Even though it was two o'clock in the afternoon, I told him to go ahead and he went up those stairs like his legs were heavy weights. Still, I figured he would get some rest and be all right in the morning.

It wasn't long before Clive came in the back door looking around for Mark.

"His hand's fine, but he's upstairs. Went just a minute ago."

"Maddie was full of questions. Asking if he'd ever acted this way before and if it was something about the wedding." Clive sighed. "Said to let her know if she could help him somehow." He didn't say what he'd told her and I didn't ask either. It didn't make a bit of difference to me. Clive acted like he was going to say something else, but he must've changed his mind because he went by me on his way to the den.

When he turned the television on to the car race, I went upstairs to change out of my church clothes. The door to Mark's room was closed and I stood there listening, but I couldn't hear anything, not even the sound of him breathing or rolling over in bed. I shut my eyes against the memory of him as a little boy, sleeping on his back with his arms flung out on either side.

Instead of going back downstairs, I went in the extra bedroom. We had four all together—the one where Clive and I slept, Mark's room, the guest room for when my sister, Libby, and her husband, Warren, came to visit, and an extra room where I kept the sewing machine and a little twin bed. Clive still had the television on downstairs and I could hear the cars roaring around the track. I straightened up the stacks of material on the shelf in the closet and put away the ironing board I'd left out before church.

For years we'd planned for that room to be a nursery. We had wanted a brother or sister for Mark, but we ought to have had better sense than that. We'd started trying for Mark not long after we were married. If my monthly time came, Clive's eyes got small with disappointment. I'd tell him "Maybe next month," and sometimes he would nod and other times he acted like he hadn't heard me. By the time I was coming up on forty years old, we'd about given up and, when my monthly time didn't come, I guessed it was the start of the big change and we had lost our chance. But one day I was standing in the kitchen putting up the leftovers from supper and hunger rushed at me so strong it almost hurt. Even though I'd already eaten, I took out a leftover sweet potato and peeled the skin away from it. I can still remember that sweetness sliding down my throat and the way I rubbed my stomach over and over again like I didn't have any sense in the world—but knowing the truth just as sure as I knew my own face.

Once I came back downstairs, Clive turned off the television. "How's he doing?" He cleaned out one of his fingernails with the knife he always carried in his pocket.

"How in the world would I know that? You can see as well as I can that he's not down here for either one of us to see how he's doing." Clive sighed and I wished I'd said it some better way. He put the knife back in his pocket and went out the back door.

Maddie called and I told her Mark was resting, that I was sure he'd call her back shortly. As I gathered up some mail to take out to the burn barrel, I thought I heard him coming down the stairs, but it wasn't anything except the old house settling in further.

Libby—whose given name was Elizabeth, but I'd shortened it to Libby when we were little and it stuck—called most Sunday afternoons, and that one was no different. The whole time she talked about her husband Warren's toothache and I didn't breathe a word to her about how Mark was acting.

"Warren's going up there tomorrow to see about it," Libby said. "But the main dentist is down at the beach somewhere. I don't know who in their right mind takes a vacation this time of year, but that's what the receptionist said. I told you she's Willa Dunn's first cousin, didn't I? Willa's family has been down here for years. Somebody told me Willa's sister was sweet on Warren when they were in high school."

"I think you've told me that before." I wound the phone cord around my finger, waiting for her to finish. Willa Dunn was somebody from up at the church. Lynette knew all those people better than I did. It didn't matter that she didn't live in Garnet and never had.

Even though she was younger than me by two years, Libby married first and left Bennettsville where we were born and raised. She moved with her husband across the border to Greenville, South Carolina—far enough away that you had to cross over the steep gorge on an awfully high bridge to get there. Not long after, I'd decided to marry Clive Caswell, the same way I'd decide to wear a blue dress instead of a yellow one. He seemed nice enough, but I barely knew him. Every so often he came up to the church in Bennettsville with his older brother Levi's widow—held the hymnal for her even though she knew all the words. He was ten years older than me, had clean shirt collars, and came from a good family. A family a lot like mine.

Garnet, where Clive was raised, wasn't but twenty or thirty minutes south of Bennettsville. They were the same kinds of places—mostly farmland pushed up against pillowy gray mountains. Places where everybody up at the church knows everybody else's business, where the gossip is passed around before morning service as quick as the peppermints.

In some places around here, the road curls around the land like fingers closing in a tight fist. But where we lived on Maranatha Road, the fingers ease into an open hand. It's not a valley exactly, but close to one. The only time I held a paintbrush was in grade school, but sometimes I wondered how an artist might paint this place—the twisted mountain roads stretching into gentler curves, letting the light in, the farms spread out on both sides of the road.

When Clive brought me to Garnet after we were married, he told me the town got its name on account of the mining. "Garnets mostly, and sometimes emeralds," he said, rolling down the window in his truck and letting in the smell of manure and fresh-cut grass. I nodded and looked down at the ring he'd given me. It was a plain gold band and I didn't need anything fancy. But that didn't stop me from imagining how a garnet or emerald ring would look on my finger. Like something a queen would wear, I guessed.

"Over there, that's where the old school house used to be, but they tore it down. Built a new one up where it won't flood." Clive pointed out the window and I saw the brick school spread wide over the hill. I thought about our children going there one day with their little legs pumping to get up the hill and their lunch boxes swinging from their hands.

Back then Clive showed me the house on Maranatha Road where he'd been born and raised and where he'd lived by himself since his parents passed on. When I saw the white, two-story farmhouse with a big porch across the front, I figured our life was about to start. I didn't know—I couldn't have known—how it would end up. Some places up in the mountains are dark, like in Wyeth's Mill where my Aunt Callie lived. But the sun could reach Maranatha Road and I thought it would be light there most all the time.

"Mark doing all right?" Libby asked, and it was like she could read my mind even though I hadn't said much of anything. I thought of telling her how he'd been after church, then imagined her calling somebody else to tell what she'd heard.

"Getting ready for the wedding," I said. And I told her I needed to get off the phone, that I had a lot to do.

When it came time for supper, I made tomato sandwiches with butter and salt because Clive favored them and I knew I shouldn't have been so hard on him before. Sometimes I meant one thing and it came out another, like I didn't have any kind of softness in me, whether I wanted to or not. Clive came in and washed his hands at the kitchen sink.

"I reckon Mark will be down to get something to eat," he said, then pulled out his chair from the table.

"He might or he might not." I closed my eyes and opened them again, trying to smooth down my voice. "I don't know." I took a bite of my sandwich without waiting on him to say the blessing and then I got up and stuffed the rest of it in a plastic bag.

————

The next morning Mark finally came downstairs. He kept clothes at the house for when he stayed over, but even though he'd changed, he was a mess. His hair wasn't combed and his face looked mashed up something awful. He drank half a cup of coffee—stirred some sugar into it with his finger and then pushed the cup away, staring at his finger like he couldn't figure out how it got sticky. After he ate a bite of scrambled eggs and half a piece of sausage, he said he'd better get on to work. Monday mornings he had to be there early. He scraped the rest of his food in the scrap bucket and left his dishes in the sink.

"Are you feeling any better?" I wanted to comb through his hair with my fingers to make it lay down. "Mark, you can tell me. Has something happened?" He didn't answer, just touched my arm on his way out, right below my elbow. I know the spot exactly.

CHAPTER 5

―――

Clive wasn't much for arguing and carrying on. Most days he did his thing and he let me do mine. But after Mark left for work that day, Clive came inside and stood by the kitchen sink, holding out his arms, one to the other, like he was measuring to see if they were the same length. I started filling up the sink with hot water. He could stand there if he wanted to, but he wasn't going to keep me from doing what I needed to do. When I shut off the water, he finally started talking.

"I guess there's something going on with Mark and Maddie then." He got out his bandana and blew his nose.

"I don't know. I don't know what's got him torn up."

"Seems like something they'll work out, I'm guessing."

"I don't know about that either." I said as I scrubbed a plate. "You know he doesn't get over things easy."

"Still, I guess it's probably best to let him see after himself. Might be something going on he needs to take care of."

"He's got cold feet about the wedding, that's all. That's what I'm guessing anyway." I felt around in the warm water for the silverware, careful of the knives. I didn't know what I was saying, but the way it came out, I thought it might turn out to be right. "Somebody just needs to tell him it'll all work itself out."

Clive shook his head. "Might be best if we give him some room. He'll figure it out."

"You know something I don't?"

He paused at the back door. "He'll figure it out," he said again and then he was gone. The truth was he didn't know Mark like I did.

The radio was on while I finished cleaning up the kitchen. Libby had been worried about the weather, but it was going to be fine for the next few days. The tropical storm down at the coast was already moving out and we wouldn't even have any wind from it, not as far west as we were.

We always kept watch on the weather on account of the river. Back in April, we'd had so much rain that some roads had washed out and somebody's car slid off the road into the river and two people drowned. Once when Mark was little, a tropical storm came in far enough to reach Garnet. Trees shuddered and fell and the lights blinked out and we thought it would never stop raining. It was so cold and wet that one of the yard cats got pneumonia. Mark carried it around for three days in a box almost as tall as he was, with that poor, sweet cat trying to scratch her way out the whole time until she didn't have any energy left. Mark always did try to help anything that needed rescuing. When that cat died, he let it weigh heavier on him than he should have, and even though the sun had come back out, he barely moved or talked for two weeks.

Eventually Mark got his energy back, but it was like he was racing to catch up on everything he'd missed. He talked a mile a minute and wanted everything he laid his eyes on. He could hardly see a rock outside without picking it up and he started stacking up leaves in his room. They weren't even pretty ones—they were dried-up things the color of Coca-Cola.

The older he got, the more Mark was two different people. Some days he was wound up tight, not able to stay still for a minute. He stayed up half the night and kept going all day. He started building things—ladders and hunting stands and bee boxes and bird houses. One time he built a dog house and we didn't even have a dog to sit in it. Most things he started building he left half-finished, already moving

25

on to the next thing. Clive and I asked the doctor if his heart was working too hard, but he said Mark was fine and we didn't know what else to ask. Then there were times when he was emptied out. He acted like blinking his eyes was almost too much work. When he was in high school sometimes he lied to his friends and all those girls who called up at the house, saying he had to stay home. The worst was when he didn't want to eat, not even when I made macaroni casserole the way he liked it, light brown around the edges.

Still, he never missed a day of school, not unless you count the time he got the stomach flu. He was always a real nice-looking boy, and girls acted like they didn't have a lick of sense, the way they chased after him. He was even Homecoming King his senior year, a silly thing if you ask me, but it showed how much he was thought of. Got an award in shop class too because he was good with his hands. And once Mark took a job with the logging company, he talked about how nice it was to be outside all day instead of cooped up.

A losing like what I'm talking about doesn't come all at once. It comes at you in pieces. You're asking "Don't you want to get up and go outside?" and then, before you know it, you're saying "Calm down, please just calm down." The whole time looking for a middle, settling-in place. Like what I thought Mark had found with Maddie.

———

The logging company office was nothing more than a trailer set up by the side of the road with a cardboard sign stuck in the ground. Shaky metal steps led up to the trailer door and inside a girl at a cheap-looking desk was talking on the phone. When she finally put it down, she asked if there was something she could help me with.

"Yes, I'm looking for Mark Caswell. I'm his mother." She looked at me like that wasn't enough, like I had to have some kind of a badge or something. Like it was some kind of top-secret government fort.

"I'm sorry, we don't really give out that kind of information. Besides the crews rotate around. They might be in this county or the next on any given day." She shrugged.

"What if there was some kind of emergency?"

"Well, I mean, I could find out if I absolutely needed to." She tilted her head to the side and looked at me. She had that stringy kind of hair that always looks dirty and she hadn't bothered to brush it. "What kind of emergency are we talking about?"

"A family emergency, that's what kind." I crossed my arms and waited. She spun her chair around and pulled open a drawer from the metal cabinet behind her. After she got out a folder of papers, she flipped through them until she found what she was looking for. Then she picked up the phone and dialed a number, keeping her finger on the paper the whole time.

"Hey, Jake? It's Yvette. Down at the office? Yeah, so there's an old lady down here wanting to find out where Mark Caswell is. Says it's a family emergency. Uh huh. Okay, I'll tell her." She hung up the phone and told me that Mark's crew was out on Halfour Road, past the strawberry farm and before you get to the Jacksons' home place. I knew exactly where she was talking about and it didn't take me long to get out there.

I'd never gone by to see Mark at work before. But I kept picturing the way he'd been when he'd walked out of the house. Whatever was going on might be something I could fix. Maybe if I promised him the wedding would go off just fine then he would settle down.

There must have been eight or ten boys out there, not counting Mark, all of them wearing long pants and long-sleeved shirts to keep from getting scratched. Mark came up to me wiping sweat off his forehead with his arm. "What is it, Mama?"

I didn't have anything planned out to say and I realized it didn't make any sense for me to have bothered him when he was working. All around us boys were pulling up their equipment and hooking up chains. "I guess I just wanted to make sure you were doing all right," I said finally.

A heavyset older man came up to where we were standing. "Everything okay here?"

"It's my mother." Mark shook his head like he didn't know what to do with me. But I could see how tired he looked, how something was different about his eyes, and I decided I wasn't going anywhere without talking to him first.

"You need to take a minute?" the man asked.

"This is my foreman, Charles." Mark said, and he rubbed his arm across his forehead again.

"Nice to meet you." I nodded at him. "Didn't mean to disturb anybody."

"No disruption at all. We've met before up at the church, but I don't blame you a bit for not remembering." He pointed over to a picnic table. "Look, if you need to talk to Mark, he's due for a break anyway. See that he gets something to drink."

Mark and I walked over to the picnic table and he opened a cooler and took out a metal thermos. He unscrewed the top and drank with his head tipped back.

"Did something happen after church? You were fine yesterday morning." He wiped off his mouth and didn't answer me. "Is there something going on about the wedding?"

He shook his head and even all sweaty like he was, I was thinking about how handsome he looked. At the wedding, the two of them—Mark and Maddie—would look like they were right out of a magazine. All those people up at the church would shake Mark's hand and tell him how good Maddie looked and she would stand there beside him exactly where he wanted her to be.

"It's all messed up," he said quietly. "I just don't know what to do."

"What do you mean?"

"You wouldn't understand." Mark looked down at his feet, digging one of his shoes in the dirt.

"This wedding is going to work out fine. You'll see."

"It's all a big mess. I don't know if Maddie's going to find out, but it's probably just a matter of time. And it's my own damn fault." He sighed. "I can't see how I've messed up this big." He closed his eyes like he could block it all out.

"Well, you can get it fixed then, whatever it is."

"I can't snap my fingers and make it go away."

"What do you mean? I have no idea what's going on, why you're acting like this."

Mark took another sip from the thermos and a fly landed on his arm, but he didn't brush it off. "Do you remember the first time the Spencers came to the house?"

"Sure I do. It wasn't that long ago." I watched the fly walk up his arm and fly away, remembering how meeting Maddie had been good for him from the start. "That day when you and Maddie met each other."

"Yeah." He closed his eyes again, rubbing his fingers over his eyelids, and when he opened them, they looked red. "You know what Maddie said to me when they left, when they were getting in the car?"

I shook my head. "I don't know what she said."

"I don't either, that's the thing." Mark sighed. "She said something to me, something like I hope to see you again soon. Something like that—something polite and nice, but more to it than that."

I didn't know what to say so I just waited for him to get out what he needed to. It didn't seem like he was finished.

He held the thermos out to me. "You want some?"

"I don't need any, but thank you."

Mark screwed the lid back on and put the thermos back in the cooler. When he got up, he stood there for a minute with his hands pressed against the table.

"The thing about Maddie—it's hard to say what I mean." Mark shook his head and frowned. "It's like how it must be to find a big garnet when you're not expecting anything but dirt."

I tried to tell him that the two of them were good for each other, but he raised his hand like he was waving to me and turned away. At least he was talking again. I guessed it wouldn't take long for Mark to get back to himself. I watched him walk away—damp with sweat, his shirt untucked on one side.

CHAPTER 6

——————

When I got back to the house, a crow squawked at me from a tree branch. Our mother had always said that meant bad luck, but I didn't know what was coming and I probably couldn't have stopped it even if I did.

Around noon Clive came in for dinner and then he left for the stockyard. He didn't say what he was going about, whether he was buying or selling. I guess he never did tell me that kind of thing, not that I ever asked him either. He reached for his cap on the hook by the back door and pushed it on his head like he always did, the same way you'd press two halves of a sandwich together. He nodded toward me and said he would be back in time for supper. The hinges of the door let out a long squeak when he went out. I heard the heavy falling of his boots going down the back steps. The metal clang of the tailgate snapping at the white truck. The truck door opening and closing and the motor starting up like something hungry.

I wiped out the skillet and set the glasses on a towel to dry. Through the kitchen window I watched one of the yard cats outside prowling around the sunflowers. Mark had named him Junaluska, after a lake he had gone to with a friend from school. Clive and Mark chuckled when I started calling him Junie. But the nickname stuck, just like my name for Libby had. He was meowing like he had something real bad to complain about, so I checked to make sure there was food in his dish on the porch. When I called him over and scratched behind his ears, Junie settled down to eat.

Vinson Keller came by shortly after Clive left—had his cap crunched up in his hand when he came up to the back door. I opened the door, but didn't invite him to come in the house. I'd known Vinson a long time and that man's hands were always dirty. That was the kind of thing I worried about then, whether somebody would leave a greasy handprint on my tablecloth.

"Mrs. Caswell, I don't mean to bother you, but I came about that wood Clive told me about." Vinson's voice was so loud, it was like gunfire, and it was all I could do not to jump back like I was getting out of the way. "Said you all had plenty and for me to help myself. Didn't want you to wonder what I was up to back there." He twisted that cap around in his hand and looked anywhere but at me. At the freezer chest on the back porch. The white curtain on the door, hanging from tiny gold loops.

"I guess that'll be fine then," I said and Vinson nodded and turned to go. All afternoon I could hear him in the back yard by the woodpile. Every time the ax hit the wood, it was like a skull cracking open.

After I finished cleaning up the kitchen, I decided to bring down some of the chairs from the attic. Even though Mark hadn't asked me to get them, I figured I knew the ones Maddie wanted for the reception and I might as well get started on cleaning them up. I could picture Mark telling her she was the bride and could have whatever chairs she wanted. When she was around him, the best Mark showed up, the real one.

I bumped the chairs down the stairs all the way to the first floor. The oak was in pretty good shape, just needed a little polishing. When I finished going over them to clean up what I could, I called at the Spencers' house in town. Even though nobody answered, I decided to go on up there.

The chairs wouldn't fit in my car and Clive had taken his pickup truck down to the stockyard. But there was another old truck out in the shed that Vinson Keller used when he was helping Clive. The back of it was dirty with mulch and I swept it out the best I could with a broom. I carried out two of the chairs, one of each kind, and tied them to the sides of the truck bed so they wouldn't fall over.

The Spencers lived in town in a big, red brick house that used to be Judge Wright's before he died without any family to leave it to—an awfully lonely thing to think about. The house was set close to the road with columns across the front and a weeping willow tree that draped over the living room window. Nobody answered the doorbell at first and I thought I'd have to give up when I remembered the flower garden out back.

Maddie's mother had wanted to have the wedding reception out there. You could tell she was right proud of it, having flowers instead of something like beans or tomatoes. But Maddie told her Mark had been going to Solid Rock since he was a baby and they wanted to keep the reception at the fellowship hall. Everything I'd been to at the fellowship hall—other wedding receptions, homecomings, reunions—was all the same. The light gray tile floor and the folding tables covered with paper tablecloths. Everybody—whose names and faces I could never keep straight—drinking lemonade so sour it made your teeth hurt. And if it was summer, those big fans blowing so loud you could hardly hear what anybody was saying. Of course, their wedding was going to be in December right before Christmas. "When everything will be like a fairytale," Maddie had said. "If it snows, that'll be even better. Only a dusting, not so much that you can't drive in it." And Mark laughed and said if he could find some way to make it snow for her, he would.

That weeping willow was so big that I had to pull branches aside like they were curtains. Around the back of the house was a porch with no roof and the flower garden, big enough to walk around in but just barely. Maddie was out there in a blue striped dress with a full skirt and short sleeves, pushing around big pots of mums. When she saw me, she lit up. "Mrs. Caswell, what a lovely surprise. I'm so glad you came out. Mark's okay, right? He's feeling better?"

"He'll be all right. I tried calling before I came out here, but didn't reach anybody."

"I'm sorry about that. I don't know where Daddy is, but Mama is down at the hairdresser's and I've been out here messing around. I can't imagine what my makeup looks like at this point." She patted at her cheek and shrugged. "I'll hear about it from Mama when she gets home, I guess."

"You look the same to me. Seems to me like you look better than some girls do if they haven't done anything more than sitting on the couch all day."

Maddie laughed. "Well, that's awfully nice of you to say. I don't know. What do you think of these mums?" She stepped back and put her hands on her hips. There must've been eight or nine pots of them, some white and some between orange and gold.

"They look real nice."

"For the wedding, I mean. Do you think they look too much like fall? Maybe some dark red ones would be better? The orange ones might not be around in December. Mama says white roses and holly branches. That's the only kind of flowers she likes for a winter wedding. I do kind of like the bright orange though. Don't you?"

"They're real pretty with all that color."

"Kind of gold like the bridesmaids' dresses, maybe? Look, I'm so sorry. Here I've been blabbing away and I haven't even offered you anything to drink. Let's go inside and sit down for a minute."

"I brought by some of the chairs to show you—for the reception, the ones from the attic."

"Oh, you did? You didn't need to do that. But I can't wait to see them. Here, let's at least get some water and we'll go take a look."

I followed her through the back door and into a kitchen that looked like something off the television. The cabinets were light wood and the countertops were some kind of black rock, the kind you'd imagine came straight from the middle of a volcano. Maddie got two glasses down and stuck them under a spigot right in the door of the refrigerator. "Do you want to go sit down in the living room? Mama should be back soon."

"If you want, I could go ahead and show you the chairs. I brought one of each."

She nodded. "Let's do that."

Outside, Maddie put her glass down on the ground and ran her finger over the carving on one of the chairs. "They're both so pretty, Mrs. Caswell. Don't you think?"

"They need cleaning up a little bit."

"You know, it was my mother's idea. She saw it in a magazine, having different kinds of wooden chairs, I mean. But now that I see them, I get it. I think they're going to be perfect. I can't wait to tell her." She pressed her hands together, smiling, with the little pearl ring Mark had given her on her finger. "You really had these up in the attic?"

"Eight of the one kind and six of the other."

"Isn't that something?"

"If you and Mark want any of them for the house after you're married, you're welcome to them." As soon as I said it, I knew I'd said the wrong thing. The Spencers had already bought a brand-new house for Mark and Maddie to live in after the wedding—on a brand-new street, one somebody put in after they tore down some old warehouses. The Spencers were probably already filling up the house full of furniture.

"If you really aren't using them, that might be nice. I can ask Mark next time I see him." She touched my arm. "It's really nice of you to offer. Both for the wedding and for after."

"Mark's been good when you've seen him lately, I guess?"

Maddie nodded. "Yes, of course he has. Yesterday was the only thing, but I think he was just tired after all the work he's been doing out at the house, don't you?" She bent down and picked up her glass.

"What house do you mean?"

"Well, he said he was painting the rental house with Cliff. But it doesn't look like they've made much progress out there and Odell at the curb market told Mama she'd seen Mark's truck out at the gray house, the other one y'all rent out. So I must've had the wrong house, I guess."

"What's he been doing out there?"

"He said fixing it up and stuff. He's been so busy lately, I haven't seen him much." She smiled and shrugged.

"Well, I'm glad you like the chairs. I'll get them cleaned up. Thanks for the water." I handed the glass back to Maddie and she stacked it on top of hers. I looked at her ring, the one from Mark. "I'm surprised you didn't want something other than that ring," I said without thinking. "It had to have been all that Mark could pay for and it's real pretty, but I don't know—" A pearl probably wasn't what Maddie wanted, not with the big diamond her mother had.

She switched the glasses to her other hand and held out the hand with the ring, looking down at it. "Oh, Daddy has his mother's ring, a big sapphire one. He said Mark could have it, but I didn't want it."

"I told Mark he could have my garnet too, one that Clive gave me years ago. We could still turn it into a ring. There's enough time."

"He picked this one out." Maddie shook her head, still looking at that ring. "And I love pearls, don't you? The way they kind of glow or something. He picked out exactly the right one."

As soon as I left, I went by the gray house. No lights were on, and when I knocked on the door, nobody came so I went on home. I could always ask Clive about it later.

It was almost suppertime when I got the call. I'd put a pot of water on to boil and was standing at the kitchen sink peeling potatoes, wondering when Clive's truck would come down the driveway. Vinson had finished up with the wood and gone on home. After all the racket earlier in the day, it was quiet then. The only sounds were the knife scraping against the peel and thudding against the plastic scrap bucket.

When the phone rang, I jumped. I dropped the knife and it clattered in the sink as I hurried to the phone, wiping my hands on the dishcloth. Before I even said hello, I heard a woman's voice. "This is Willa Dunn calling."

"I'm here. What is it, Willa?" I put the dishcloth down on the counter and stared at the striped material.

"I was driving home not five minutes ago," Willa took a deep breath, "and I saw Mark—your Mark—out on the bridge."

Not sure what she was talking about, I didn't say anything. Instead, I stared at the green and white stripes on the dishcloth, the way the green ended and the white started. The red spot that looked like tomato juice, darker on the green part than on the white.

"Something about it didn't look right to me," she said. "He was pacing around and shaking his head. He looked upset."

Already I wondered how quickly I could get out there.

"Out on the bridge," Willa said again, and I saw in my mind the height of it and the long dizzy drop to the ground below. I stared at that dishcloth, at the red spot on it, and right then it looked like blood and nothing else.

PART THREE

*Tinley Greene, Mark Caswell,
and Clive Caswell*

SEPTEMBER–OCTOBER 1998

CHAPTER 7

— *Tinley Greene* —

As I head up to the Haughtrys' house, I practice what I'll say to Mrs. Haughtry. Now that I'm a senior I can start applying to college. The guidance counselor said I might qualify for a scholarship, but for now I have to fill out the financial aid form and I need Mrs. Haughtry's help.

Even though I can't do much work around here because of school, the Haughtrys have let me stay at the trailer. Mr. Haughtry said I should move into their house, but Mrs. Haughtry assured him I'm fine where I am.

Five hazy months have passed since my parents died—day after day of putting one foot in front of the other, of pulling back from my friends who can't understand, of wanting nothing but to hide in the trailer by myself sniffing around for hints of Mama's hand cream and Daddy's aftershave.

I knock on the Haughtrys' back door, but no one answers. Mrs. Haughtry isn't in the old dairy barn and I don't see her on the path around back. I check the tomato patch and the garden. On my way back up to the house, I pass the chicken shed where I waited for Mama and Daddy. I can't make myself open the door, but there's no way Mrs. Haughtry is in there anyway.

I'm almost back to the trailer when I remember the tool shed. An overgrown, prickly blackberry bush partially blocks the door and it's like a sign telling me not to go in, but I push it aside and pull open the door.

Mr. Haughtry shades his hand over his eyes from the light I've let in.

The work lamp shines on the table, but the rest of the shed is cloaked in darkness.

I clear my throat. "I was looking for Mrs. Haughtry, but I couldn't find her."

Mr. Haughtry puts down the rusty piece of metal that he's working on—a motor or a fan, something big enough that he holds it with both hands.

"Well, she's off visiting her cousin in Atlanta, if you can believe that," he says, shaking his head. "Got a call in the middle of the night. Some kind of an emergency or something and she left before it was even daylight this morning." He comes toward me, squinting. I've never been afraid of Mr. Haughtry before, but now I feel like running and I don't know why.

"It's just me and you," he says. "What do you think about that?"

"I'll just try to find her some other time."

Mr. Haughtry wipes his hands on an old rag and stuffs it in his back pocket. Then he takes another step toward me. "Come to think after all this time, all those years and we've never been alone until now, just you and me."

What he's saying feels flat wrong, even though the words are true. Somebody else has always been around. My mother or father or Mrs. Haughtry. Instead of saying anything back, I shrug, imagining I can shake off the bad feeling in the room. Like I could move the right way and whatever Mr. Haughtry means would fall away.

I remember a time when Daddy helped Mr. Haughtry fix a water pipe at their house. They spread their tools out on the floor and Mr. Haughtry rubbed his fingers over the wood. I pictured a splinter going right into his finger and I must have gasped out loud because Mr. Haughtry asked me what was wrong.

"Nothing," I said. "I thought you could get a splinter."

Mr. Haughtry laughed and wiped his chin. "Well, then I guess you'd have to bandage me all up, wouldn't you? Might do a thing like that to get me a pretty little nurse like you."

Daddy shook his head and marked off a square with a pencil. When

Mr. Haughtry started using the jigsaw, the wood dissolved into sawdust. Under the floorboard, more wood appeared, and underneath that, a gray cloth glued to another piece of wood. I thought of our trailer and the place by the refrigerator where the plastic floor was peeling up. Watching Mr. Haughtry cut through the wood, I had a sick feeling about that smooth yellow floor in the trailer, like there wasn't anything under where we walked except plastic and then dark air until you got to the ground, which belonged to the Haughtrys.

"I'll come by later after Mrs. Haughtry gets back," I say now, inching backwards toward the door. "I didn't mean to bother you."

But before I know what's happening Mr. Haughtry grabs my waist, then pulls me toward him.

"I need to go, Mr. Haughtry." I strain to get away from him. My heart stutters and speeds up and I can't look at him. "I need to go," I say again, louder this time.

"You don't need to be going anywhere." His breath smells sour.

I try to break free of his arm, but he's too strong. "What are you doing? Let me go. Turn loose."

Mr. Haughtry takes my hand and presses it on himself, on his private area, and I start to panic, struggling to break free of him, remembering the way he once pulled my bra strap up from where it had slipped on my shoulder, his cackling laugh when Mrs. Haughtry gave him a stern look.

"Let me out of here." I try to yank my hand away, but Mr. Haughtry pushes it down harder. Through his pants he moves like a throbbing heart until I grow dizzy. The wooden walls covered with black tar paper seem to sway sideways and the back of my throat burns like I'm going to throw up.

Seconds later, Mr. Haughtry shoves my hand away from his pants, but he holds onto my wrist. With his other hand he unbuckles his belt.

"You have to let me go. You can't do this." My voice cracks as I plead with him.

"Where do you think you're gonna go off to? Seems to me you've got no place to go. Now am I wrong about that?" Mr. Haughtry unbuttons and unzips his pants. "You tell me, am I wrong? Besides, you owe me a fair amount seeing as how I've let you hang around—eating my food, running my water. And you haven't so much as lifted a finger. Don't you see it that way?"

When I don't answer, he drags me closer to him, his breath so spoiled that my eyes water.

"Don't tell me you don't have a boyfriend you do this with. A pretty girl like you with that figure of yours."

I shake my head, grinding my teeth, still struggling to get free and gulping in air that smells thick and oily. In the dark, the walls seem to spin around me and then, from out of nowhere, a light flashes.

CHAPTER 8

— *Mark Caswell* —

"Is anybody in here?" I clear my throat and peek in. Toward the back of the dark shed, a man looks up, his arm clenched around a girl. When he sees me, he lets go of her arm and she scurries to the corner where an old rake leans against the wall.

"I was heading up to the house," I try again, "but I thought I heard somebody in here."

The sound of the man zipping up his pants makes me shiver. I don't know what I've walked in on. I wasn't even supposed to be here. I'm not usually the one who goes to talk to the landowner.

The girl starts to cry and I move closer. "What's going on in here? Is everything all right?"

The man looks at the girl in the corner, then back at me. "Hey there, son. What can I help you with?" Even though his voice booms like somebody on the radio, his hands shake as he tilts the work lamp away. The weak light falls on the back of the shed where I can make out some metal tools hanging on hooks.

Right up to him—no other way to do it. Reaching out to shake his hand, I mumble an explanation about why I'm here—access for the logging company, his driveway. The words don't make any sense. Everything seems different now because of this girl. She's why I'm here. I've walked in on this and now I have to save her.

"How long are y'all gonna block my driveway?" He looks at me with his arms crossed.

Staring at that girl, I can't come up with how to answer him.

"How long?" he asks again.

I bite my lip. "Won't get started 'til early next week and then it won't be more than an hour. Maybe two."

"They go to the trouble of sending somebody out in advance like that, says to me it's gonna be blocked for quite some time."

"No sir. They do that just as a courtesy." It's not usually me. I'm out in the field, not going to see people. Not until today when Hanson called in sick. Maybe because I was meant to be here instead. The girl crouches in the corner, her legs pulled up under her, like she wants to disappear. "Is it Mr. Haughtry? That's what the paperwork said."

"You've got the right place then." He wipes over an oily place on the worktable with a dirty towel.

"I'm wondering if—I feel like there's something going on here. Something I walked in on. I'm not sure."

Mr. Haughtry comes out from behind the table and points toward the door. "Maybe the best thing is for you to be going."

"Are you okay?" I ask the girl, but she's still crying and doesn't answer. When I head toward her, Mr. Haughtry puts out his arm like he'll stop me.

"Don't you bother yourself over nothing," he says. "It's none of your business."

I ignore him and draw closer to the girl. It's all I can do. He can come at me or not. Doesn't matter to me. I'm getting to that girl. With her eyes glued to me, she stands up and grabs the rake.

"Why don't you put that down and come with me?" I plead with her. "We can get out of here if that's what you want."

Behind me, Mr. Haughtry says, "You need to worry about your own self, son, and don't waste time on somebody else's business."

My eyes stay on the girl until she lets go of the rake and it falls to the floor. Once I reach for her elbow, she falls into me. Now we have to get out of here. There are all sorts of ways Mr. Haughtry might try to stop us. He could grab her and push her against the wall. He could punch me in the stomach or grab the metal scythe from the wall and bring it down over our heads.

But he stands still and doesn't move to stop us. The door is behind him, open enough that I can see a wedge of green grass outside. I nod at the girl like I'm telling her to keep going. We come right up to Mr. Haughtry and he stares at the sawdust on the floor and doesn't budge. Once we're past him, we run until we're outside in the sun and already this girl is mine and I am hers.

CHAPTER 9

— *Tinley Greene* —

The boy holding my elbow looks like he's built out of something different than the rest of us—like some part of him is made from the sun. We run past the fig tree in front of the Haughtrys' bedroom window toward a truck I've never seen before. It's dark green like a Christmas tree, this truck I'm going to ride away in—shiny and clean with the sun glinting on the metal parts. The figs rotting on the ground give off a sweet smell. Down the road, cars pass by like they would any other day—people heading to the feed store or the corner stand where gourds and pumpkins are piled up for sale, the ones on the bottom damp under the weight of the ones on top.

I'm convinced he will take me somewhere. It doesn't matter where, as long as it's not near Mr. Haughtry. I don't want to see Mrs. Haughtry either, or the trailer or the school. I've been walking around asleep for months, thinking my parents aren't really gone, imagining that any minute now Daddy will walk through the door of the trailer and hang up his keys on the hook near the stove. But Mama and Daddy are lying in the ground and they aren't ever coming back. And nobody can help me except this boy who can take me somewhere new. Now that I'm awake, there is no old place I can go to again.

When we get up to the truck, he lets go of my elbow and it feels like the next impossible, terrible thing in a long line of them. But then he shakes his head and leans down close to my face and I want him even closer. "Are you okay?" He touches my elbow again and I breathe in deep, like now I can take in air. "I mean, I don't really know what happened back there or what that was all about, but do you think you're okay?" "I'm okay." *I'm whatever you want me to be.*

He points to the passenger side. "You want to come with me? Do you want to get in?" Nothing I could say would be big enough and all I do is nod. He opens the door for me and I climb in. After he closes it, he pats it like you'd pat a child on the back. I watch him walk around to the driver's side. He's a little older than me—tan and solid and wearing pants that hang long over work boots.

As he starts up the truck, he asks if I'm okay. "Where do you want to go? He didn't hurt you, did he? I could take you home or something. I—I don't know. I don't know what to do." He sweeps his hand like he can erase everything. "I mean, this is crazy, all of it. He—he must be—has anything like this ever happened to you before? How do you know Mr. Haughtry?" He twists around to face me. "Did he hurt you? Would you tell me if he did?"

"No, he didn't hurt me. But only because you came in there right then." I look back toward the shed—no sign of Mr. Haughtry.

"Where do you live? Where can I take you? What's your name?" He shakes his head and laughs. "All these questions." He covers his mouth with his hand. "I didn't mean to laugh. I mean, nothing's funny. I just—"

"It's okay. Tinley Greene. I live in the trailer behind the Haughtrys' house. But I can't go back there."

He nods, his eyes a clear minty green and his dark hair curling thick over his forehead. "I forgot to tell you my name. I'm Mark. Mark Caswell." As he pulls out onto the main road, I say his name over and over again in my mind, tasting its sweetness.

"How long have you lived with the Haughtrys? On their land, I mean? I could take you to your parents if you want. I don't remember us ever meeting—I went to school at Garnet High. Graduated three years ago.

Never had anything like this happen," Mark says, talking fast like he's behind in a race and talking is what will catch him up. "Nothing even close to what happened today. I mean, what almost happened. I can't even—you must have been so scared."

"My whole life, that's how long I've lived with the Haughtrys. So seventeen years, I guess. I just turned seventeen." I ignore the offer to take me to my parents.

"You're so young. I can't believe he would do that to you. I just can't believe it. Are you sure you're okay?"

"I promise. You got there in time."

"Where should we go? Where do you want me to take you?"

"I—I haven't really thought much about it, I guess."

Mark looks at the road, then at the radio and back at the road again, tapping his fingers on the steering wheel and all of him seems wound up. "I mean, I can take you wherever. Wherever you need to go."

"The thing is, I don't really have anywhere."

"What about your parents?"

I shake my head. "They passed away." It's enough to tell him that, but I take a breath and decide to tell him how they died because I want him to know everything about me. "Their car got swept off the road in a big storm. Earlier this year."

What I've told him settles around us like a bad smell. Mark shakes his head. "Oh no, I'm so sorry. I can't believe that. That's awful. I mean, I heard about the accident. Everybody did. I guess I didn't think about—I didn't know who—you'd think in a small town we would all know each other." His voice cracks as he pulls up to a stop sign.

"It's different when you don't go to church with everyone. My parents didn't go to Solid Rock or the Methodist church either. So I've never gone—I don't know." I shrug, feeling a tiny bit invisible. Then Mark looks over at me and I'm real again.

"What kind of bad luck, what in the world?" He shakes his head.

Now he knows the worst things that have happened to me. But everything is different now. It has to be. We pass a pasture with a barbed wire fence and some Holsteins in the back corner chewing on grass, their tails flicking back and forth.

"I'm going to take care of you, okay, Tinley? I mean, anything I can do, I'll do it. You let me know."

And even though I just met him, some part of me already knows we're going away from everything and starting over. He's driving down the road like he's sure about where to go. The radio in the truck is on—a guitar and a man's strong voice—and the gray vinyl seat of the truck feels warm from the sun beating in. A pair of men's work boots rests on the floorboard and a can of WD-40 rolls around whenever we slow down or speed up. I line my foot up next to one of the boots, pressing right up against it until there is no space in between.

"We'll get something set up for you. I'll think of something," Mark says.

"I just need somewhere to sleep. But you don't have to—I mean, I guess if you don't mind taking me up to the church—" I shrug. "Even though we aren't members, they could probably help me out."

Mark shakes his head. "I wouldn't feel right doing that, not if you don't know people up there. I can take care of it. I can get you whatever you need."

"I knew you'd say that."

He laughs. "You just met me."

But I know him already and I end up laughing too. And that's how he is—so full of light that, at least in my mind, he can make people like Mr. Haughtry, with all their darkness and sourness, fade away.

He takes me to a gray wooden house with a front porch. "I was supposed to come clean this out, but I think it'll be okay for you to stay here. You won't be bothering anybody. And it's sitting empty otherwise."

"Are you sure? Is it yours?"

"It's my family's. We rent it out sometimes but there's nobody in there right now, probably not until the spring when it's planting time." Mark opens the truck door. "Let's go check it out."

I follow him across the yard and up to the porch. The wooden steps stained the color of watered-down iced tea creak under our weight. Mark flips around the keys on his keychain until he finds the right one and, when he goes to put the key in the lock, he stops. "I promise it's fine for you to be here. It's no problem at all, okay?"

"If you're sure, thank you."

"But let's not tell anybody that you're here. For right now."

"You don't need to worry about that. And I don't have anybody to tell anyway."

He stares at the dust curling around his shoes. "Well, let's check it out then." The door opens into the living room—brown carpet, a low navy couch, a coffee table, and a rocking chair with a cream-colored cushion tied on with strings. On the other side of the room I spot a TV on a stand and the doorway to the kitchen.

"It's kind of dusty." Mark runs his finger over the coffee table.

"That's okay. I don't mind cleaning."

"Are you sure?"

"If you're sure I can stay here."

"Yeah, I'm sure about that part." He smiles and looks at me, then tilts his head like he can figure everything out by looking at me the right way. "Let's go see what we can find in the kitchen. Maybe there are some paper towels."

We find dust rags and spray cleaner and he shows me bath towels and sheets. After we've cleaned, we go back to the kitchen to get something to drink. The cabinets are stocked with white dishes and pale pink plastic cups. Even though we're only drinking water, the color of the cups reminds me of the strawberry lemonade they have in glass bottles at the bakery on Main Street.

"How'd you know all that stuff, like how to get those stains out of the bathtub?" Mark goes to the sink and fills up his cup again.

"I guess I figured it out from watching my mother. She worked for the Haughtrys, cooking and cleaning. I don't know how to cook much though." Thinking about the soft insides of her biscuits, the way they gave way when you pulled them apart, and the crispy edges of her squash casserole, I'm hungry in a way I haven't been in a long time. I watch the way Mark drinks, how he closes his eyes when he puts the cup up to his mouth.

Even though he promises to come back the next day, a deep—almost smothering—emptiness settles around the house after he's gone. When I lie down to go to sleep, I remember Mr. Haughtry rising up in the dark and I shake my head to make the image disappear. He didn't hurt me. I don't have to see him again and maybe he isn't even real. Maybe the only thing that's real is Mark standing close to me and drinking from a cup that glows.

CHAPTER 10

— *Tinley Greene* —

Mark comes by the next morning, just as he promised.

"Did you sleep okay? I forgot that you'd need stuff like a toothbrush and soap and things like that." He holds up grocery bags, two in one hand and one in the other. "Can I come in? I got some things, stuff for breakfast and the others I just guessed. I mean I didn't really know what kind of toothpaste you'd want." He frowns. "Maybe I should've waited and taken you with me, but I had the idea and I thought I'd go on to the store while I was thinking about it."

"I don't know how—I mean—thank you. Thank you for everything." I reach to take the bags from him. "That was really nice of you."

"I put the bathroom stuff in one bag. A toothbrush and comb and all that. I guess you have your own, but I didn't know when you'd want to go get it, if you wanted to go back there. Yesterday you—"

"I guess I'll need to go get the truck sometime, but that's it."

"We can go by there later and get whatever you want," Mark says, nodding.

"I don't want to be there long. The key is always in the same place and I can be quick."

"Sure, I can come get you after work and we'll go over there right then. Is that okay? Will you be all right in the meantime? I brought you some bread for toast and stuff like that."

In the bags, I find a loaf of bread, eggs, orange juice, two apples and a banana, a jar of mayonnaise, a package of sliced cheese, two boxes of crackers, a jar of peanut butter, a big clump of green grapes so light I can almost see through them, a pack of mint-flavored gum, a chocolate candy bar, one yellow tomato and one red, and lunch meat—turkey and ham— wrapped in white paper and masking tape. Mark stares at me like he hopes I like what he's brought. I want to tell him that everything is perfect. He is the perfect answer to everything.

"I didn't know what you liked—" he starts to say and I touch his arm, just below the elbow. He looks surprised and his neck turns red, like he's rolled a strawberry over his skin and some color is left behind.

"I like everything. I can't believe you got all this for me." I'm still thinking about what it was like to touch his arm, how I could almost feel his bones and his blood moving beneath the skin, how he's strong and warm and more alive than anybody else. He watches me put the groceries away with his hands behind him on the counter.

"Will you be all right here?" He pushes himself forward and falls back like he's on a playground swing and his eyes roam over me the whole time.

"Yes, it's a beautiful house."

Mark frowns. "Well, it should be safe at least. I'm just glad you're doing okay."

"I'm good, I promise. Thank you for letting me stay here."

"I'll come by after work and we'll go out to the trailer if you want to, okay?"

"Thank you. Just to get the truck. That's all I need."

"You don't have to say thank you. I want to do it."

When I smile at him, he smiles back, then bites his lip like he's embarrassed.

The rest of the day I finish cleaning up the house. Behind a set of folding doors in the kitchen, I find an almost brand-new washer and dryer. A screen door separates the kitchen from the back porch and I run my fingers up and down it. I've always wanted a door like that. When I open it and let it go, it slaps shut and I smile and do it again just because I can.

Throughout the day, I try not to think about the trailer or the Haughtrys or even my parents. It's like when you have a sore and the slightest thing, even just brushing up against your clothes, can make it hurt again. But if you leave it alone, if you don't look at it or touch it, you won't feel it. If you can slide through the whole day without touching anything, you can almost forget you're hurt.

As I dust the shelf above the stove, I think about the things I used to have that I might never see again—unless I get them at the trailer. My Emily Dickinson book with the black and white drawing of a bird on the cover. My kite, tangled up with Daddy's in the plastic storage chest. The cinnamon-scented candle my mother gave me for Christmas. My good summer sandals, the ones that look like leather at least from a distance. If I hurry, I could get all these things and stuff them in the suitcase that my parents kept under their bed.

When Mark comes by after work, I'm waiting for him on the porch. He gets out of the truck and I gasp at how handsome he is.

"Do you want some water or something?" I can't stop thinking about how he was the day before. His eyes closed and his mouth opening, his tongue on the edge of the cup waiting to get wet. My cheeks start to burn and I wonder how pink they've gotten.

"Maybe later. I'm ready to head out there. Not that there's any hurry, but I guess you want to get what you need to." Mark holds out his hand and I start to take it, but he drops it and looks down at the ground. "You're doing okay? I mean, is the house okay and the food and everything? I got some more stuff on my way over here." He tilts his head toward the back of the truck where I notice a bag of mulch and black containers of mums, dark red with little yellow flames licking up from the centers.

"They're beautiful."

Mark looks down at the ground and turns the keys around in his hand. They clip together and come apart again. "You're beautiful," he says. He says it softer than what he's said before. His voice is deeper and I barely hear it, but I do. I hear it over and over again, the way a river sounds slipping over rocks.

On the way to the trailer, Mark talks like he always seems to. He says he can wait by the truck ready to go or he'll help me in the trailer, whichever I want.

"We could take several trips so you get whatever you want," he says. "I don't want you to leave anything behind that you might need. You shouldn't have to feel like you're rushed or anything."

"I just hope he leaves us alone."

Mark knows who I'm talking about without me saying it. "I bet it'll be okay. I don't think there's anything to worry about, not really. And if Mr. Haughtry does come by, then we'll just tell him it's your stuff. You're entitled to it, every bit of it."

"I don't want to see him, that's the main thing. I could probably forget about the truck, maybe leave it there. But it's the only thing I have that's worth anything. And I'll need it to get around." Since my parents died, I've been driving it back and forth to school, my father's smell still lingering around the driver's seat.

"I don't think he'll bother us. He'll probably be busy working outside somewhere. If he comes down there, I'll talk to him." Mark sits up straighter. "I'll wait by the truck if you want and that way I'll see him if he does anything to bother you, okay?" He looks over at me and then back to the road. There's a warm smell in the truck, like yellow leaves in the sun.

Mrs. Haughtry is probably back in town. If she comes down to the trailer, I don't know what will happen. I remember the apron she always wore, white with red apples around the hem, and a red and white checked sash that tied in the back. She's always been nice to me, but she must know how her husband really is.

Mark tilts his head at a little white house off the road. There's no porch and it looks naked, like something has been ripped off. On one corner of the house the white paint has been scraped until the light brown wood color shows through.

"That's where I live with this guy I work with," Mark says. "Nice guy but sleeps all the time and he's about to get fired if he misses another day of work." He shakes his head and laughs. "Cliff's messed up. When he's got a day off, he's supposed to be painting the house for us instead of paying rent, but you can tell from here he's a little behind."

All the times I've been by that little house and I never knew he was inside it—walking around with bare feet and his work boots lined up in his closet, spreading butter on toast, standing at the sink brushing his teeth—what I wouldn't give to see him doing all of those things. I want to see what he looks like when he's tired and what he does when he's mad—if he ever gets mad—and whether he combs or brushes his hair or doesn't do anything to it except run his fingers through it on the way out the door.

"How long have you lived there?" I ask finally, embarrassed to imagine him reading my thoughts.

He turns the radio knob and holds up his long fingers to feel if air is coming through the vents. "Not too long. And I guess I won't be there too much longer." He frowns the way someone does when they have a cramp in their side.

"What's wrong?"

"Nothing. It's okay. It's nothing."

He's still frowning and I wait for some sort of explanation, but instead the silence grows between us. When I can't stand it any longer, I ask where he grew up, if it was somewhere around here. Mark nods. "Down on Maranatha Road. The big white house."

I can picture the house—one of the prettiest farmhouses in Garnet, maybe even in all of Wynette County, one of the prettiest I've seen anyway. I've always wondered who lived there. There are usually red flowers in the little pots on the porch and ferns hanging above them. It's some kind of a sign, the way I've wondered about that house and the whole time Mark was there. My mother always said if you look, you can find signs everywhere.

"Yeah, I still stay over sometimes with my parents. I keep stuff there for now and kind of go back and forth." Mark shrugs. "Sometimes I don't like being around Cliff if he's got a bunch of people over or whatever."

When we get to the Haughtrys' house, I don't look at it. Instead I stare at Mark, at his tan arms and his shirt sleeves rolled up.

"I don't see any cars," he says. "That's a good sign. I bet we're going to be just fine. I'll pull over here around back. It's down there behind the house, right?" The potholes in the gravel road bump under the truck and we come to a stop under the big oak tree in front of the trailer. One of the tree's branches taps in the wind against the side of the brown trailer and Daddy's truck is parked by the door, the same color as the washed-out sky.

Breathing fast, I hurry to the door, expecting one of the Haughtrys to come down the hill any minute. It's unlocked and in the kitchen Mama and Daddy's old keys dangle from a hook by the stove. Right away I find the keychain for the truck—the dark green rubber diamond with rubbed-off white stamped letters that used to say Dell's, the body shop where Daddy bought it. I grab the keychain and count up what else I have time to get. I check outside the window, part of me expecting to see Mr. Haughtry in his dirty overalls with his cap pulled down. But nobody is there except Mark pacing around the yard with his arms crossed.

I take one last quick look around since it's the last time I'll be here. I glance over at the row of Daddy's caps on wall hooks and the jar of molasses on the counter. Everywhere in the trailer the smell of fried eggs and corned beef lingers, things Mama cooked when it was just the three of us, when she didn't have to be up at the Haughtrys' house. Her work shoes are still by the front door, one more untied than the other.

Down the hall, my parents' bed is made up with the blanket pulled over the pillows. I can still see the way Mama did it, how she tugged up the blanket and stabbed her hand under each of the pillows to make the blanket go where she wanted. The brown plaid suitcase slides out easily from under the bed and I carry it down the hall.

In my room, the bed sheet hangs out from under the bedspread and I take a minute to tuck it under again. The metal blind on the window is bent so that it never closes all the way. The nightstand isn't anything but a cardboard box turned upside down with a placemat on top of it—empty except for a plastic alarm clock.

With the suitcase unzipped on the carpet beside me, I throw open drawers of the chest as fast as I can. Jeans, my four sundresses, a long-sleeved knit dress, t-shirts, a pullover sweater that's a little too small, and a thick cardigan. I sigh, remembering the way I used to flip through the stacks of my clothes, wishing they were new, wanting something with tags I'd clip off instead of what Mama made with material the print works plant threw out. I add socks and bras and panties to the suitcase. My three other pairs of shoes. My brush and comb. Lip gloss. Tampons. Nail clippers. The little sample of face cream Mama got in the mail and the velvet jewelry case I got for my birthday. My robe off the plastic hook on the back of the door. The barn jacket hanging by its hood from the doorknob.

My candle and books are on top of the chest. As I reach for them, I hear something outside and I zip up the suitcase and run, leaving everything behind except the truck key and what I have in the suitcase.

Once I'm outside again, my breath catches like a bubble in my chest when I realize there's nobody but Mark. I don't see the Haughtrys anywhere.

"I thought I heard something," I say, trying to catch my breath in the afternoon heat. "But you were right." I hold up the suitcase to show him. "They didn't bother us." Maybe Mark is always right. Maybe there is so much good in him that whenever he guesses about something he turns out to be right.

"Let's get out of here. Did you get what you need? You're okay? I knew it would be okay."

I follow behind him in Daddy's truck, checking in the cracked rearview mirror to make sure the Haughtrys don't come after us.

CHAPTER 11

— Tinley Greene —

Driving back to the gray house, there's no sign of the Haughtrys and I remind myself to breathe easy. Already I ache to be back with Mark again. I remember telling my mother about the first boy I ever liked, Greer Campbell. He sat next to me in sixth grade, and when we were supposed to be doing worksheets he would pull out a book from his backpack and hold it under his desk reading. He'd look up at me and smile like the two of us were in a secret club. One day Mama was rolling out dough for biscuits in the Haughtrys' kitchen and I told her that Greer knew all the state capitals, even the hard ones like Pierre.

"He sounds like a really nice boy," Mama said, and I felt my face going hot, but I held onto what she said like it was a present.

Later I told her about Brooks Gayton, who held my hand at Candy Evans's fifteenth birthday party, and Chase Honeycutt, who looked like he could be on a soap opera and asked me to the school dance. Now I imagine telling her about Mark, leaving out the pieces of the story involving Mr. Haughtry, the parts I want to forget.

Once we're back at the gray house, Mark and I plant the flowers he brought. Kneeling in the dirt, he pats mulch around the plants and asks if I think Mrs. Haughtry wonders what's happened to me.

I shrug. "I guess she probably does. But surely she knows how her husband can be." When Mr. Haughtry had mentioned me moving into their house, it was Mrs. Haughtry who changed his mind. Maybe she worried something would happen. Maybe she suspected she was married to a monster.

"Well, it doesn't matter now. I'll get you whatever you need. Anything at all. I can bring you more food. It's no big deal."

"You can't keep doing that." *But you have to keep coming here some way.*

"It's really no problem. It's on my way home anyway."

"But it'll start getting expensive."

"Don't worry about it. I've got a good job and—" Mark stops and frowns, picking at one of his fingernails.

"Look, Mark, I'm going to get a job no matter what you say, okay? I need to keep gas in the truck and stuff like that. And I need to pay rent if you'll let me."

"No way on the rent." He shakes his head. "And we'll figure out something for you to do, a way you can make some money."

"Maybe I could clean houses or something. I've watched my mother take care of the Haughtrys' house since I was little."

"Are you sure you wouldn't mind doing that? I mean, if you want to, I could ask some people. But I want to be sure you're okay with it."

"I don't mind at all. I like taking something messy and making it neat again, the way it should be."

"It needs to be something you can do after school. I'll need to talk to a few people. I can tell them a friend of mine is looking for work."

"I'm not going back to school."

"I thought you had another year to finish up." Mark wipes the dirt off his hands and leans back, looking at the flowers. "You were just taking a few days off after what happened, right?"

"I'm not going back there." I can't explain to him what I mean, how I didn't want to go back to school after my parents died, but I had to because everyone told me I should. And I was walking around in a daze anyway. Now that I've woken up, I'm not going to have anything else to do with the Haughtrys. Instead, I'll be a new person doing different things and going different places. Mark and I will do our own thing.

He crosses his arms, watching me.

"Look, I promise I've thought about it." I start tugging off the gardening gloves he brought.

"Are you sure? I just don't know about this. I'm not sure what to tell you." The glove on my right hand gets stuck and Mark reaches for my arm. He picks up my wrist so gently it might be made of glass. Then he peels off the glove for me, clears his throat, and hands it to me. We're standing close and I can't stop looking at him. He takes a step closer and then clears his throat again before turning toward the driveway.

"Are you leaving?" I wring the gloves as I watch Mark go.

He hurries towards the truck and calls out, "I better be going." I wait for him to turn around, but he doesn't.

———

When Mark comes by the next day after work, he says he doesn't want to come inside so I walk down the steps to him.

"I can't stay," he says, holding up his hand and not looking at me. "But I wanted to tell you that I've already found three guys from work who'll pay for help with cleaning and laundry. They don't know how to do laundry, or they've been dragging it up to the Laundry Express out by Roses." He looks down at his feet and touches the toe of one foot with the other shoe. "And you should see how messy some of their places are. Apartments, some of them, and a couple of the guys share a house they're renting. But they're in real bad shape. Dirty dishes in the sink and dog hair on the carpet, stuff like that."

"I don't mind, I promise. I can't believe you're doing all this for me."

He shakes his head. "I wish you wouldn't worry about it."

"Well, I appreciate your help. I really do."

"I bet some people up at the church could probably use some help too." His hair is curled over his forehead, damp-looking, and I want to touch it. "I mean, I probably shouldn't go around asking, but—"

"It's okay, you don't need to do that."

"Okay, then. I'll swing by tomorrow—or sometime, I guess. And you can make me a list if there's anything you want me to get, to bring by for you." Mark's eyes meet mine and he glances away.

He walks back to his truck, and if I could do anything to make him stay, I would do it. If he would only stay here beside me, I could reach up and hold his hair off his forehead. I could tuck a piece of it in my mouth to see what it tastes like.

CHAPTER 12

— *Tinley Greene* —

The next morning I hear a knock at the door and I don't know whether to open it or pretend I'm not there. It's early and I'm in my robe because I've just gotten out of the shower. Daddy's truck is in the driveway and whoever it is will know I'm there, so I pull the door open. Mark is standing there, because who else would be? Nobody else knows where I am. It's like the two of us are the only people in the world. His hand hangs in the air like he was about to knock again and he laughs when he sees me.

"There you are."

"Here I am." My hair falls in front of my face and I push it back behind my ear. "I didn't know you were coming."

"Your hair's wet." Mark reaches out like he's going to touch it, but he lets his hand fall to his side.

"Just a little."

"I'm sorry. You just got out of the shower. I can come back later. It's no big deal."

I shake my head, silently begging him not to leave.

"I'm not sure why I keep coming here. I really shouldn't."

"I'm glad you came. Don't you want to come in?"

He leans against the doorway looking at me and biting his lip.

"Come in. I mean it. You don't need to just stand there."

"I don't know." Mark laughs again and clears his throat. "I don't know what I should be doing." He looks at me without blinking, at my legs and stomach and mostly at my chest where the robe dips open. "You are so—I can't—" His eyes stop at my face and he covers his mouth with his hand.

I touch his waist and pull him, just a little bit, into the house until he's so close to me I can feel him breathing. He reaches behind him to close the door.

"You tell me where you want me to be," he whispers. "And what you want me to do and I'll do it."

Mark keeps whispering, but I can barely hear what he says. The words float toward me, out of order, and barely making any sense. The one word I keep hearing is want. And it's what's underneath everything else, the humming heart of everything.

"I'm not sure if this is a good idea," he says, but his hand is reaching for me when he says it, touching my robe where it clings to my still damp shoulder.

"I'm not sure either," I tell him, but it's a lie because right then I can't imagine stopping him. No part of me can imagine being anywhere else or moving any way other than closer to him.

Mark lets go of my robe and holds his hands up, laughing a quiet, small laugh and shaking his head. "What are we doing here? Who are you?"

Whoever you want me to be. That's who I am.

"Come here." Mark's voice sounds lower than it has been before. He holds me at my waist and pulls me closer. Heat drifts from him and his chest heaves up and down. His belt buckle presses into my stomach, but it doesn't hurt. No part of me can hurt anymore because I'm made out of air, something that has nothing sharp or hard about it, something that moves when and where it needs to.

"Tinley," Mark says, and it's the first time somebody has said my name, because I'm being born all over again.

I press my face into his chest, a sweet taste in my mouth. One second

I'm holding my breath and the next I'm breathing deep. Hot and cold at once. Sweating and shivering. I stare up at him and he looks so perfect—so boyish and sweet, so chiseled and strong—that this might not be real. Maybe in another second I'll have to turn away or something bad will happen. He'll turn to stone or he will fly away like a bird or some other kind of magic.

Mark's other arm wraps around my waist as his hand presses into my back. I reach up to touch the back of his neck. The tiny hairs feel rough like they've been shaven and started to grow back again. He rubs his thumb on my side, a warmth I feel through my robe. When I close my eyes, he reaches for the belt, tied loosely below my stomach, and, with my eyes still closed, I sense it slide through the loops, then hear the satin fall to the floor like a drop of water.

When I open my eyes again, he's staring at my mouth and my lips open and the desire to taste him is something I can feel in my stomach, a kind of wanting that moves and feels alive and hungry. *How close, tell me how close.* The taste of his breath lingers on my lips until there's the sure slip of his tongue against mine.

When we're lying on the bed afterwards, the window is open and the air drifts in through the screen and I breathe in the bright smell of detergent from the sheets. Mark rests his hand at my hip with the sheet draped over his legs. I put my hand on top of his. Nothing that has happened is enough and nothing that will ever happen after this will be enough, not unless it's us coming together again.

After a few minutes, he sits up. "I have to go," he whispers. He grabs the edge of the bed, leaning like he's getting up. "I don't know what I'm doing." His voice shakes in a way I haven't heard before and he jerks his pants to straighten out the legs before he tugs them back on.

"When are you coming back?"

"I don't know. I really don't." Mark slides his feet back into his boots. "Do you need anything? Oh my God—" He presses his finger on the sheet. "There's some blood. I didn't think about it. You're so young, I should've known."

"It's okay. I'll clean it up." They told us in school how it was like that your first time. Part of me feels like I know what I'm doing, and the other part thinks none of this can really be happening.

Mark pulls on his shirt and I want to lift it up again to touch his stomach, but somehow I know it's not what he wants, not now. Instead, I stay in bed, propped up on my elbow, the sheet covering me. He comes up and kisses me on the forehead, the way you'd kiss a child.

"I'll come by later this evening or tomorrow sometime." He picks up his keys from where they've fallen on the floor. As he walks out, he closes the bedroom door and then opens it again. "Tinley—"

"What?" My voice sounds sleepy and I snuggle down into the covers.

"Never mind." Mark pats the doorway and disappears into the hallway. The front door opens and closes, and he's gone.

———

The next day I'm sure he's coming back and I wait for him all day. It's close to five o'clock when I hear footsteps on the porch steps. He is taller than I remembered and his green eyes find me again.

CHAPTER 13

— *Mark Caswell* —

The second time I do wrong by Maddie, it's late afternoon and I have dirt caked under my fingernails and sawdust mixed with sweat in my hair. But Maddie has never been a bit bothered by me showing up after work and this girl isn't either. Both of them are good through and through— Maddie, who I'm set to marry in December, and this girl who needs me.

After what happened last time I shouldn't have come back here. I should have found Tinley somewhere else to stay. We could've gone our separate ways.

But she's impossible to let go of. Lord, this girl. The sweetness in her, even with what she's been through. And curves everywhere you look. I start sweating whenever I think about her.

Right now her hair is pulled back from her face and her legs are twisted up with mine in her bed. She reached for me this second time like she was drowning and I was air and dry land both. Tinley needs me like nobody else does.

"You're something else." I kiss the side of her face, my hand holding her warm, full breast.

She sighs and rests her hand against my arm. "I think this might be the happiest I've ever been."

Since I brought her here, Tinley has acted like this is some kind of mansion instead of just an empty old rental house Daddy told me to look after. When I asked her not to tell anybody where she's staying, she shrugged.

"Nobody to tell," she said.

When she says stuff like that, it cuts me to the quick—the way she doesn't have anybody looking out for her. Nobody but me.

In some other place, somewhere with tall slick buildings made out of glass instead of Garnet with its weathered gray fences and white farmhouses, Tinley would be a girl that people would pay to look at in magazines—wearing a dress cut low in the front and diamonds around her neck or a two-piece swimsuit with sand dusted on her shoulders.

If I hadn't shown up when she was in trouble—if she didn't look the way she does—everything would be different. I'd be out fly fishing in Green River right now, easing up on some trout. When I was done, I'd tip the water out of my waders and head back up the gorge to my truck— breathing heavy but wanting to touch all the trees I passed, to feel the roughness of the bark, to rest for a minute under the shade of rustling leaves.

I've always liked the way Garnet is an in-between place. Coming up from South Carolina, the railroad grade rises so steeply that back before there was diesel, they had to bring in helper engines to push the trains up. And if you head down to Garnet from the north, from Wyeth's Mill where Mama's Aunt Callie used to live, the road cuts through the mountain—steep with rocks on one side and trees down to the river on the other. But the steepness eases off a bit in Garnet, especially on the road where I was raised—gives people a rest.

Tinley runs her hand down my arm and hooks my fingers with hers. "I can't believe you," I whisper, closing my eyes against being here—with the wrong girl. Through the open window, the smell of smoke drifts in. Somebody outside is burning leaves, I guess. Once something is burned up, you can't get it back—same as the mistake I've made.

She moves in bed, closer to me. The mattress shifts—a creaking sound—and then Tinley leans her head on my chest and it should be quiet. But I hear something moving. Something outside. A car—in the driveway or near it. *Oh my God.* I sit up fast, brushing Tinley off. "This can't be happening." I have to get out, have to move fast. Out of bed, my clothes on the floor. Lunging, reaching, I yank up my pants and throw on my shirt and leave it unbuttoned. When I tear into the hallway, Tinley scurries after me with the sheet wrapped around her.

The wood floor feels smooth under my bare feet, and through the living room window a truck backs up in the driveway and turns onto the road. White. I think the truck is white like Daddy's. But nothing has much color—not now. It seems like the color has drained out of everything all of a sudden, leaving only gray and white behind.

"It's nothing," Tinley says from behind me. "Nobody's here. It's nothing," she says again. I turn around in time to see her turn back toward the bedroom, the sheet dragging behind her like a long train on a wedding dress.

Following close behind her, a sour taste comes up in my mouth. "Look. I don't know what I was thinking, how I ever thought—"

"Would you be in trouble if somebody found out you let me stay here?" She turns around, a concerned look on her face.

I don't answer her. I just laugh and it comes out like a dog barking. Where are my shoes? I have to find my keys and get out of here. Then I'll go find Maddie. There could never be a good reason to do something like this to her. Somebody else can save this girl. Not me. I can't do it anymore. Never should've tried. I shouldn't have let it get out of hand like this.

"I could pack my stuff. It wouldn't take me long at all. Is that what you're worried about?" Tinley leans against the bed. "You could take me up to the church and when I find a new place, I'll call you." She lets the sheet slide down, pulling on her dress from where it's draped on the footboard, then nudges her underwear up from the floor with her big toe.

"That's not it." I shake my head. "It's not about the house." If it was, I could fix that. The thing about an evened-out place surrounded by mountains, I remember, is that before long, you're headed back up or back down.

"It's okay. Whatever it is." She scoots her underwear up over her skinny legs and brushes her dress back down. "And nobody was out there anyway, if that's why you're worried. I'm sure it's fine."

"You don't know that for sure." It's the truth, but an ugly thing to say all the same. Maybe this is who I am now. Somebody who takes things too far, who gets in too deep before he knows what kind of water he is in. My fingers are shaking and the buttons on my shirt won't fit in the holes.

"Do you need some help with that?" Tinley reaches toward me, but I pull back.

"I can get it."

"Are you okay? Mark, what's going on?"

"This isn't a good idea. I have to get out of here." I slide my work boots on, not stopping to lace them up. My hand lands on the back of her neck, the hair on the top of her head ticklish under my lips. "I'm sorry," I whisper, something hollowed out already, something inside dried out and past growing back. Tinley doesn't follow me out of the bedroom, but she looks up when I turn back toward her.

CHAPTER 14

— *Clive Caswell* —

When I saw Mark's truck over at the gray house, I couldn't think of what he might be doing there. And the light blue truck parked next to his—I didn't recall ever seeing it before. Maybe I should've stopped and gone in. But Mark was a grown boy and I thought—I knew—he could take care of himself. When I was his age I wanted to figure things out on my own, even if I made a mistake or two along the way, and Mark deserved the same.

Not long after that, I was up at Dell's body shop having him replace the brake pads on my truck. Dell gave me a cup of coffee while I waited and paced around watching him work. Eventually the conversation came around to all the cars and trucks he'd bought and sold over the years, and I asked about a light blue Chevy truck, nine or ten years old, give or take.

"That blue's a color you don't see too often," Dell said. He scratched his head, then nodded. "Would have to be the one I got off of the Honeycutts."

"Who'd you sell it to?"

"Turned around and sold it to somebody who worked over at the Haughtrys' place. Last name Greene."

I took a sip of coffee. "Not that couple whose car went off Beulah Road last spring?"

"That's the one. Awful mess. Their girl is still with the Haughtrys, last I heard."

"There was some talk of her after the wreck, I remember. High school or thereabouts?"

"Probably sixteen, seventeen. Don't see her around town much, not that I ran into her parents too often either. They kept to themselves mostly, unless they needed something."

As soon as Dell was finished with the truck, I paid and left. I didn't have any reason to suspect Mark of anything. I didn't have the time or inclination to go by the gray house again. I had to get home anyway. We were running behind on the last hay cutting, and I had cattle to get ready for the stockyard. Any farmer worth his weight knows two things. You don't ever rest—you've got to stay on top of everything. And the other is that you have to be patient. It sounds like a contradiction, but it's not. After you've planted, as long as you keep up with the weeding and the stakes and runners, there's not much left to do except wait for rain—and trust that, come spring, what you planted shoots up through the dirt.

CHAPTER 15

— *Tinley Greene* —

"I don't know, Tinley. About any of this," Mark had said, standing in the bedroom doorway. "I don't know what I was thinking."

"What are you talking about?" Still in my bare feet, I followed behind him through the living room and watched him go out the front door. When I called out after him, he shook his head.

He didn't come the next day, or the next. The guys he worked with left their laundry in front of their doors. When I picked it up, I imagined running into Mark with one of his friends, coming over to watch some game on TV. But I never saw anybody, only a yellow lab who licked my hand when I held it out. One day at one of the apartments, there was a note for me from one of the logging guys, asking if I could start cleaning for his mother, Mrs. Price. He'd written down the address for me. Two weeks went by and I needed to see Mark in a way that felt a lot like starving.

By the next Sunday I decide what I have to do. I've washed my hair and I put on my nicest sundress, the yellow one. Even though it's from the Bargain Box, it's my favorite dress. The waist is fitted and flares out slightly at the hips. The straps are trimmed with lace. As soon as Mark sees me, I'm convinced he'll break out in a big smile.

At first I have the radio on in the truck, but the music makes me too nervous so I turn it off. I roll down the window a little bit, enough for a breeze but not enough to mess up my hair. Outside, the air is practically buzzing with the smell of golden hay drying in the sun. Even though the leaves are changing, the summer's heat keeps hanging on.

On the way to the house Mark showed me, I wonder how surprised he'll look when I knock on the door, how happy he'll be to see me. Before I get out, I check my hair in the mirror and put on lip gloss that smells like peach candy.

I knock on the door, my chin raised even though my palms have grown slick with sweat. The door opens to a guy with long hair the color of dirty dishwater.

"Are you Cliff? Mark's roommate?"

"Yeah, you guessed it." He puts out his hand for me to shake. "You want to come in or something?"

After we shake hands, he looks me up and down and tucks his hair behind his ear. "I don't believe we've met. Are you a friend of Maddie's?" I hear what he says, but I'm not thinking about it, not really, because I'm full with the thought of finding Mark and him kissing me and there's no room for anything else. "I'm a friend of Mark's. Is he here?"

Cliff looks at my chest and down to my feet. "Mark's friend, huh? What a nice surprise."

"Do you know where he is?"

"He doesn't really fill me in on all the details. They've got a big list of things to do, I guess." He scratches his chin, scruffy with the start of a beard, and leans against the doorframe.

He might as well be talking in a foreign language. "Who are you talking about? What do you mean?"

"Who do you think I'm talking about?" Cliff lifts up his jeans where they've slipped down.

"I'm asking about Mark. Mark Caswell. I just want to know where he is. Do you know? Can you tell me?"

He laughs, "Yeah, I guess they're still at church. That or they're up at the house for dinner. His parents' house. Anything else you want to know? Want me to take you up there?"

"No, I know where it is."

"I can't wait to hear all about it," he calls out after me. "Almost makes me want to go up there and see for myself."

When I turn back to ask Cliff what he means, he's already pushing the door closed with his bare foot. I brush him off like I'd flick away a mosquito and climb in the truck.

CHAPTER 16

— *Tinley Greene* —

Everybody knows where the church is, not far from the Haughtrys' house. A red brick building with a little porch and a pointy white steeple, and a square red brick building beside it where they must have birthday parties and things like that. The parking lot looks full so I find a spot in the gravel lot across the street.

Waiting on Mark to come out is too hard. I decide I might as well go inside. All these years living here and I don't think I've ever been inside. I remember passing by the church and thinking everybody in town went there except us and the few people who were Methodist. Still, it's never hit me until now, this feeling of being outside and having to push my way in to be noticed.

Inside the heavy doors, there's a blast of cool air. Light gray walls and tall windows trimmed in white and a multi-colored window at the front above where the choir sits showing Jesus on the cross. I find an empty seat two rows from the back, and as soon as I sit down, I look around for Mark, searching up and down each row until I finally see him up near the front. The back of his neck is a little red from the sun and he's wearing a nice blue dress shirt. My cheeks start to feel hot. Beside Mark sits a tall, gray-haired man and a woman with gray hair pulled back into a bun. I wipe my sweaty hands on the seat cushion as I realize they must be his parents.

"Come get right with the Lord," the preacher says in a loud voice that makes me jump. He comes down the step at the front of the church and marches up and down the middle aisle. "You know who you are," he says, waving a Bible in the air. "Come get right with the Lord. All it takes is one step. Make that first step out into the aisle, brother. Take that step on faith, sister." He nods as the choir stands up and the woman at the piano leans forward to start playing. "Let's all rise and join in on hymn number three hundred and seven."

The songbook gets heavier in my hand until I'm not sure I can hold onto it any longer. Everybody sings, looking down at the words. Across the aisle, a woman bends down to hush her baby. Every now and then, I can see the woman at the piano up front closing her eyes.

"Just as I am," the words go. "Without one plea, but that thy blood was shed for me." I think about all that Mark and I have done and about how real it is, and how he's sitting up there with his perfect parents and it feels like we're so far away from each other. There might as well be an ocean between us instead of rows of caramel-colored wooden pews, and I need to be closer to him, to talk to him, to hear him say he still wants me, that he's wanted me since the day we met.

As soon as the service is over, people gather up their purses and bulletins and candy wrappers and Bibles, shuffling down the aisles. I wait for Mark to turn around, but I can't see him through the crowd of people and I don't have a choice but to move out of the pew with everybody else.

People line up to speak to the preacher on their way out. Instead I sneak down the side aisle and outside, keeping my head down the whole time, suddenly conscious of my old dress and scuffed shoes. From the parking lot I see Mark's parents coming down the front steps. Mark isn't with them. All around me people are saying, "good to see you," "is that a new dress?" and "how sweet of you to notice." And "God bless you" and "how well you're looking" and "I haven't heard anything else on Abner, but I'll check in on him sometime this week." When Mark's father touches his mother on the elbow as they come down the steps, I stop walking, telling myself that I belong with them. His family is the kind of family that I want.

Mark's mother carries a black leather purse hooked over her wrist. Behind them are some people I don't know, and finally coming down the steps there's Mark. He's handsome in a stop-what-you're-doing kind of way. Brushed and clean in his navy blue suit pants and his light blue button-down shirt and his cheeks that are pink from the sun. The people between Mark and his parents walk off in different directions and Mark comes up beside his father. That's when I see the girl beside Mark. I've met her before. Back in the summer she and her parents came up to the Haughtrys' house about some church committee. Maddie Spencer, standing right up close to Mark—maybe even touching him. Her dress is dark pink, the color of fruit punch, and her blonde hair lays on her shoulders like a cape made of pure gold.

People crowd around the bottom of the steps, but I push through them to get closer. "Excuse me," I say. "I just need to get up here for a second." I shake my head like I can erase her, but when I look again she is still beside Mark, and I remember Cliff asking about Maddie. Maddie who is standing close to Mark, whose bare arm brushes his. She wears gold earrings, tiny bows with a pearl in the middle, and her narrow belt is made out of the same pink material as her dress.

"You'll just meet us at the house then? Your mama will have the chicken ready, won't be but a minute," Mark's father says.

"Yes, sir." Mark nods, squinting in the sun. "We'll be right behind you."

Maddie smiles up at him and they walk quickly toward the parking lot. And they don't stop even when Mark sees me. He looks away, but I know he sees me.

CHAPTER 17

— Mark Caswell —

We're almost to the truck in the church parking lot when Maddie touches my elbow and I let out a yell same as if a bobcat snuck up on me in the woods.

"Are you all right?" She squeezes my arm and I blink. Once. Twice. Maddie is still there, still squeezing my arm. Pale, pink, pretty, perfect Maddie. Her hair smells like honeysuckle. I don't see Tinley anywhere. *Breathe. I've got to breathe.*

"I'm all right. You just startled me, that's all."

"Well, I'm sorry about that." Maddie reaches into the front pocket of my dress pants. Her fingers scratch my leg through the material, teasing.

I reach for her wrist. "You better watch it, or the gossip will be that we were going at it in the church parking lot." I raise my eyebrows daring her to look around. Trying to act like nothing is wrong. The Honeycutts' Taurus is parked two spaces over, and Mr. Honeycutt opens the door for his wife, waiting for her to squeeze in before he shuts it.

Maddie pulls the truck keys out of my pocket and holds them up, laughing. "You worry too much, Mark. All of a sudden." She checks the truck doors, finds them unlocked, and climbs in the passenger side. When I close my eyes and open them again, she's still there. Small and blonde. Waiting for me. How a girl like that is waiting on me—

She rolls down her window. "Hey, are you looking for something out there?"

Reaching in through the window, I lift up her hair from her shoulders. "Did I ever tell you how pretty your hair is?"

Maddie shakes her head. "Maybe. I don't know."

"I want to take care of you. You know that, don't you?" I kiss her face right by her ear.

"We take care of each other, Mark. That's how it is." I nod and pat the door of the truck. Walking around to the driver's side, I hear Maddie rolling the window back up, the little whine the handle makes. She shouldn't have to take care of me.

When I climb into the truck, Maddie looks over and smiles. There's a can of WD-40 by her foot and I bend down to shove it under her seat so it won't get her shoes dirty. She rubs her thumb on the back of my neck and for a second, only a second, I let my head rest on her lap. *You can take care of me. Please.*

But I have to sit up again, have to see all the people in the parking lot, coming and going. Talking and laughing. Swallowing hard, I start up the truck. I don't see where Tinley has gone. She must have left. The way she was just standing there, looking at me—did she come by looking for me? And she saw Maddie too, right by me. Still, I couldn't have expected to keep it a secret forever. If Tinley had asked anyone in town about me, they would've told her that Maddie and I are getting married. How did I think she would just disappear and not cause any trouble?

A car door slams and somebody yells out their window that they're going to swing by on Tuesday and somebody calls back, "See you then." I remember the truck turning around in the driveway at the gray house, how close Tinley and I came to being found out then. But I don't think Maddie noticed anything today. She didn't see Tinley staring. Then again, in a place like Garnet, everybody eventually finds out everybody's business.

I remind myself to keep breathing. Someone around town might have seen me with Tinley. If they told Maddie about it, I'd have to think of some excuse. And I don't know if she would believe me. I don't know how I've gotten to this messed-up place, how I got so lost right when I had everything I wanted.

Idling at the parking lot exit, I take my hands off the wheel to yank a thread off the sleeve of my shirt. Twisting it around my finger, I watch the skin turn red and then white. Then I let the thread go. Unraveling. I almost say the word out loud. This is all unraveling right here, right now.

On the way to Mama and Daddy's, Maddie talks about the wedding and our new house and I nod and tell her we can do things however she wants. White walls everywhere sound fine. No, I don't think they'll get too dirty. If they do, Maddie, I'll clean them off for you. I grip the steering wheel, wishing I was scrubbing something clean right now. Wishing I could go over and over a blank stretch of wall until my arms shake from being tired.

We turn onto Maranatha Road and I tell myself I'm almost home. Safe. Mama will have dinner about ready. Tinley wouldn't ever come by the house. I told her which house it is, but she'd know better than to do that, wouldn't she? The radio switches from bluegrass to the race and Maddie turns the dial before giving up and turning it off. We ease off the blacktop onto the gravel driveway.

"I've always liked how your parents' house is set back from the road." Maddie looks out the window where the driveway cuts through the corn fields. Up around the big white house are old pastures and fences made out of weathered wood, just this side of crumbling rotten, running across the front yard and stopping where the fields start. Years ago Daddy's family moved the cows down to some land by the river, but they kept the fences up anyway. I was six, maybe seven years old, when I started climbing on those fences. Back then, all I had to do to right myself was lean a little bit the other way.

CHAPTER 18

— *Tinley Greene* —

If I went up to the house, I could talk to Mark and find out what's going on. But I keep picturing Maddie Spencer on those church steps—all coolness and strawberry pink and perfect teeth when she smiled at him. In the truck mirror I look nothing like her. I'm red-faced and my dishwater-colored hair needs combing and won't ever lay down flat like hers or be as blonde as hers. And I can't go up there and have them stare at me—Mark pushing back his chair and putting his napkin on the table, looking all surprised that I'm there.

Back at the gray house, I pull the curtains closed, lock the door, and crawl into bed. When I wake up later, I'm mad at myself for sleeping all afternoon. What if Mark came by and I didn't hear him knocking? But after I eat some crackers straight from the box, I fall back in bed.

The next morning I have to be at the Maybins' house before noon and the Prices after that, where Mrs. Price wants me to pull up the weeds in the front flowerbed. The whole time I'm yanking those weeds up out of the ground I imagine they're pieces of Maddie Spencer's blonde hair.

When I get back to the house, Mark's truck is in the driveway, the engine still running. I suck in my stomach as I go up to the driver's window, waving. When he sees me, Mark turns off the truck and gets out. He moves slowly, like his legs are stiff.

"We should probably talk, I guess." He sighs and rakes his hand through his hair, using his fingers like a comb.

"Do you want to come in?"

Mark shrugs, but he follows me inside and into the living room.

"Do you want something to drink?" I ask him. "I could get some tea."

"Tinley, I can't do this anymore," Mark says, his eyes not meeting mine.

Something twitches in my chest. Maybe he means the house and I offer to move my things out, promising it won't take long to pack, but he shakes his head, his arms dangling by his sides.

"I saw you yesterday at the church," I say quietly.

Mark nods and sits down on the couch. He looks down at his lap, a dullness in his eyes that might be close to tears, and it's impossible to be mad at him.

"It's okay." My voice cracks and I clear my throat.

"It's not, though. It's not okay, Tinley."

"You can talk to her. You can tell her what's going on, what's happened between us."

Mark makes a face like he's hurting somewhere.

"If you can just tell me what's going on—"

"I'm not sure what we're doing. But I've messed up. I wanted to help you and you—I mean, look at you. God. I've never seen any girl like you." Mark drops his eyes to his lap again. "But I didn't mean—we can't—we can't do this anymore." Then he looks up at me—looks me straight in the eyes—and that's when I start to panic. The whole thing is impossible. It can't be happening. I ease onto the couch beside him and reach out to touch his arm. His skin feels warm under my fingers.

"Tinley, I'm not sure what you think's going on here. But Maddie can't find out about this, how I've messed up, okay? She can't. We have to pretend it never happened. I'm sorry. I don't want you to feel like you haven't got anybody, especially now, after everything that's happened to you."

"You're not making any sense." I try to laugh like this is all a joke, but it comes out like a gasp. *I do have somebody. I have you.*

"I never meant for this to happen. This thing with Maddie, it's not something I can throw away."

I let go of his arm and let my hand fall to my lap until my fingers press against my stomach. Like I can somehow protect myself. My heart beats fast, out of control. The house around us sits still and quiet, the only sound the refrigerator humming in the kitchen. But I feel like there must be an invisible storm blowing closer and closer.

"We're supposed to be getting married, me and Maddie."

The words punch me in the stomach. "You'll find a way to fix it." *You have to.* "You don't have to marry her. Nobody's making you." I reach over to touch Mark's knee, but he tilts it away from me.

"I know." He nods. "But I want to."

"How can you say that?"

"Tinley, I don't think—I don't think you get what I'm saying. I don't—I'm not trying to find a way out of marrying her. If I could turn things around and do it all over, I'd have gone ahead and married her the day she said yes."

"But she isn't—" *She's not me. She can't love you like I do.*

"I only wanted to help you, but every time I got close to you—"

"That's real, Mark. What we have is real."

"I should've dropped you off at the church and been done with it." Mark bites his lip. "I'm sorry. It's an awful thing to say, that you were some kind of a mistake."

Mark stands up and before I know it, he's at the front door, reaching for the handle, and I have to say something to keep him here. Something, anything. There has to be a way for me to keep him.

"I'm pregnant." The lie comes out on its own before I can even consider it. I cover my mouth with my hand. I might throw up.

"What did you say?" Mark stares at me, frowning. "What?"

I pause, not sure whether to keep going with the lie. What could I say to make him see it—that we have to be together?

"We're supposed to be together," I finally say. "We're going to be a family, you and me and the baby." If I can get him to see how we would be as a family, then he'll go back to the way he was before. And later I can explain that I was wrong about being pregnant and it will be okay because we'll be together. I have to try to keep him from slipping away because he's all I have.

Mark stares at me without blinking.

"Look, this is going to be okay, right? Tell me it's going to be okay." I beg him.

He shakes his head. "The truth is, Maddie is the first thing I think about every morning when I wake up," he whispers.

I reach out to grab his arm, but he jerks it back, like you'd jump back from a hot stove, and then he's outside, the front door flung open behind him, heading for his truck.

I chase after him, trying not to cry, but I'm too slow and Mark gets in the truck and backs out of the driveway and into the road. As he drives away, I finally let myself cry, my arms crossed over my chest like I'm hugging myself. I sink down to the ground, the grass prickly under my legs, and rock back and forth, still crying and trying to decide what to do. I could grab my keys and try to find Mark. Or I could let him go. The choice swirls around me until I'm dizzy. The trees in the yard seem to be the only solid thing in the world. I crane my neck to look up at the sky, even as the clouds break apart and float away.

PART FOUR

Tinley Greene, Clive Caswell,
and Sadie Caswell

OCTOBER 1998–JUNE 2001

CHAPTER 19

— *Sadie Caswell* —

I told Willa I'd get to the bridge as quick as I could and I slammed down the phone. I don't know how I got in the car, but I was still wearing my old house dress and I hadn't even stopped to put on shoes. The gas pedal was rough under my foot and I pressed down on it harder, speeding up as I passed the Watsons' home place, then around the big curve and by Solid Rock, the red brick church and the fellowship hall beside it. The closer I got to the bridge, the more the mountains pressed into me on the one side, making it harder and harder to breathe. I prayed and then prayed some more. Up ahead the sun started to slip down behind the trees and I drove faster, looking to where I knew the bridge would be.

When I got there, I turned off the road and onto the dirt. Mark's truck was parked to the side of the bridge and I pulled up beside it. I looked inside, but the truck was empty. At first I couldn't see anybody around anywhere and I thought it was all a big mistake. I'd misheard what Willa said or she was wrong. Or they had fixed things up and left—Mark with his flushed cheeks and his long fingers and his hair probably flopped over his forehead, damp with sweat. By now, he was probably somewhere laughing about it all.

Rocks covered the ground by the railing. When Mark was little, he might have liked to throw them over, waiting to hear them land way down below with an echo. "Again, again," he would have said, swinging his tiny hands.

Breathing hard, I looked around again, trying to figure out where Mark could be. He wasn't in his truck or near the bushes off to the side. I made myself dizzy turning around in a circle looking for him. The asphalt road curving away toward South Carolina. The dirt pull-off where Mark's truck was parked. The metal railing of the bridge, almost as high as my hip. Birds soaring in the airy gap between the bridge and the wavy, blue mountains way off in the distance. Mark wasn't anywhere.

My legs shook as I ran to the bridge. I screamed Mark's name and waited for him to answer me. I didn't hear anything except cars going by on the road behind me, and they all sounded the same until a tractor trailer came by that was louder than all the rest put together.

The railing of the bridge was warm from the sun. When another car went by, the metal buzzed against my leg. I tried to catch my breath. Looking out over the bridge was like being inside some kind of an oil painting. The sky was spread out above the mountains. No wind, so the air was still. Clouds hung in the air, strands of white—mostly see-through—against the blue. Far off in the distance the uneven line of mountains, the trees sponged with orange and red.

Heat built up in my chest as I looked out over the railing. I studied the rocks scattered on the slope before I let myself look down. Down and further down the gorge's sheer drop.

And there below on the ground—how many hundreds of feet?—nothing more than a smudge. A smudge shaped like Mark. The dark brown of his hair, the blue of his pants and his legs bent like he was about to take off running. Run baby, I wanted to say, except I knew it was too late for that. Overhead a bird called and it sounded like a cry. Hush now, baby. Hush.

CHAPTER 20

— Sadie Caswell —

Behind me a car pulled off the road, but I didn't turn around. It didn't matter who it was. The next thing I knew, a girl ran up to the bridge, screaming Mark's name. Her face was red and sweaty. A stranger, some girl I'd never laid eyes on before.

"I tried to follow him and I saw your car so then I followed you." She shook her head and wiped her nose. "Why is Mark's truck here? Where is he?"

I made myself breathe in and out. But I couldn't make myself answer her. She wasn't anything to me anyway. I couldn't see how much of anything mattered anymore, not when my boy was down at the bottom of the gorge like he was.

The girl saw him too. I don't know what made her look, but she did and she let out a loud scream and bit her hand so hard it drew blood.

Minutes or maybe hours later, EMS showed up and some boys picked their way down the slope with a folded-up stretcher between them. By that time, the girl had folded herself up small and was wedged halfway under a bush off to the side.

While I waited for them to bring up Mark, I went over to where the girl was whimpering like some kind of hurt animal. I asked who she was and what she had to do with Mark, why she was following him. She wouldn't answer me. When I yelled right in her face, she picked at the knee of her tight jeans and mumbled something about trying to keep him.

"What did you say?"

"We might have argued and maybe he wasn't sure, but he loved me," she said finally. "I know he did."

I knew then what she was about, some girl who wanted Mark but couldn't have him—the way she must have been after him, bothering him, following him around town, pestering him.

When the EMS people came up from the gorge, they took it slow, stepping over rocks and pressing into the steepness like you'd lean into a strong wind. One of them carried an orange bag over his shoulder and it bumped against his hip as he moved.

"Watch it," one of them said. Another one said, "Just a minute," and reached down to adjust the stretcher between them with a white sheet draped over the top. The sheet was loose, but nothing was moving under it. I knew it was there because Mark wasn't fit to look at. I knew it, but just the same I wanted to climb over the railing and lift up that sheet to see for myself.

When I thought about how he was gone, I was almost sick to my stomach. I flung my hand over my mouth. The smell of those potatoes was still on my fingers, the smell of dirt and bitter skin. I would've given anything to be standing back in the kitchen. When I didn't know.

Birds flew overhead making a ca-ca sound, and the noise echoed out over the gorge. Some boy from the sheriff's department came up holding Clive by the elbow. He stumbled around like his legs weren't working right, like he couldn't feel the ground underneath them, the way you feel for a step in the dark. The boy from the sheriff's department led him up to me.

"I don't think it can be right, what they're saying." Clive looked at me and shook his head.

"I guess it is. I saw him myself."

Clive grabbed hold of my hands. It was starting to get dark and a little chilly, the Indian summer finally letting go. He faced me and kept his back to the bridge where they were bringing up the stretcher. He didn't even turn around. That's how Clive was, I guess. Once I'd told him it was true, he didn't have any need to see for himself. He looked down at me and closed his eyes, swaying back and forth. Below us something bumped as they moved the stretcher up and over the railing. It jostled when they set it down on the ground and I let go of Clive's hands. I reached out like Mark was going to fall off that stretcher, like I could do something to keep it from happening.

One of the EMS workers saw me. "We've got him strapped in, ma'am." He patted the straps buckled over the sheet like that solved everything.

The sun had disappeared behind the mountain by then. A boy from the sheriff's department was talking to that girl, and he called out for somebody to bring him a blanket. He wrapped it around her like she was something that would break, and it was more than I could stand, seeing her petted and coddled and fussed over, that girl who must have caused all of this. Otherwise, what was she doing there? Clive put his hand on my arm, but I ignored him and walked over to them.

"She's the reason this happened." I said, pointing at that girl sitting there shivering, wrapped up in the blanket. "She said they argued, that she was following him. She had no reason to be doing that." The sheriff's boy looked at me like he didn't know what I was talking about, like he hadn't heard me right. "It's her fault." The more I talked, the louder I got. "You need to listen to me. You need to get her out of here and charge her with something."

"I don't see that she's at fault, ma'am." He patted the girl on the shoulder and stood up with his hands at his waist and his stomach puffed out over his pants. He couldn't have been more than twenty-two years old.

"What do you know about anything? You weren't here, not anywhere close," I told him. The girl pulled the blanket tighter around her, staring at me.

The sheriff's boy shook his head. "Ma'am, I hear what you're saying and I understand where you're coming from. I really do."

"You don't understand anything."

He looked down at the ground. "Not about losing somebody like that. You've got me there."

"Well, then you do your job and get her out of here." I pointed to where the girl was bent under the blanket crying, shaking her head and biting her hand.

"Look, Miss Greene is just as upset about this as you are."

"Miss Greene?"

"Yes," he looked down at his notepad and flipped back to an earlier page. "Tinley Ann Greene."

I guess I started screaming then. I told him I didn't need to know her name and that if she was upset, then it was her own fault.

"No, ma'am, that's not what happened here." He said it wasn't possible, not when you looked at how high the railing was. A person would have to climb over it. A girl her size couldn't have picked up somebody his size or pushed him over. "I'm sorry," he said. "It just couldn't happen that way. You have to look at the facts of the situation."

It wasn't what I meant. He didn't understand. How if it hadn't been for her, Mark wouldn't have done what he did. Mark would have still been alive. Clive came up with his arms crossed telling me to calm down. But I kept screaming at the sheriff's boy and that girl. I screamed louder than I ever knew I could. If you listened hard enough, I guess you could hear me screaming in every part of Garnet, all over Wynette County, clear down to Haird, and up to Yates County, in Wyeth's Mill and all the way up to Bennettsville.

CHAPTER 21

— *Tinley Greene* —

Mark's mother screams at me and, even though I cover my ears and pretend to be somewhere else, I still hear her. Part of me wants to scream back at her, but mostly I want to wrap my arms around her and tell her I understand. That I loved Mark too. That I can't imagine him being gone. Someone pulls her away and somebody else from the sheriff's office says he needs to ask me a few questions about how I came to be there.

"I went by the house he lives in now, but Mark's truck wasn't there," I explain, remembering how desperate I was to find him. "So then I tried the house where he grew up and his mother was tearing down the driveway and I worried something had happened."

"So you followed her out here?"

I nod, tugging the blanket closer.

The officer writes something down on his little note pad, no bigger than a stack of cards.

A sheriff's department car is parked by Mark's truck and the blue lights keep flashing and it's like they should be making noise, but they're broken and there's no noise at all. A few feet away next to the bridge an ambulance waits with its back doors open. The writing on the side says "Wynette Rescue Services." It's too late for rescuing though. There's nothing left to save.

I bite down on my knee, feeling the sharpness of my teeth through my jeans. "That's all I know."

He nods. "What happened? How did you know Mark Caswell?"

"He was upset. I don't know." I shake my head.

"What was your relationship with him?"

"I loved him."

"Okay." He frowns and purses his lips. "Were you his girlfriend? Look, I'm sorry. I haven't been back here for long. I don't know—"

"Yeah, I was. At least I thought—I mean, yes, I was."

He squats down on the ground beside me. "I'm going to need you to tell me everything you can remember, okay?"

At first I don't answer. I can't think of what to say except that the only goodness in the world showed up when the two of us were together. That I remember when I first met Mark, when the brightness in him made all the darkness disappear. When it was like magic.

"Look, you take all the time you need, okay? But you're going to need to tell me what you know. I need to take it all down." The officer taps his pen on the note pad. "Do you have a way home?"

"No, I don't have anybody."

"That's okay. Once we finish up here, we'll run you home if you don't feel up to driving."

I don't even have a home, I want to say. The house where I'm staying is his. It belongs to the Caswells. But I can't think of anywhere else to go and it's the place Mark would want me to be. It's where he would come to look for me. Even though I know he's not coming, I still catch myself thinking he might. He might even be there waiting on me, sitting on the front steps flipping his keys around in his hand, wondering where I am and what's taking me so long.

This is all a bad dream. It has to be. I'll wake up and it will be a different day, brand-new and nothing like this one. Daddy will be shaving in the bathroom. I'll hear the razor scrape across his neck and the tapping as he hits it against the edge of the sink and the water running when he rinses it off. Mama will be at the stove cooking breakfast, the biscuits wrapped in a towel to keep warm on the table. I whisper the words *Mama* and *Daddy* and *Mark* out loud, imagining that I can summon them back, that the sound of my voice will drift across the sky to reach them.

"Is the blanket helping at all? You feeling any better?" The officer clears his throat. "We've got all the time in the world, okay? You just take your time."

I make myself force the words out. We argued. I tried to stop Mark from leaving. I tried to keep him. He was mine.

CHAPTER 22

— *Sadie Caswell* —

Libby and Warren got up to the house late that night. As soon as they came in the door, I grabbed Libby by the arm and buried my face in her chest. She held on to me until I pulled away to get them something to eat.

For days after Mark died, Clive didn't go outside. I'd never known him to be inside so much, not even when there was snow on the ground. But after Mark died, Clive sat in the den watching the television.

Even though people from the church brought casseroles, I stuck them in the freezer and made things I knew Clive favored. One day I made chicken pot pie, something he always liked. The first pie came out doughy in the middle and burnt on the sides, so I threw it in the scrap bucket and made another one. But it never got brown like it should so I dumped it in a bowl to make soup with later and started over again. The third one was light brown all over, like they all should've been, and I brought a plate for Clive in the den and held it out to him. He acted like he didn't see me, just stared at the television where there was an advertisement for a vacuum cleaner. I put the plate on the floor beside him with the fork on top.

Clive nodded right as I turned to go. "Appreciate it."

I didn't say anything back because I didn't have anything to tell him, and there were things I needed to do. Hymns to pick out, the songs Mark would've wanted, the ones he used to like singing at church. He used to stand beside me in the church and mark the place in the hymnal with his finger.

Markinson's had said three o'clock for the visitation the last time I talked to them, even though I'd asked for four o'clock. Libby and Warren were off getting something to keep coffee hot for when people came to the house afterwards, but they might need to go back for extra cups and napkins because we didn't have enough, not if a lot of people came. The florist had left a message that white lilies were too hard to get this time of year. Once I dealt with her, I had to make sure Pastor Mason would speak at the funeral, not that Pastor Weaver who didn't know anything and looked like he was about twelve years old, even with that beard of his.

Maddie's parents had said they would take care of canceling everything with the wedding, that we didn't need to worry about that on top of the funeral. Whenever I saw Maddie, her eyes were red and she kept twisting her pearl ring around her finger. Right after we'd gotten home from the bridge, the Spencers were waiting at the house in that fancy car of theirs. All three of them looked pale and tired. They kept shaking their heads and Maddie tore up a tissue until it was nothing but little pieces. I never breathed a word to her about the girl who'd been with Mark. Eventually she probably heard it around town. But the only thing I could think to tell her was that Mark loved her. If I could've thought of any way to make what she was feeling ease up, I would've done it.

When we were getting ready for the visitation, Warren kept Clive company and Libby followed me around the house. She kept talking about every other funeral we'd had in the family just like they were all the same. Mama's and Daddy's and Aunt Callie's. She didn't have anything better to do than to tell me about all the wreaths they had at Daddy's, so many they wouldn't all fit on the coffin. I told her I didn't care one bit how many wreaths there would be at Mark's, but she needed to write down who sent what on account of the thank you notes.

"Sadie, you know I'll do anything you need me to," she said.

"You can keep the list and do the notes too. I don't know all those people anyway."

"Let me do it. You've never been good with keeping names straight. I'm not saying there's anything wrong with it. You're better at other things, that's all."

"Names or faces either. Just go ahead and say it, Libby. You know that's how it is."

"It doesn't matter. I'll talk to people who come up to the house too. You don't need to worry about that. Here, let me do the sweeping." She tried to take the broom out of my hand, and I turned away from her. Libby might have thought she was helping, not that I'd asked her to and not that I needed any sort of help. She was only in the way, I decided, bumping into me in the kitchen and following me around in the hallway.

"I'm doing it and when I finish down here, I'm going to do the upstairs too," I told her. "First the wood floors in the hallway and then I'll get the mop to do the bathroom floors. You can go sit down with Clive and Warren."

"Sadie, it's probably best if you get some rest." Libby frowned. "Don't you want to get some rest?"

"You don't need to treat me like a child, not now, not all of a sudden." I shook my head and started sweeping. There were crumbs everywhere, some cobwebs too, especially in the corners.

"You're going to do what you want to do. But I wish you'd let me help. I wish you'd let somebody take care of you. If you're not going to do it, I mean." She reached again to take the broom out of my hand. "Here, give me that. Let me have it and you go on upstairs. Get some rest."

"I don't need to rest."

"You do. You're more tired than you think. It's going to sneak up on you."

"Libby, I'm sixty-two years old and I can take care of myself. But I thank you for your concern and I'll have you mind your own business."

"At least let me get you some tea or something. Have you eaten?"

"I've eaten and I'm not the least bit thirsty. I'm going to get these floors done first thing."

"Sadie—"

"I'm telling you to leave me alone. That's what I'm telling you to do."

"I'll just do the dusting," Libby insisted.

"I wish—" My voice started to crack. "I wish you'd leave us alone. I have a lot to do. Go on up to your room. Get unpacked. Get some rest. Go back and see about Warren. Something."

Libby headed for the kitchen. I followed and watched her open the cabinet under the sink and tear off two paper towels. She started to reach for the bottle of furniture polish and I'd had enough.

"You put that down right now. I'm telling you. I have enough to do without having to worry about you not listening to what I'm saying."

Libby ignored me, acted like she hadn't even heard me. I gripped my hands, one with the other. "Just get out of here."

She stared at me. "Sadie, you aren't thinking right." She looked toward the den, where Clive and Warren were keeping to themselves.

"I'm as serious as a heart attack, Libby." I told her that when her daughter, Tricia, and her husband got into town, they could stay at a motel together.

She folded the paper towels into a square and put them on the counter and she put the furniture polish back in the cabinet. Then my sister turned around, real calm like it was an ordinary day, and walked down the hall and out the front door. When she was gone, I threw the broom against the wall. It fell to the floor, leaving a mark across the paint as it went.

CHAPTER 23

— *Tinley Greene* —

The funeral home parking lot is full of cars. The announcement was in the paper: visitation for friends and family, four o'clock at Markinson's Funeral Home, 122 Church Street, and I knew Mark would want me to be there.

It's a short white building between the flower shop and the gas company. The sidewalk with high black railings slants down from the doors to the street. When my parents died, there wasn't a visitation. I only remember being outside at the county cemetery, the grass wet with leftover rain and the ground soft and smelling like black dirt. That day, people I barely knew squeezed my hands and said things like "My prayers are with you" and "You poor, sweet girl."

Today, a man in a dark suit stands at the front door like a guard. He opens the door for me, and another man inside shows me to the right room. The floor is covered with thick burgundy carpet, and people crowd around the cushioned chairs. Everybody is waiting to get to Mark's parents, who stand stiffly at the front of the room by the piano.

I join the line, and when it moves, I notice the casket on a stand covered with a velvet cloth the color of moss. There are so many people, lots of dark suits and long dresses and hands clutching tissues. One woman wears a black hat with a see-through black flower glued to it.

At the back of the room, the tables overflow with flowers, mostly white but some yellow and purple. A few people glance at the cards that say who the flowers are from and a heavyset woman in a dark purple dress writes things down in a small notebook. The smell of the flowers mixes with the smell of furniture polish, peppermints, hairspray, and perfume. My stomach hurts from all the smells, but I'm trying to act the way Mark would want me to because I'm convinced he is looking down at me.

The man in front of me turns around and I nod and say hello. He says "Afternoon" and turns back around. His white hair sticks out over the back of his shirt collar, but he's bald on top. Mark had so much hair and it was so thick and dark. When I think of how it smelled, and how the back of his neck felt when I touched it, all the air goes out of the room. I'm trying to catch my breath when I get a good look at Mark's parents.

Mr. Caswell's head is bent down, like his neck can barely hold it up. Mark's mother stands beside him, her back straight. Her gray hair is pulled back into a bun like it was at church. She wears a black long-sleeved dress with a pearl necklace and shoes with low heels. It makes me tired the way she stares at everything, hard and without blinking.

We inch forward and the man in front of me turns around again.

"How did you know Mark?"

His breath smells like pretzels, and white hairs sprout out of his ears. As he waits for me to answer, my eyes fill with tears. I can't say anything so I just shake my head. He pats me on the arm before he turns back around. The line creeps forward and the closer I get to Mark's parents, I can hear what people are saying—"It's such a shame" and "Nobody should have to go through that" and "Bless your heart" and "I'm praying for you." "If there is anything, anything at all, that I can do, you let me know, you hear?" Mr. and Mrs. Caswell nod, letting people hug and pat and squeeze them. Neither of them cries, but Mr. Caswell's eyes are red. I don't know what I'll say to them, but it will be something about how much I loved Mark. They don't know me, not really, and I'm sure Mrs. Caswell didn't mean those things she said on the bridge. They will see how much I loved him. Maybe we'll even help each other like a family. I can hope for that anyway. Some goodness might come from all this hurt.

When I reach the casket, I want to run my finger along the brass handle. The lid is closed and Mark is in there, but he isn't really. His body may be there, but he doesn't need it anymore. He doesn't need anything anymore. I imagine pressing my hand on the shiny brass and leaving my fingerprints up and down the handle. Mine. He was mine.

When I reach the front of the line, Mrs. Caswell smells like lavender and she stares at me with her dark blue eyes. It's okay to blink, I want to tell her. I feel almost like she is my child and she needs me to take care of her. Almost on their own, my arms go around her and her body feels small and rigid under my grasp. As I step back from hugging her, she glares at me like she wants to set me on fire.

"You get out of here." Mrs. Caswell fakes a small step away from me. Even though she's shorter than me, now it feels like she towers above me. Every second I shrink smaller and smaller.

"I know you're upset. I am too," I try again.

"You. Get. Out. Of. Here." Her eyes dart to the person behind me in line and then back at me. "Or I will call the law over here," she says in a hissing whisper.

Mr. Caswell stands next to her, talking to the man in front of me. "It was good of you to come," he says and I imagine him saying it to me, the same words in the same way. As I tiptoe out of the line, I keep imagining it. *It was good of you to come, Tinley.* I search for the door, for any way out, looking everywhere but at Mrs. Caswell. *It was so good of you to come.*

When Maddie Spencer walks up, my legs tremble and I'm frozen in place. Her shiny black round-toe shoes don't make a sound on the burgundy carpet. She wears a black dress with sleeves that come to her elbows and her blonde hair is pulled back from her face with a tiny black headband. Her father holds her arm and her mother stops to talk to someone. When Mr. Caswell sees Maddie, he raises his arm and motions for her to come stand up there with them—with the family. Mrs. Caswell looks over and nods and Maddie heads toward them.

To get out of the room, I have to go right by her. As we face each other, I imagine that I'm nothing but a big block of ice. The thick carpet makes everything quiet, my footsteps too, and all these people around me are nothing but dark blue water, still and cold. My fingernails dig into my palms and I float past Maddie, smooth and easy, and I don't start crying until I'm back outside and the cool air hits my face.

CHAPTER 24

— *Tinley Greene* —

Mark is gone and he stays gone, but somehow people still walk around and talk and do the same things they did before he left. It feels impossible, all of it. I don't know how I can do anything, even something like putting one foot in front of the other. Sometimes I hold my arm out and stare at it. What is it doing there? What is it good for, and how is it still attached to my shoulder when everything else around me is coming apart, or ought to be?

When I think about how maybe it was my fault, how I might have made him so upset because I didn't want to let him go, my lungs seize up and I dig my fingernail into my skin. The sharpness wakes me up. It feels alive and it hurts, which seems right because I deserve to hurt. I don't deserve anything except the squeezing in my chest that makes each breath hard to get and a stinging pain on my arm or chest or neck or leg. No pain is enough to take away what I've done. And nothing I can do will bring Mark back. His whispering in my ear grows softer every day, and before long I won't be able to hear him anymore. I'll listen for him the way you listen for a train coming in the distance. But I won't hear Mark or anything else because the whole world will have gone silent and I won't be able to move in it.

The funeral is two days after the visitation and I wake up dizzy and weak. I get up and try to get dressed because I have to be there. Even though Mark's family and Maddie and her family might wish I hadn't come, it's my last chance to see Mark, to say goodbye to him. But as soon as I pull my dress over my head I know I'm too sick to go. I can barely stand up straight. I'm so light-headed with missing Mark that I'd probably tip over in my chair.

"I'm sorry," I whisper to him. "I'm so sorry I can't be there."

When I'm in bed with the covers pulled up, I find myself talking to him again. "Mark, I would've been there today if I could have. I should've been there for you."

"It doesn't matter," I imagine him whispering. "It doesn't matter who was there and who wasn't. I want to be with you more than anything else."

"Tell me how it was so I can see it for myself."

"The women's shoes sunk into the mud," he says. "And the preacher lost his place in the book. He licked his finger when he flipped the pages."

"And the other day? What was that like? The last day."

"Oh, that day. I can't tell you what that was like. I can't describe it. I can't think of the words to make you feel it."

"Was it like flying?"

"That's what it was like. It was like flying."

"Why didn't you take me with you?"

"You could've come with me if you wanted to," Mark—or his ghost or at least my memory of him—says, as real as if he is in bed beside me. "You could still come."

CHAPTER 25

— *Sadie Caswell* —

Our mama used to say when you lose one thing, you gain another, but I've never put much stock in that. The way I see it, things are going to happen when they're going to happen, when the good Lord wills it. Sometimes you might have a whole handful of good things all at once, so sweet you can hardly stand it, and other times, things are ripped away from you and you feel so empty you think there's nothing left to take, not until the next thing is taken away.

All I could see was that girl Tinley. Sometimes I saw her on the bridge screaming at Mark and Mark shaking his head no, wanting her to stop yelling more than anything else. Even if she hadn't been there when he went off the bridge, she made everything harder on him. The way Mark was with Maddie, he wouldn't have paid any mind to a girl like that. He would have been desperate for her to leave him alone. But she kept on after him.

After the funeral, Clive went back to spending most of every waking day outside. He always took care of the fields, getting wood for the winter, patching up the roof, and seeing that the renters paid on time and had hot water. He'd always taken on anything that needed doing outside, and the money part of things too. Every month he took stock of who owed us money and what we needed to pay. Between the different areas he farmed and the fields and houses he rented out, we'd always been lucky in that way. Or more likely it was due to Clive being smart about things. For the most part, we'd always left each other alone, and if we didn't find much to say to each other, that was fine.

Back when we hadn't been married for long, Clive showed me the different places where he farmed. I remember telling him how the hill out on the south end would be a good spot to plant some apple trees. Nothing was out there but a few walnut trees and some bushes. I don't know what put it in my head, but I could picture what apples trees would look like, how pretty they would be. Clive didn't do anything but shrug and say it was good like it was. I told him that was fine—and it was. It was his decision to make. But sometimes I couldn't keep myself from thinking about how those apple trees would've looked out there, rows of them with their puffed-out blooms.

After Mark died, there wasn't room in the house for both me and Clive. We had the same space in the house that we did before. The narrow hallway stretching from the front of the house clear through to the back. The den and the living room. The dining room with its long dark wooden table. The kitchen and the sleeping porch with its freezer chest and rows of canning jars: pole beans, butter beans, okra, tomatoes, and pie apples in sweet syrup. And the bedrooms upstairs, one right after the other. Quiet and empty and the beds made up with quilts and cool white sheets. But not enough room for both of us. Whenever Clive came inside to take his meals, I felt like he was bumping into me even though he never got close enough to touch me.

One day after Clive came inside, I couldn't stand to be in the kitchen with him. When I passed him on my way out the back door, I told him there was food on the table and he didn't do anything to stop me. It must've been close to an hour that I wandered around outside, out to the hill on the south end where there was nothing worth seeing—no apple trees, nothing—and through the old pastures clogged with weeds and dried-out stumps. It was cold, and once it started to sleet, I had to go back to the house.

Those days after the funeral, Clive hardly slept. He'd never been much of a sleeper—usually came to bed late, woke up early, and got up in the middle of the night. One night right after we were married, I went downstairs after him and saw him outside walking around with his hands in his pockets and his work boots unlaced. After I told him I was expecting, and when Mark was younger, there were some nights when Clive rested easier. Sometimes he even slept the whole night through. But once Mark started having his ups and downs and especially once he was gone, Clive wouldn't hardly touch the bed before he got up to check on something outside.

We got Mark's truck back and I watched Clive clean it out. He threw away some plastic containers from the back and rinsed it off with the hose and dried it carefully with an old bath towel.

The next night at supper Clive watched me cut my ham into five pieces and then ten and after that I put down the knife because the pieces were too small to keep on cutting. Then I put my napkin over the ham, pressing into the pinkness until the napkin felt wet, and Clive gripped the table hard. The ice rattled in his glass and he sighed and looked at me, not giving me any room.

Don't you see how wrong everything is? That's what I wanted to ask him. *Everything?* But he wouldn't understand. When a bad thing happened, Clive acted like it was a rotten piece. All you had to do was cut out the black parts and then you could go on with what's left. But I wasn't like that. The way I saw it, it was all black, every last part.

Or maybe he wasn't that way. Maybe I was wrong and it seemed big to him too, so big he couldn't get his long arms around it. Maybe Clive felt the blackness all the time like I did. Something like drowning. We couldn't talk about it. There just wasn't a way.

CHAPTER 26

— Tinley Greene —

It seems like all I do is sleep. For days, I sleep so much that I'm confused about what's real and what's a dream. I wake up to eat what I can, usually a little bit of peanut butter right out of the jar. The saltiness coats my tongue and throat and it's the only thing that feels good when I'm awake, that and the cold water I drink after. Mark keeps asking me to come with him and I close my eyes, not knowing what to do or how to get from one day to another.

One day, I'm lying in bed and I hear a noise at the door. I don't have the energy to get up and I wait to see if it's one of the Caswells coming to kick me out. But the noise doesn't come again and I go back to sleep.

By the time I get up, it's gotten dark. I open the door, realizing the weather has turned cold and the air feels minty in my mouth. Somewhere a dog barks and another one howls back. On the steps by the door I find a brown paper grocery bag and, when I pick it up, something shifts inside.

In the kitchen, I unpack what's inside. Two apples. A banana. A loaf of dark brown bread. A small plastic container of butter. A half dozen eggs, the carton split down the middle with a jagged edge. A jug of whole milk sweating but still cold when I touch it. There's no note, no clue about who brought it, not even a receipt at the bottom of the bag. Before I put the things away, I stand in the kitchen staring at them, running my bare foot back and forth on the chilly vinyl floor. Then I take out the skillet and start melting butter. The egg yolks stay whole when I crack the shells. And when they're done, the fried eggs taste so good—salty and buttery and full of everything—that I can't imagine having eaten anything like them before.

The next morning, I make myself get out of bed. After I get dressed, I call up to see if the Maybins still want me to come clean. Mrs. Maybin tells me to come around eleven o'clock so that's what I do. I put one foot in front of the other and I think about taking something dirty and making it clean again.

Cleaning houses is the only thing I know to do and the gray house is the only place I know to stay. I don't have anybody now that Mark is gone too. It's like he's still with me, though—at least sometimes. One evening when I get back from work, he's sitting on the steps waiting for me. He's dressed in his work clothes and his hands rest on his knees. He looks like he could wait for me all night, like he doesn't want anything except to hear how my day has been. When I see him, I smile, even though I know it isn't really Mark. But he seems so real that I believe it, at least for a minute. Then a black cat streaks across the yard—a bad sign that breaks the spell.

It seems like every day will be just like the one that came before it. I get up early to start on the wash and when it's done I go wherever I have a cleaning job, first the wet work, the mopping and cleaning the bathroom toilets and sinks, and then the vacuuming, saving the dusting for last. If I sometimes wish I'd stayed in school, I remind myself how it was when Mark and I were together, about my idea to start over and become a different person. Someone who didn't lose everyone she loved.

At night, I dream about a time when I was with Daddy. I can't tell where we are. The sun warms my shoulders and the wind whips my hair in front of my face. I don't know what we're doing or what Daddy says. It's something I want to hear, but even though he is right beside me, I can't hear him. *Tell me, Daddy. Tell me what to do.*

When Mark's ghost doesn't come back, I'm so alone that I feel the need to force my eyes to stay open so I don't go blind from the darkness swirling around me. I try to conjure up the images of my mother and father, eventually giving up when all I can summon are meaningless snatches of memories that hurt even worse than the blankness I felt before.

One day, I'm out at Lynette Barnes' house to do her cleaning. Some people leave when I get to their house. Others stay to watch me clean, and they point out if I'm not doing something the way they want. Some are nicer than others and with Mrs. Barnes, it all depends on her mood.

Today when I'm squatting down to wipe behind the sink, she stands in the doorway of the bathroom with her arms across her chest and her eyebrows raised.

"Gotta be careful down there," she says. "You knock one of those pipes loose and it'll flood us clean out of here."

"Yes, ma'am, I'll be careful." I wipe so carefully around those pipes you'd think they were made of butterfly wings. I go around the faucets with an old toothbrush and Mrs. Barnes checks to make sure I rinse off the brush marks.

She has left greasy, dirty pots and pans in the sink even though I'm not supposed to have to wash dishes. By the time I start mopping the kitchen floor my stomach rolls with sudden queasiness. But I make myself keep at it. Every time the sharp smell of the cleaner hits my nose, I press my arm over my stomach like that will keep the sickness in. Mrs. Barnes watches as I wring out the mop and swipe it across the floor, trying not to breathe in the smell. I think I'll be okay until I bend down again. Then I drop everything and run past Mrs. Barnes for the bathroom.

CHAPTER 27

— *Tinley Greene* —

As soon as I come out of the bathroom, hoping to avoid Mrs. Barnes, she appears, asking if I'm going to clean it again.

"Yes, ma'am. Of course I was planning to. I'm sorry about that. I don't know—I haven't been eating right, I guess."

She stares at my chest and stomach and then shakes her head. Something in her face softens. "Can't be helped, I guess. Not with you in this situation."

She's not making any sense, but at least she isn't upset. Back in the kitchen, I pick up the mop again and finish the floor, wondering what she means. When I pass by the den with my bucket, Mrs. Barnes is picking up things from the mantle and putting them back down again. After I clean up the bathroom again, I go out the back door to dump the water. By the back door, I rinse out the bucket with the garden hose and hook it over my arm. Back inside, she waits for me with her hands stuffed in the pockets of her apron.

"Mrs. Barnes, I'm sorry about before, I really am. I've cleaned up the bathroom."

She shakes her head. "I know how it can be. It's just like when I had Lester. I was sick as a dog some days, couldn't even get out of the bed. Couldn't keep anything down except some soda crackers. Thought for sure that baby would come out too small to live, but he was all right. Had the colic and I liked to never get an hour of sleep, not until he was two years old. He's living up in Richmond now."

Not sure if she's ever said this many words to me in one day, I stare at her.

"Now Lou Ann, she didn't do me that way. I wasn't sick a single day with her, not like you are. Of course, once she came out, it was another story."

My heart races and I have to get out of there. If I can sit down somewhere by myself, I can think through what she's saying. She's not talking about me, or maybe she is. She can't be right, but I don't know for sure. My mother would know. What does it all mean, I'd ask her. What if I'm only a month late? What if we only did it two times?

Mrs. Barnes shakes her head and wipes her eyes. "She didn't make it past the first day, Lou Ann didn't. Sometimes I think about her nearly all day. It's been a long time, but you never get over something like that. I guess you don't."

"I'm so sorry, Mrs. Barnes."

She hands me a piece of paper with some writing on it. "You go see Dr. Trantham. He delivered Lou Ann and Lester both. His son is in with him now in the same office. Either one of them will take care of you."

"I don't know—I mean, thank you."

"Don't you worry about the bill either. I don't think the Trantham boys keep up with their billing too much anyway, but even if they do, I think it's the law that they've got to take care of you. You and the baby both, at least at the start." She taps her chin with her hand like she's thinking something over. "But if they say one thing about it, you tell them to send the bill over here."

Mrs. Barnes opens the door for me and hands me the bucket, which I must've put down while she was talking. As soon as I climb in the truck, I lean my head against the steering wheel. My brain knows it's the same truck I drove here, but it doesn't seem possible that anything can be the same as it was before.

My hands shake as I drive, thinking about what Mrs. Barnes said, going over the words in my mind again and again, to see if they fit. The wind blows hard and I take the curves slow, trying not to think about the wind pushing me off the road.

Beulah Road winds around following the course of the river, and the mountain laurel and rhododendron bushes have grown so far over the road that in places they scratch the sides of the truck. I'm almost past the curve where my parents went off the road when a gust of wind rushes through the truck, even though the windows are closed. I take in a deep breath, leaning up close to the windshield to see the road outside, telling myself I don't believe in ghosts. Even so, the wind that I swallow carries Mama's and Daddy's voices in it. The truth burrows deep inside me, telling me I'm going to have Mark's baby. Once I say it to myself, it's so real I can't believe I didn't know it before, that there was ever a time when it wasn't part of who I was.

That night, I lie in bed snug under the quilt whispering to Mark. I tell him what I said that last day was true. If only I'd known for sure, he says over and over and he touches my cheek. I fall asleep thinking about how our child exists because of what we had together. Something good that will last. The lie that became the truth.

———

After I've been to Dr. Trantham and he tells me what I already know, I decide to go see the Caswells. They're the baby's grandparents and they will know what to do. At first they'll be surprised, but I'm sure Mrs. Caswell will help me because deep down she must have a good heart. After all, she was Mark's mother and you can't give birth to somebody that good without having a little bit of it yourself, even if it's deep down, the way clear water can run in an underground spring.

When Mrs. Caswell answers the door, her eyes widen.

"I need to talk to you." I inch closer to the door.

She takes a deep breath, holding the door barely open. "You ought to have known better than to come here. I told you before." She goes to close the door.

"Please, I just want to talk to you. I promise." *Let me tell you how much I loved him. Let me tell you about the baby we're having, about the lie that became the truth.*

Mrs. Caswell looks up at the sky, which is turning gray like it's about to rain, and then back at me. "I don't need to hear anything from you, not now, not ever."

"I know this is a hard time for you and I just—" She moves again to close the door and I start to panic. This isn't who she is. It can't be. She's Mark's mother. She just needs to look at me. She needs to hear me. "Mrs. Caswell, please, if I could just come in for a minute—"

"I don't know what it is that you want, but you've caused enough trouble around here already. First time I laid eyes on you, you admitted you'd been arguing with him. You were chasing after Mark and he was so anxious to get away from you—the way I see it, you drove him to it."

I can't help it—I start to cry, covering my face with my hands. "I loved him. I loved him so much."

"You listen to me. I don't know what happened the day he died or who you think you are, but—"

"And I'm having his baby and he's gone and I don't know what I'm going to do."

"What did you say?"

I'm crying so hard that my ears are ringing. I can hardly answer her, but I tell her again that I'm having Mark's baby, that I didn't know it before, but I do now. That I loved him. I loved him then and I love him now.

Mrs. Caswell shakes her head. "Not my Mark," she says like she has a bad taste in her mouth, and she shivers and crosses her arms. "You don't know what you're talking about."

"Yes, ma'am. Mark is the only person I've ever been with. He and I would have been happy together." I wipe my eyes and try to stop crying. "We would have been a little family."

She grabs the frame of the door. "That can't be right, not when he was getting ready to get married."

"Mrs. Caswell, I'm not making a mistake. I know exactly what I'm talking about. I know all about Maddie. Mark was going to talk to her. I'm sure he would have. He was confused. He didn't know what to do." She raises her eyebrows and steps onto the porch, letting go of the door behind her. "If he was lost, then it was your fault, every bit of it," Mrs. Caswell says quietly, and even with the ringing in my ears, I hear her just fine.

I stare at the house, trying to settle the sudden dizziness I feel. Mildew has crept onto some of the white wood around the bottom of the windows. Through the half-open front door a hallway stretches down the middle of house. The old wood floor, scarred in places, is beautiful—almost as dark as coffee.

"You think you know anything? Here's what I know. Mark was happy until you came along." Tears stream down Mrs. Caswell's face. "You came and ruined everything. That's what you did."

I shake my head but it makes the dizziness worse. Hurrying, I trip down the porch steps. In the yard, I realize it's cold and the sky is so gray that it might rain any minute. I need to start this over somehow. This is all wrong.

"I don't want to ever lay eyes on you again. Not ever again," Mrs. Caswell yells after me before she stomps back inside, slamming the door behind her.

When I get to the truck, things are still spinning and I feel like I'm reaching for her, for something just out of my reach. For a second, I watch the porch swing moving in the wind. The sky darkens and I wish the rain would go ahead and start. The water could cover me up, drowning everything that has happened—and me with it.

The front door opens again and Mrs. Caswell hurries down the steps. She holds something in her hands, but I can't tell what it is. I wait for her by the truck, thinking there's a chance she has changed her mind. When she comes up to me, her chest heaves with her uneven breath, but she has stopped crying.

CHAPTER 28

— *Tinley Greene* —

"Here." Mrs. Caswell throws dollar bills at me and they flutter to the ground. "You get that baby taken care of and it'll be like none of this ever happened. Except I won't ever have him back, you understand that. He's not ever coming back."

"I don't—I don't want your money."

"You get this taken care of. Maybe down in Greenville. I don't know where. You figure it out. And I don't want to hear another word from you. I can't hear anything else you've got to say." She flicks her hand through the air like she's pushing something away and turns back to the house. I don't even call after her. She stumbles on the stairs and almost falls, but she makes it to the door and slams it closed again.

I take big gulps of air, still standing by the truck. It starts to rain, and water falls on me and on the money scattered on the ground. There's no way I could do what she's saying. I couldn't kill our baby any more than I could have killed Mark. As I gather up the money, the rain washes all over me like it's going to make everything clean.

We're going to be a family, just the two of us, I tell my baby once I'm behind the wheel of the truck. We will live in a house that's cool in the summer and warm in the winter. Every spring, daffodils will push up out of the ground. You'll like watching the birds flying outside the window and stopping to rest on a tree branch. You'll find a cat wandering around and you'll ball up some yarn for it to play with. I will take you to school, buy you pencils and spiral notebooks, whatever you need. Some days you'll come home upset that your friends aren't being fair and I will say, "Sweetie, sometimes you can only count on yourself in this world."

The rain tumbles down hard as I drive through Garnet. The truck wipers sling back and forth as fast as they can, but they can't keep up, and the rain is so loud, I can barely hear the radio anymore. I slow down to see what's ahead, trying not to wonder if the rain was like this when my parents died. Tabor Road may not be as dangerous as Beulah, but it's narrow, especially on the curves, where mirrors on wooden posts are supposed to show if a car is coming from the other direction.

I stay clear of the steep bank, which I know leads down through the trees to the river. And I try not to think of my parents drowning in that same river. My heart thumps in my chest as I ease around the next curve, leaning into it, staying as far away as I can from the river side until I realize I'm sliding off the road and barreling toward the trees.

My foot slams down on the brake and I try to steer back toward the road. I jerk the steering wheel as the front of the truck clips a tree. The tires skid in the mud, a horrible wet grinding sound, and the back of the truck smashes into another tree. Clenching my teeth, I jab the brake again and again until the truck shakes and stops moving.

Raindrops hit the truck windshield, the sky almost as dark as nighttime. I force myself to breathe in and out, then in and out again. I rub my stomach. No pain, nothing hurts. I straighten my fingers and pat my knees and stretch my neck. Nothing hurts anywhere. Like someone can see me, like it will help us be okay, I nod furiously. The baby is fine. I'm fine.

My purse is on the floor of the truck wedged between the brake and the clutch. When I pull it out and open the door, the rain soaks me almost immediately. I toss the purse strap over my shoulder and push my hair out of my eyes.

Stumbling and slipping in the mud, I inspect the truck. The front end is banged up—one tire knocked halfway off—and the back is ruined, crumpled against a tree. What now?

Through the trees the road twists and turns. Breathing hard and trying not to cry, I look up and down the road for help.

Seconds later, headlights pierce through the rain. I wave my arms, yelling "Help!" even though there's no way anybody can hear me. But a pick-up truck roars closer and slows down. The driver looks like he's leaning up to see through the rain. I scramble closer to the road and he turns on his turn signal and stops with the engine still running. As I get up to the truck, the turn signal blinks on and off again. The driver motions for me to get in and I open the door. He looks older than me, with wide shoulders and brown hair. Tan, like he spends a lot of time outside in the sun.

"This rain's not letting up a bit. You come on in if you want to catch a ride."

Not quite believing what I see, I nod and get in. Once I'm settled beside him, I get a good look and I can tell for sure. This man looks like Mark and that's my sign.

CHAPTER 29

— Sadie Caswell —

That girl's truck tore back down the driveway. I stood just inside the house listening to it, feeling the cool wood of the door behind me and making sure the truck didn't stop until she got all the way to the road. My hands were clenched into fists, thinking about what she'd done to Mark. How she messed everything up right when he was doing better.

When I was sure she was gone, I tried to do what I needed to around the house. I pulled the cushions off the couch to clean them, but by the time I dragged the vacuum cleaner up from the basement, my legs were shaking and I could barely stand up.

Upstairs, I laid down on top of the bed—didn't even pull the covers back. My shoes fell to the floor, first one and then the other. Outside, the rain came down heavy. I put my hands on my chest and tried to take deep breaths, tried to make my heart slow down.

Everything that girl had said, it was all lies. Mark wouldn't have had a thing to do with her, not when he was getting ready to marry Maddie. She had no business coming up here like she did. She probably wanted money and that was it. There wasn't any way she was expecting a baby, and if she was, it wasn't Mark's. That part couldn't have been true. When I asked myself why I told her to get rid of it, I could only come up with one answer. If she was really having Mark's baby, then that wasn't the

Mark I knew, not the Mark I ever wanted to know. But Tinley was probably lying about the whole thing anyway.

I wondered what Clive would say when I told him and I couldn't imagine it. I guessed he would be upset at her for lying about a thing like that. He would probably tell me to come get him if she came up to the house again and to keep the door locked even during the day. The same way he'd talk if there was a bear coming up in people's yards.

After a little while, I got up and went over to the windows where the curtains were pulled closed. Those chintz curtains must've hung there since the room had belonged to Clive's parents. They were always dusty, even after I washed them, and the material was starting to fray on the edges. I dragged over a chair and climbed up, reaching to unhook the curtain rods. Behind the curtains were white metal blinds and we didn't need both anyway. After I climbed down from the chair, I pulled the rods out from the material, propped them up against the wall, and folded the curtains into tight rectangles. Somebody down at the Bargain Box could probably use them. I started to open the blinds, but it was still pouring rain and there wasn't any light to let in.

Not long after Mark was born, Clive had given me an old garnet, the one I'd offered to Mark for Maddie. Clive found it plowing outside one day—a smooth, round rock the same color as the dirt. But he recognized it as a garnet right away. Come Christmas that year we took it down to the jewelry store on Main Street and they cut it up and polished it. We never had it made into a ring or necklace or anything, didn't have any reason to. But I kept it in an old pillowcase in the top dresser drawer.

That day, I took out the stone and turned it over in my hand. It was hard to see and I didn't bother turning on any lights. But I sat down on the bed and held that garnet for a while, feeling the weight of it.

When I heard Clive come inside, I knew I should go downstairs. He would want something for supper, some sandwiches anyway. Even though darkness was settling into the bedroom, I stayed on the bed. The water came on downstairs and I figured Clive had hung up his raincoat and was washing his hands.

If I were to go down there, I would put my shoes back on first. Then I would smooth down my hair. The stairs would creak in that one spot where they always did. The den would be dark when I went past it, but I'd still be able to see Clive's lumpy chair, the color of oatmeal and the brown couch with the cushions still on the floor where I put them earlier. When I got to the kitchen, Clive would turn around from the sink and I would say—what? Could I tell him what that girl had said? Or about me sending her away? I didn't see how I could tell him any of that.

Clive and I hadn't even talked about Mark or what happened on the bridge. He had to wonder about it just like I did, but he'd never asked if I knew who she was or why she showed up there. Maybe he didn't want to know. Mark was gone and he didn't need to know any more. Or maybe he couldn't know any more. Maybe knowing Mark was gone had filled up Clive to where he couldn't take on anything else on top of it. Whether Tinley was lying or telling the truth, it wouldn't make Mark come back either way.

The television came on downstairs and I let the garnet drop on the quilt, pressing my fingers into my eyelids. I laid out flat on the bed and listened to the rain outside while the bedroom got darker. Without sitting up, I started feeling around for the garnet and when my hand touched it, I put it under the pillow. Then I rolled onto my side, bent my knees like a baby does, and closed my eyes.

CHAPTER 30

— *Tinley Greene* —

"Where are you headed?" the man asks and when I shrug, he says he's going back down to Haird—almost at the South Carolina border, smaller than Garnet and without a grocery store or mall or movie theater. I remember on one of our Sunday afternoon drives seeing a sign for it between tall gray rocks slick with water.

"I've never been," I tell him. "But I've heard it's real pretty."

"You want me to drop you off somewhere on the way?"

"Well, the thing is, I don't have anywhere to go." I try not to think about how I had this same conversation with Mark.

He turns the truck around a curve and picks up speed. The rain has stopped now, but it's left behind a chilly dampness and water still drips from the trees. "You needing work or something?"

"I guess so, yeah. I mean, I've been cleaning houses, but if I could go some place else—"

"I'm not talking about any handout." His voice is deeper than Mark's, with more dirt and gravel in it.

"I know. Me neither."

When he says his name is Travis Beddingfield, I nod, sorting through the people I remember from school for a Beddingfield and coming up empty. It's better that way. We can start over without anything from Garnet bringing us down. Daddy once took me swimming up at Lake

Summit and the weeds under the water wrapped around my legs, making me think I'd forgotten how to swim. Maybe I can pull off the Haughtrys and Sadie Caswell and everything else rotten about Garnet the same way I kicked free of those weeds.

Every chance I get, I sneak a look over at this man who has rescued me. He is built heavier than Mark was and he's older—too hard to tell how much. When he sees me shivering, he points toward the vents. "Turn up the heat if you want. Won't bother me a bit." I push the dial over toward the red line and warm air gushes in. When we cross over the bridge, I close my eyes and lean back against the seat.

"We run a camp called Emerald Cove. Maybe you've heard of it?"

"I'm not sure. It's a pretty name though. It sounds like—I don't know—some kind of a fairytale place." I can already see it—the walkways lined with rocks, the hills sprinkled with flowers, me swinging in a hammock strung up between two trees, rocking my baby in a basket with my toe.

"Been in Leigh's family for years. Ever since the Cherokee lit out."

I open my eyes. "Who's Leigh?"

"My wife." He nods. "Maiden name of Justus. Do you know some of them?"

"I've heard the name." I swallow hard, rolling over the word wife in my mind. It doesn't matter, I remind myself. He's not Mark, not really. Without thinking, I lift up my hand to touch his cheek, to turn his face toward me so I can see how much he looks like Mark, and at the last second I catch myself and let my hand fall back to my lap.

I could go back to the gray house—but it belongs to the Caswells. And I can't imagine what Mrs. Caswell would do if she found me there.

Maybe I could ask Lynette Barnes for help. She was nice enough about the doctor. She might let me stay with her or she could give me some money for an apartment somewhere. But you never can tell what kind of mood she's in, not until you're right up in it. And I know what she would say about me staying at her house, about how she wants to help, but she can't have me underfoot all day. My cheeks burn when I picture the way she would shoo me out like a dog off the street. Maybe she would give me money and maybe she wouldn't.

If only I'd stayed in touch with a friend from school—but I made a clean break when I dropped out. I haven't called or written anybody, even the girls I used to eat lunch with. This man could take me back if I asked him to. He could turn the truck around, spitting up mud from the back tires, and head back toward Garnet. But I imagine the road draped with all my bad memories hanging from the silvery, wet trees like ghosts.

"Can I see the camp? Can you take me there?"

"It depends on what you're wanting with it."

"Look, I might as well come right out and tell you that I'm pregnant."

"Well, would you look at that. You married?"

I shake my head.

"How old are you, girl?"

"Seventeen."

Travis sighs as we pass the old mill. Shaking his head, he turns down a dirt road and we bump over potholes, splashing up water as we go.

"Where's the daddy?"

"He's—he's not around." I take a deep breath. "And my parents aren't either," I say, because I know that's the next question coming.

"Well, it's a shame all the way around. Good Lord. Listen, I'll take you up to the house and Leigh will see about doing something for you."

I bite my lip, suddenly six years old and waiting to see if I get a piece of chocolate sheet cake for dessert.

"That all right by you?"

"Yes, I'm sorry. I really do appreciate the help."

When we drive up to a gate, Travis hops down out of the truck and drags it open. After we drive through, he grunts and points his thumb back over his shoulder. "You mind getting it? Off-season we keep it closed."

I pull the gate and latch it closed, then climb back up in the truck. Travis tells me about the camp as we bump and slide down the narrow road. He points to the log cabins off in the woods—boys' on the left side of the road and girls' on the right. Some of the cabins have a big light hanging down over the door with rusty metal like a cage around the bulb. He explains that's where the showers and toilets are.

"We'll start back up again in the spring," he says. "We get some for spring break but mostly it's a summer operation. A lot of youth groups. Some from Raleigh, some from the South Carolina coast. Looking for some place cool in the summer."

I imagine groups of girls, all friends, climbing up the hill, barefoot on the carpet of pine needles. Travis points out the dining hall, where two long clotheslines stretch across the front yard and a heavy-looking gray bell hangs on a wooden stand. Even now a light shines over the back door and dish rags are draped over the wooden railing. On the steps, I spot a jug of bleach and a mashed-up bag that says "crinkle cut fries" in square letters.

Travis parks the truck under an overhang running between the dining hall and a cabin made out of lighter wood than the rest. The roof of the porch has steep sides that meet in a point at the top like the letter A.

"We built a new cabin for ourselves a couple years back." Travis points out the window. "You let me handle Leigh. Keep quiet for a second and let me do the talking."

"Yes, sir." I cringe. "I don't know why I said sir. It's not like you're my father."

"Well, I can tell you were raised right anyway." Travis reaches behind him on the seat of the truck and shrugs on his coat. "We don't have any children of our own—just the campers coming and going."

Inside the dining hall, Leigh is skinny and flat all-over with long curly brown hair. She takes one look at me and asks Travis what in the hell he was thinking bringing me there. I back up, wishing I could melt into the wall and disappear. The dining hall smells like ammonia and detergent and fried chicken, and underneath everything else, iced tea cut with lemon.

"Are you kidding me with this?" She jabs her finger at his chest. Even though it's chilly outside, the ceiling fan clicks around, flipping the stack of napkins on the front table. She and Travis are both wearing jeans and flannel shirts. They're younger than Mama and Daddy, but older than me by a good bit.

"It's not like that," Travis says. "She doesn't have anywhere else, that's all."

"That's the story she told you?" Leigh laughs a hiccup kind of laugh and pushes her hair with the back of her hand. "I can see from here why you'd pick her up, why any man would."

"Leigh, come on. She's expecting." Travis shakes off his coat and drapes it over a chair.

She raises her eyebrows and looks me over again, top to bottom.

I put my hand on my stomach. "I mean, not right away. But come June—God willing."

"Is that right? Who's the daddy? Anybody we know?"

I shake my head and show her my left hand, the fingers naked as the day I was born. "I'm not married, just so you know."

"That doesn't bother me." Leigh shrugs as she steps closer with her hand on her hip. "But what do you think you're doing here?"

I stare at the floor where a paper straw wrapper is tied up in a knot. "I don't know. But I can help y'all out, you and your husband. Cooking or cleaning, stuff like that." I raise my chin and look at her straight on. "A big place like this, I don't know. Maybe you could use the help?"

She frowns. "When's that baby due again?"

"June, I guess. If he's on time."

"It's a boy?"

"Well, I don't know for sure. It's just a feeling I have. You ever have feelings like that, kind of deep down?"

"Yeah." She pulls a cigarette out and puts the pack back on the table. "Yeah, I do. I know what you're saying." She sighs and lights the cigarette with a lighter from her pocket.

Travis offers to show me where I can stay, but Leigh holds up her hand.

"I'll take care of this," she says. "You can stay right where you are."

Travis shrugs. "Makes no difference to me."

"Yeah, I bet it doesn't." Leigh rolls her eyes.

"Like I said—never mind, you've made up your mind not to believe me anyhow." Travis grabs a rag from a bucket and starts wiping off the front table.

Leigh says, "Come on then," and I follow her out and down the hill.

Inside the cabin, bunk beds are jammed together on one side of the room and Leigh points to a single bed on the other side, like the top bunk has been snapped off.

"I'll have to go get some sheets and a blanket unless you brought some with you."

"Sorry, I kind of left in a hurry."

She frowns and peers at me with her head tilted. "Is somebody coming to look for you?"

"No, nothing like that. I promise." I hold up my fingers twisted around each other and she shrugs at the gesture. Feeling like a kid in pigtails, without a clue about anything, I shove my hand in the pocket of my jeans, where the dollar bills from Mrs. Caswell are still damp.

CHAPTER 31

— Sadie Caswell —

The next day, I woke up and realized some of Mark's things were still down at the rental house where he stayed sometimes with the boy from work. As soon as I got dressed, I went down there. The boy who answered the door said his name was Cliff. He was one of those boys who can't keep still. He kept pulling up his pants and messing with his hair. When I asked him if I could get Mark's things, he walked me down the hall.

"Let me know if you need any help. I guess I can carry stuff out for you or whatever." He shrugged and I thanked him and said I could get it myself.

Mark didn't have much there, as it turned out, less than I would've thought. In the closet some work shirts were hung up, and in the drawers nothing more than socks, underwear, and pants. For a minute I sat down on the bed, picking at the edge of my coat. I wanted there to be more of him to see, to take back with me.

When I got up, I checked under the bed but I didn't find anything except some dust. In the hallway bathroom, I packed up his toothbrush, toothpaste, deodorant, and comb. Some of his dark hairs were still caught in the comb and I left them there.

On my way out, I asked Cliff how Mark had been right before he died, if he'd noticed anything different. He was sitting on the couch watching television with his feet propped up on the coffee table.

"He was pretty much the same, I guess. It's not like we really talked about stuff. Maybe the cable being out, or the power bill. Things like that." Cliff shrugged and turned down the television. The table was cluttered with a crunched-up soda can and an open bag of chips. "I'm not really sure."

"Did Maddie Spencer ever come by here to see him?"

He nodded. "Sure, she did. She came by all the time. Don't know that she ever liked me much, but she's pretty cool with everybody it seems like."

"Did any other girls come around looking for him? Somebody like Tinley Greene?"

"Oh, is that her name? Little thing? But curvy?"

I sighed. "I guess so. So you've seen her around here then?"

"I met her, but only that once." He stood up from the couch and pulled up his pants.

"She came by here? When? What did Mark do?"

"She was looking for him, but he wasn't here that day. To tell the truth, I don't know what was going on with them."

I asked Cliff a few more questions, but there wasn't anything else he could tell me. And it didn't matter anyway. He hadn't told me anything I didn't already know. That Tinley had been chasing after Mark. That she'd come here looking for him when she had no business doing it. The more I knew about her, I could see exactly how she'd swooped down just in time to mess everything up, right when things were settling, the way a bad storm can blow in on a sunny day.

After I left, I went by the other rental house too, the gray one. The driveway was empty and the front door was locked. I'd have to ask Clive for the key. I peeked in the front window and didn't see anything out of place. The house looked to be in good shape—there were even some nice mums planted by the front sidewalk.

On my way home, I ran by the store to pick up coffee and bread. As soon as I walked in, I saw a woman carrying a tiny baby in one of those pouch things. The baby had its eyes closed until the woman leaned over to pick up a bunch of bananas. Then the baby opened its eyes and looked around before shutting them again and I turned away before I saw anything else.

That evening when Clive came in, he was worked up about the new barn the Honeycutts were putting up.

"That kind of cheap sheet metal they got will rust something awful." He reached for the dish of butter and split open his piece of cornbread. "Looks shiny now, but it won't take but a few rains or even damp days before the rust starts coming. I don't know what they were thinking. They ought to have known better than that."

"The bottom of that pot's still hot," I told him, setting down the beef stew. Clive spooned some in his bowl and broke up another piece of cornbread on top of it. He didn't ask what I'd done that day and I didn't offer it up. I was too tired to ask him for the key. What did I expect to find at the gray house anyway? Some old furniture we cleaned out years ago?

That night when I went upstairs before Clive did, I didn't go to our room like I normally would have. Instead, I chose the room with the sewing machine where we stored an extra twin bed. I kept a quilt on top of that little bed, mostly pink colors. I didn't even turn on the light. I knew where the bed was and I made my way over to it. When I laid down, the feather pillow smelled musty, but I closed my eyes and tried to forget about it.

The next morning, Clive didn't say a word about where I'd slept. I wanted him to ask, but at the same time, I didn't want him to mention it. He thanked me for his coffee and started eating his eggs. He always liked them over easy, and my stomach twisted as I watched him, the way he swirled his fork around in that yolk like he was some kind of artist going to paint something with it. *Just eat it and be done with it.*

———

After we got through Christmas and the start of the year, Libby came up to visit in March. When it came time for her to head back to Greenville,

I had my suitcase ready to go. I asked if she minded if I went back with her, if it would be okay if I stayed with her and Warren for a while. She didn't say anything, which wasn't a bit like her. She grabbed the suitcase from me, even though I could carry it fine, and shoved it in the trunk of her car.

"I can drive myself. There's no need—"

"You get on in the car, Sadie. I'll drive. You won't need a car down there anyway."

When I told Clive I was going, he took his bandana out of his back pocket and wiped it over his face. "I wish you wouldn't." He stuffed the bandana back in his pocket and then took it out again, twisting it around in his hand.

"I guess I'll be back before too long," I told him while Libby stood there watching us. I thought of saying I didn't have a choice, that if I didn't get out of the house and away from him, I might never get out of bed. I might end up too tired to even take another breath.

I went up to Clive and patted him on the back and blinked away tears. Then I followed Libby out to her car.

CHAPTER 32

— *Tinley Greene* —

When I wake up the next morning, a chill hovers over the cabin and I pull the blanket tighter around me. "They're letting me stay here," I whisper to Mark's ghost beside me. "They want to take care of me—me and the baby." I don't know what it means that people are always having to let me stay or tell me to go—the Haughtrys after Mama and Daddy were gone, Mark at the gray house, Travis and Leigh.

First thing, I walk around the whole camp, the rows of cabins, the lake hidden in the trees with a wooden dock and fog lifting up around the edges. Everywhere I hear the quiet sound of pine needles dropping. Daddy always said pine wasn't worth anything, that it burned up too fast to keep you warm and if you tried to make anything with it, it would scar if you so much as ran your fingernail across it. But I like the way the pines out here are spread apart so you can see the sky between them.

Up at the dining hall, Travis spoons out oatmeal with butter and salt in paper bowls and we eat without talking much. Then I take a quick, cold shower and get started on what Leigh tells me to do. Sweep out the cabins, careful about the cobwebs around the doorways and in the corners. Mop out the bathroom in their cabin, bleach in the toilet but not in the shower because it eats away at the grout. "There may be some painting later on," she says.

———

A few weeks later, Travis goes back to Tabor Road with his cousin who has a tow truck. While I wait for them to bring Daddy's truck back, I remember its warm, spicy smell, the way the seat was cracked along the sides, the old piece of waxed paper stuffed between the seat and the door. When Mama made saltine crackers with peanut butter for Daddy, she wrapped them in waxed paper folded over the top like a Christmas present.

But when Travis and his cousin get back to the camp, they don't have Daddy's truck. Instead, Travis is driving a little white car.

He explains that when they got the truck out, it was too damaged to be worth anything but scrap. If I want, he'll work out a trade for the white Toyota. "It'll last longer than I will." Travis puffs out his chest and hooks his fingers through his belt loops like he's proud of helping me. All I can do is say thank you, whether I mean it or not. Thank you for doing that for me. But that night I cry myself to sleep over this new loss. When will they ever stop?

———

Some days I can't remember Mark, can't piece together in my mind what he looked like or how his voice sounded. Little parts of him float around in my memory. The way his eyebrows looked, the way he sat with one hand on his lap. But I can't press them together to make a full picture of him. When he came up close to me, he smelled a certain way, but I can't bring it back, and even when I envision the times we had together, I can't come up with the way his voice sounded whispering my name. It doesn't get any easier lying down or closing my eyes or running my hand up and down my arm imagining it's his. It never gets easier.

At Christmas, we open presents in the living room and Travis and Leigh give me two packs of diapers and a folding playpen for the baby. When they see how overcome I am, they pat me on the back and tell me not to cry. Saying thank you over and over again, I hug them both. On

Christmas I should be with my parents, or Mark, or someone who loves me. But I ignore the lump in my throat and try to be grateful for what I have. I tell myself things can work out.

Once the weather starts warming up, Leigh and Travis have more chores for me outside and I do whatever they ask me to. The only part I worry about, that burrows inside my head when I'm trying to fall asleep, is the painting, because I don't know if I should breathe in paint fumes. What if it messes up something with the baby's brain, or his lungs or eyes?

But a few weeks later, when Leigh hands me a paint brush and a metal can with yellow-white paint the color of butter dripped over the sides, I nod and back away from her. I'll just have to hold my breath.

I lay down plastic tarp all over the floor of the first cabin like Leigh said, and I'm propping up the ladder when Travis shows up out of the woods, bundled in a jacket with his cap pulled down over his eyes.

"Leigh told me you were fixing to start painting." He adjusts his cap and looks over at the tarp. "You've studied about it?"

"What do you mean? About the baby?" I rest my hand on my stomach, swollen slightly, pushing against my dress. Now that I've gotten bigger, I can't quite pull my sweater closed.

"You ought to know we wouldn't ask you to do something that wouldn't be right. Not after what we've been through ourselves."

"I don't know." I shrug. "There's a smell to it, but it probably doesn't even get to the baby." I consider asking what they've been through. But I guess they must have wanted children of their own, that instead the campers are all they have.

Travis frowns and reaches for the paintbrush in my hand. "Listen, hold on and let me talk to Leigh."

I hand him the brush, swallowing hard. "I'm happy to do it. I promise. Just don't make me leave." I follow him to the doorway of the cabin.

His back is turned toward me as he walks back down the hill, pulling aside tree branches to make way. "I know." Travis waves over his shoulder. "You've told me. You don't have anywhere else to go."

No matter what, I'm never moving back to Garnet—too many people I don't want to see, too many memories. But sometimes I remember the trees there, how the leaves are all different shapes, the different sounds they make when the wind blows.

Leigh says I'm being dumb about Garnet. "You can't always be looking around for ghosts, Tinley."

"I don't have to look," I tell her. "They're around anyway."

But the closest grocery store is in Garnet and she keeps asking me to go, not buying my excuse about not wanting to see people I used to know. Finally I agree, guessing I need to do whatever errands Leigh suggests if I want to stay at the camp. She hands me an envelope of money and a list, which I shove in my pocket.

I drive past the old mill and up the mountain with steep rocks on both sides of the road. Before I get to the bridge, I turn off, choosing instead to go the long way through town—praying I don't see anybody I know, counting seconds at red lights wanting them to turn green.

At the grocery store, the doors slide open and shut and people walk out with their bags over their arms or push carts with whiny, wobbly wheels. Even though I've waited until late in the afternoon when it won't be as crowded, there's still the chance of seeing one of the Haughtrys or the Caswells. Or Maddie Spencer.

Right before I get up to the doors, something moves in my belly. I move over to the side with my hand on my stomach. The doors swoosh open and closed in front of me. In my belly, air bubbles up, almost like wings flapping. The baby. Mark's baby is moving inside me. People hurry in and out of the doors and a girl I used to go to school with walks by, but she's flipping through coupons and doesn't see me. And it doesn't matter anyway because I still feel the baby move.

Later, on my way out of the store, I spot Lynette Barnes in the parking lot. She has a plastic rain bonnet tied around her head even though it's not raining, just cloudy.

"Tinley, I haven't heard a word from you." She points her sturdy black purse at me. "Not since that note you sent about the doctor's."

"I wanted to say thank you at least."

"Well, where have you been?"

"I'm sorry I hadn't told you. I'm down in Haird now. With some friends at Emerald Cove."

"I don't know anybody down there." She frowns, looking me up and down. "Are they taking care of you?"

And finally I have a good story to tell. Somebody is taking care of me. I tell Lynette how to find the camp and I invite her to come by to see for herself. On the drive back down the mountain, the baby turns inside me again. He twists around and reaches, the same way a flower lifts up to the sun.

CHAPTER 33

— *Sadie Caswell* —

The bed in Libby and Warren's guest room had a good firm mattress. A white and yellow quilt and two feather pillows. A white cotton dust ruffle. There was a dresser in front of the bed—solid oak—with a matching mirror hanging on the wall. The blinds on the window kept out the light from the street outside, the street light and the cars going by. Otherwise I guess I couldn't have slept. I wasn't used to any light getting in from outside at night unless it was coming from the moon. Libby said I might've slept fine with it that way. She said sometimes you surprise yourself. It was a bunch of nonsense and she knew it. I knew myself better than anybody.

On the right side of the bed stood a chest of drawers. At first you'd think it matched the dresser. It was made of oak like the dresser was, but if you looked closer, they weren't from the same set. The floor was covered with carpet and I pulled out the vacuum from the hall closet every week to keep it clean. You have to watch carpet or it'll get dirty and you don't even know it.

Warren went off most days, during the week anyway. He was supposed to be retired, but he taught shop up at the high school, woodworking and I don't know what else. He always carried a big tackle box with him when he left. Maybe he had to get out of the house on account of all Libby's talking. Every day he dressed smart in a short-sleeved dress shirt tucked into khaki pants with a brown belt.

"You let me know if you need me to pick up anything for you on my way home," he always said when he left. "Anything at all." I never did bring up anything. There wasn't anything I needed, not that he could get me anyway. But you could tell he was a good man.

At first I didn't know what to do with myself down at Libby's. Ever since Clive and I had been married, I'd always taken care of the inside of the house, the cooking and the cleaning. Even after all those years in Garnet I never had many friends, and I guessed some people thought I considered myself too good for them. I could imagine what they'd say— that I sat up in my big white house thinking nobody else was as good as we were. They would be wrong if they thought that. I just didn't know how to talk to people, not really.

"Why don't you come with me to visit the shut-ins?" Libby asked me one day when I hadn't been in Greenville but a week. "You used to do stuff like that and I don't know why you ever quit, but now is as good a time as any to get back to it."

"You know I stopped with all that back when I had Mark. Years ago."

Libby shook her head, laughing that little laugh of hers, the one that sounded like she was blowing out air. "I don't mean anything by it," she said. "But that was a long time ago and it would be good for you to get out and see some people. Especially now."

"I'm not like you, Libby. You do what you need to do and I'm fine right here." I patted the edge of the kitchen counter. It was made of some kind of plastic, a light tan color, and she always kept it shiny and cleaned off except for a fancy coffee maker.

After Libby left, loaded up with grocery bags full of magazines and books of crossword puzzles, I thought back to the last time I'd done something like that, gone to see somebody from the church. The truth was, I hadn't stopped doing it because of Mark coming along. I'd quit getting mixed up in other people's business because of what happened with that one woman.

Right after Clive and I were married and I moved to Garnet, Libby said I ought to start volunteering up at the church. She thought it would be a good way for me to meet new people. I don't know why I listened to her, but one Sunday after service I signed up for the meals committee. We took food when something happened to a member of the church—a baby was born or somebody died. That's usually what it was. I made the food up nice in a container wrapped in an old towel to keep warm and dropped it off on the front porch, somewhere they would be sure to see it and take it inside. Most of the time that worked out fine. Once or twice somebody pulled up in their car to visit. When they tried to get me to come inside with them, I shook my head and said I didn't want to bother the family.

But one time I got pulled into the house. I had made my chicken and dumplings and it was good weather, enough chill in the air that I could leave the food on the porch and not enough cold to make it freeze. I didn't mean to stay, just wanted to leave the food like I always did and get back home.

The front door of the house was painted a real bright red, the color of a flower. Right when I was setting the dish down on the porch, the front door opened. I stood up holding the dish. The woman standing there wore a floral house coat and brand-new looking slippers. Her hair was the color of a penny and it was down loose over her shoulders—a little curly but not the kind that looks messy. Even though she was about my age and must've gone to the church, I'd never met her before, not that I remembered anyway. Then again, I'd never been good at people's names or faces.

I held up the casserole dish and waited for her to take it. But she put out her arms like she was going to hug me. I took a step backwards.

"I'm so glad somebody's come." The woman said as she took the dish from me. "The choir's starting back up again and with the bridge group on Tuesdays, nobody's been by all day. Lester's at school and Howard's gone back to work, even though he said he wouldn't go until a week after the funeral."

"I'm real sorry for your loss." I held out that dish. *Please take it and let me leave.*

"Won't you come inside?"

"Oh, I don't want to keep you."

"Please. I don't want to be by myself."

I followed her inside because I didn't know how not to.

"I'm not usually like this," she said, putting the casserole dish in the refrigerator. "Always thought I could take care of myself." The kitchen smelled like burnt coffee. The cabinets were brown and the floor was olive green linoleum. The only light came from the hallway and neither of us turned on the kitchen overhead. I didn't know who had died. It wasn't any of my business. Her name was on the list and that was it.

The woman reached for a stack of papers on the counter and flipped through it until she came to a picture, the kind the camera spits out while you're looking at it. When she held it over to me, her hand was shaking something awful. It was a baby wrapped up in a blanket that could've been white or pale pink. It was hard to tell. The baby looked like she was sleeping, but I got a bad feeling. It was like a hole came in my stomach.

"That was my baby," the woman whispered. "Lou Ann."

I didn't know what to say. The kitchen was quiet except for her crying and the refrigerator kicking on.

"She looks real peaceful," I finally told her, when it seemed like I had to say something.

"I just don't know what to say or what to think or what to do." She shook her head and her hair fell from behind her ear. "I don't see how I can keep going."

I stared at the floor and tried to think of what to say. "I guess it's all right to be that way with what you've been through," I finally said. She dabbed at her eyes but didn't say anything. "And getting over it just takes time." I started to leave the kitchen. All of a sudden I was so tired.

"I don't see how," the woman said, and she reached out her hand like she was going to stop me from leaving. I didn't know anything—what to say to her, how to get out of there, how it would feel to be in her shoes. What I did next wasn't really my doing. It must have been the good Lord reaching down and moving me closer to her, knowing what she needed and that I couldn't do it myself. I reached out and hugged that woman, and it was like something in her broke loose. She cried and cried and I kept my arms around her, half of me still wanting to leave before I did or said the wrong thing. Not even remembering her name. Not realizing that one day I would know what it felt like to have a child ripped away.

———

After Libby got home from doing her church visits, she asked me if I wanted to go with her the next week.

"I don't think so," I said. "You can go on ahead without me."

CHAPTER 34

— *Tinley Greene* —

Dr. Trantham says I can have an ultrasound to find out if I'm having a boy or a girl, but it's an extra fifty dollars I don't have and I won't ask Lynette or Leigh and Travis for it.

"It's not medically necessary." The doctor shrugs and closes the folder he's holding. "So you can decide and let the gal at the front desk know." On my way out, I tell her in a bright voice—like it doesn't matter—that I don't have the money for the ultrasound, and she goes to answer the phone that has started ringing.

Even though I don't know for sure, I still think the baby will be a boy, like I told Leigh. When he's born, I'll be able to tell right away that he looks like his father. Most babies are born with blue eyes, but from the start he'll have green eyes like Mark did. A light green, something cool you'd fall into on a hot day. His hands will be curled up at first, like he's holding onto something, but when he stretches out his fingers, they will be long like Mark's.

For a while, he won't ask about his father and I won't bring it up. He'll have his days and nights mixed up and some days I'll be so tired it will hurt to keep my eyes open. He will find my breast with his little mouth and that will be enough. That will be the easy time.

When he is older, he'll start noticing how there are fathers all around him, but not at his house. He won't ever call Travis anything but Uncle

Travis. He'll wrinkle up his eyebrows when he thinks about it, but he'll go back to playing with his fire truck. Maybe a few years later, he will be digging in the creek with a stick, something that has nothing to do with parents, but he'll ask me then all the same.

"Where's my daddy?" He'll poke the stick in the creek bed and dirt will rise up in a drowning cloud. I won't be able to give him the truth. I won't say that when I met him, his daddy was getting ready to marry somebody else.

"Sweetie, he was a great man," I will say.

"But where is he?" He'll look up at me with those green eyes and I'll bend down to get closer to him.

"He can't be here right now, honey. But he's in heaven looking after you. Looking down at you from way up high." I'll point up to the sky. "See those pretty clouds?"

He will look up and nod. Then he'll see a frog and drop the stick he's been holding, leaning forward to get a closer look. When the frog starts to hop away, my son will squeal and jump up and down.

And I will watch as the creek becomes a river, its banks growing taller until I see how things could have been different. The gorge is still deep with high, almost vertical sides. The rocks are jagged and the trees are still because the wind isn't blowing. The metal railing of the bridge lets off a small pinging sound, baking in the sun. But I'm with Mark this time. He listens to me and I promise that we will figure something out. That the baby makes a difference, or that it doesn't. Whatever will make him come down from there.

————

Most days, I only see Leigh and Travis for breakfast and supper in the dining hall. Travis cooks and I help Leigh clean up. During the day, I do whatever they tell me to do, even when my stomach gets so big I have to stay still for a minute just to take in enough air. Leigh asks if I've been to the doctor and if I need anything and one day she goes up to the Bargain Box with me to see about some bigger clothes. A musty smell hits us when we open the door, and we wander around the stacks and stacks of cheap clothes.

Leigh holds up shirts, pressing her fingers into my shoulders and leaning back to see if they'll work. But she doesn't say much of anything, and on the way back she turns up the radio. Emmylou Harris, Mama's favorite singer, sings about rocking her soul in the bosom of Abraham. "I would walk all the way from Boulder to Birmingham," she sings. "If I thought I could see, I could see your face."

———

One day coming up on June, the first campers due in less than a week, I tug the mattresses off the bunk beds because Leigh wants them aired out. It rained for five days straight and now the sun is out, hovering heavy at the bottom of the sky, but enough to warm things up. Leigh is worried about mildew. She says she wakes up at night wondering if they ought to put a de-humidifier in every cabin.

"But do you have any idea how much that would cost?" She coughed and took a sip of her coffee. "The mattresses might get the worst of it, all that foam. It'd be a big help if you could drag them outside first chance you get." She doesn't think about how heavy they are, how it makes my back ache even to stand up straight.

I've already pulled three of them outside when Travis walks up whistling. He says he'll get the rest for me and I thank him, rubbing my stomach and feeling the baby kick like he wants out. After all the mattresses are lined up outside, I ask if there's anything else I should be doing and he says to take a load off. So I lie down on the closest mattress and close my eyes against the smell drifting from it—something between pee and spoiled milk. If Mark were here beside me, he would reach for me and put his arms around me.

Travis' boots crunch as he starts to walk away, and then the sound stops.

"I ever tell you I was up in Garnet for a spell?"

The image of Mark fading away, I open my eyes and shade them with hand. From where I'm lying on the mattress, Travis looks as tall as a giant, especially from the waist up, bending down toward me with a dirty white t-shirt hanging out from under a gray one and his arms brown from the sun.

"You never told me." I close my eyes again, wishing he would be quiet. He didn't need to tell me about who he knew back in Garnet. I couldn't think of anybody worth hearing about.

"Worked up at the curb market for that Kurkendall fellow. Willie Kurkendall. Had a home place over off Balsam Road, best I can recall."

"That name doesn't sound familiar." I squeeze my eyes closed tighter.

"I worked there for coming up on two years, until I met Leigh. Lord knows how many times I came close to getting fired though. You been up there before?"

I nod, remembering when Daddy took me. The rows of tables set up under a tin roof and people selling tomatoes and squash, dried-up money plant, and pinecone wreaths.

"I helped unload stuff, get it set up in the right place. You know people paid Willie to be closest to where you come in. Cheapest was at the back. One time I got Ricky Shelton all fixed up, fast as I could. But come to find out that man was a cheat and the spot where he'd pointed was already paid for by the Honeycutts."

"I don't know them either. Might've gone to school with one of the Honeycutts, I guess." I keep my eyes closed.

"Ricky Shelton's mess liked to have got me fired, but Willie was in a good mood that day on account of his daughter's baby being born. He could've let me go when I spilled that bushel basket of half-runners too, if it hadn't have been for Clive Caswell and Vinson Keller."

I ease my eyes open until the sun stings. *What else, tell me what else.*

"Willie's passed now. Read it in the paper."

"What did you say about Clive Caswell?"

"What now?" Travis picks something out of his teeth.

"Clive Caswell. What did you say he did?"

"Oh, he fixed me up good. Squatted down and scooped up as many of those half-runners as he could grab. Kept at it with me until we had it all cleaned up and Willie never saw what had happened."

As Travis leaves, he unhooks the thermos from his belt and tilts it toward his mouth, and I whisper, "That can't be right. The Caswells don't help anybody. Mark is the only one who ever did." He doesn't hear me, but I don't mean for him to anyway.

CHAPTER 35

— *Sadie Caswell* —

I wouldn't have thought that Mark was what held me and Clive together. We'd had all those years without him, before he was born, and we stuck together then. But sometimes when a piece is wrenched off, the whole thing comes apart at the seams. The pieces don't fit together any more. You can't see how they ever did.

Libby couldn't understand how something could get so broken. "You need a little time, that's all," she kept chirping. But she and Warren never had to go through what Clive and I did, what nobody should have to suffer through.

On their anniversary, Warren brought home Libby's favorite sweets wrapped with a flimsy pink bow. "A Whitman's sampler every year," she bragged, like everything rose and fell on a box of chocolates. She treated everything Warren did like it was more important than if someone else had done the very same thing.

While Warren was out, Libby spent most of her time talking on the phone, mostly to her daughter, Tricia, who was married and living in Knoxville. When she wasn't on the phone, she went to church or watched television in the den. I did a little quilting and some knitting, mostly so I could ask Libby to leave me alone. "You'll make me miscount," I told her.

Truth be told, I was used to tuning Libby out. I could think over what I wanted to, most days remembering something about Mark. The way he'd stab his fork in his food, especially something like pot pie. He'd poke tiny holes all over the crust and lean back to let the steam escape. Or the way he'd stand in the kitchen sometimes, not doing anything but watching me, wanting to be close by. He did that even when he was in high school and later on. He would stand there messing with some fishing fly he was making, flipping it around in his long fingers.

Some days remembering Mark hurt like the devil. Then I'd force myself to think about something else. Like the way that secretary at Libby's church would like the pink blanket I was making for her granddaughter or how Libby said the vets' group wanted more of those knitted hats I'd sent in.

All through March and April, Libby said I should go up to Garnet to see about Clive. She said he would expect it. I tried to imagine going up there. Seeing the house again and Mark's empty room. Sitting with Clive in the den, just the two of us and neither with much of anything to say. I remembered when Libby and I were growing up, when we'd go out to Wyeth's Mill to visit Aunt Callie. Back then, Libby always did enough talking for us both. But when Clive and I went up there after we were married, the logs shifted in the woodstove and the water slid over the rocks in the creek, and Callie didn't do anything but nod at us from her rocking chair. Made me wish Libby was with us, but I never told her that.

"I'll think on it," I told Libby. "But I talk to him every week and he's doing fine." Part of me wondered if I should go, like it was some kind of duty since I was still married to him. One day I went so far as to get my suitcase out. I put a few sweaters in it and a house dress and some stockings. But it wasn't any use. I couldn't make myself go up there no more than I could make myself grow a pair of wings. There was something impossible about it, that was all.

Later on, Libby started saying I should invite Clive to Greenville. I didn't figure he would come, but I finally asked him toward the end of April and he said he would be down the next weekend.

When he knocked on the door, I was checking on the ham in the oven and I found myself holding my breath. The next thing I knew he was in the kitchen with Libby and Warren. He was half a foot taller than Warren, so tall it seemed like the ceiling could barely keep him in the room. He must've felt it too because he wasn't standing up straight. He stood with his head bent and his cap in his hands—didn't say anything, just looked at me and then at the stove. Anybody could see the weight he'd lost, the way his belt was cinched up.

"Well, I guess you can go wash up," I told him. "We've already set the table." Clive went out of the kitchen without saying a word and came back in after a few minutes without his cap, smelling like the orange soap from Libby's bathroom. When we sat down to eat and I was right beside him, he looked different. He almost had a yellowed look to him, especially in his eyes. He didn't eat like he used to, and when I asked him about it, he said he wasn't that hungry.

"Everything tastes real good though," he said and Libby got going about the new cobbler recipe she was trying out.

When I said I was going to bed, Clive said he needed to step outside for a minute. There wasn't anything for him to do, but I guessed he needed to stretch out.

I got ready for bed just like I would have if he hadn't been there. Let my hair down and combed it through before braiding it. Went to the bathroom. Brushed my teeth and washed my face. Went back into the bedroom and changed into my nightgown. When I was ready for bed, I turned out the lights and climbed into bed. But the room was dark and Clive wouldn't know where the furniture was. He'd only been in there to put his suitcase in the closet. I got back up and opened the closet door. I pulled the string to turn on the closet light and left the door open so some of the light came into the room, enough for him to see his way without bumping into anything.

Before long, Clive came into the bedroom. He opened the closet door and bent down to unzip his suitcase. He got something out—his toothbrush, I guess. He zipped the suitcase up again and left. I waited for him to come back. The toilet flushed and the water came on and turned off again. I heard the light switch click and his footsteps in the hall. He came in and closed the door.

In the light from the closet, I watched him fold up something and lean down to put it away. He pushed the suitcase further back in the closet with his foot and pulled the string to turn the light off. The bed moved when he got in and he crossed his arms over his chest. He started praying then, like he always used to. He wasn't saying anything to where I could hear it, but it got to me all the same. When he was done, I reached across the bed for him and he turned toward me, not saying anything except my name.

The next morning, Clive wasn't in the bedroom when I woke up. I grabbed my housecoat from the hook in the closet, and on my way to the kitchen I pulled it on over my nightgown. The hallway smelled like coffee mixed with all the food we'd cooked the day before. The ham and beans and potatoes. I pulled the housecoat tighter around me and went into the kitchen.

Clive and Warren sat at the table drinking coffee. They both had plates of toast and Libby was getting something out of the refrigerator. I let out my breath and put my hand on my chest, like that would keep my heart from racing. Clive's hair was combed and he wore blue jeans and a burgundy flannel shirt. The front of his neck was red the way it got right after he shaved. His napkin was still wadded up on the table beside his plate.

"Clive said he's heading out, just after breakfast, I guess," Libby said. She set a jar of preserves on the table and pulled out her chair to sit down.

Clive swallowed and wiped his hand over his mouth. "Better to beat the traffic." He nodded at me like he wanted me to agree.

"Good thing you got up in time to see him off." Libby dumped sugar in her coffee. "I told him about the construction in Chesnee, but he said he went around it on the way down. They're putting in some car dealerships up there, a whole row of them. It'll be a mess for a while with all that equipment."

The way Clive was sitting there, dressed and ready to go, it didn't look like he would ask me to go back with him. Not that I would have anyway. I couldn't go back there. But it was pretty clear he was doing his own thing.

"I guess he knows the way," I said and turned to open the cabinet above the stove, keeping my back to them as long as I could.

CHAPTER 36

— *Clive Caswell*—

The other day when Vinson was over here working, we got to talking about Sadie and when she might come home.

"I was surprised she didn't ride back with you." Vinson looked toward the house like any minute Sadie would carry us out some sandwiches and tea. It was already turning hot, especially in the middle of the day, and the truth was, I could've used a drink of something cool myself. But I hadn't thought to bring anything out. If Sadie had been home, she would've made up a cooler for me before I went out. I didn't notice some of those little things she did until she was gone.

I shook my head. "I thought of asking her outright, but you can guess she doesn't like to be pushed into anything. She'll come back on her own when she's ready. You want to hand me that rake?"

Vinson handed over the rake and I wiped the sweat off my forehead before getting to work. With two cows about ready to calve, we had to clean out the barn.

"Where'd you go this morning?" Vinson dragged a wooden crate over from the corner and tipped it over to empty it.

"Oh, I spent half the morning working on a little something." I shrugged, not ready to share the particulars. The checkbook was still wedged in my back pocket. Sadie would be surprised at what I'd done. "Didn't mean to keep you waiting though," I told Vinson.

We worked for a while without speaking, until I asked Vinson if I'd ever told him about when I first met Sadie.

Vinson shook his head. "Don't know that you have. She was raised in Bennettsville, best I remember?"

I nodded. "I'd go up there to check on Abigail, my brother Levi's widow, every now and again, mostly on the weekend. The Deals—that was Sadie's maiden name—went to the same church." I took a break from raking and leaned back against the rough wood of the barn. It smelled like manure and hay and specks of dust floated on the air from where I'd been working the rake. But for a minute I was back in Bennettsville, dressed for church in a coat and tie. So young I still had a spring in my step and hair black as coal.

The weather was sunny that day with the wind picking up. After church let out, the congregation milled around the front steps, talking and carrying on. It wasn't my first time up there, and by then I knew Sadie by sight, just not by name. When I asked Levi's widow to introduce me, she nodded and spots of pink showed up on her cheeks. Playing matchmaker already.

Sadie was slight, but with a sturdiness about her you mostly see in larger women. Back then her hair was chestnut brown, the same color as her eyes, and she already wore it pulled back and out of the way. My sister-in-law muddled through some kind of introduction, and up close I noticed Sadie didn't wear rouge or lipstick or any of that mess. I liked that about her from the start. No fuss. A group of us stood around for a minute shooting the breeze. It didn't bother me one bit that Sadie was quiet. You should've seen the way she listened. She nodded and looked up at me like whatever I said belonged on the front page of the paper.

The next Sunday, I was running behind. As I came up on the turn to the church parking lot, I saw two things at the same time—Sadie and her family on the church sidewalk and, in the ditch beside the road, a brown and white animal of some kind. I couldn't tell what it was from the truck. As soon as it started to move, Sadie did too. She dashed into the road, her skirt flying, waving her arms. The animal—it turned out to be a pup, just a little thing—ran every which way. Into the road, then to the ditch, then back to the road. Scared as it could be.

I jabbed the brake and swerved just as Sadie jumped into the road and scooped up the dog. She scrambled into the ditch cradling it in her arms. I saw her bury her nose in the pup's fur as I eased the truck into the church driveway. Still shaking, I rolled down the window and called out to see if she was all right. From time to time since then I've asked Sadie why she did it, and she always says the same thing—that she knew I would stop.

CHAPTER 37

— *Tinley Greene* —

When the baby is born, it's all wrong. I'm by myself in the hospital except for the nurses who keep coming in to move tubes and turn dials and pick up paper spat out by a machine. The baby is a girl, not a boy like I expected, and she has blue eyes, not green. She comes screaming into a world that isn't real, that I feel like I left a long time ago.

She cries and keeps crying and opening her eyes that are blue and not green. She doesn't want my breast, only the little bottles a nurse left with plastic wrapped around the top. And I hurt all over, not just inside, but my neck and arms and legs too, like I've been running and carrying something heavy for days.

Early that evening, a burning feeling starts in my back and spreads until I'm on fire all over and I smell something burning in the room. But when I call for help, the nurse tells me I'm imagining it. She comes back half an hour later with a wet washcloth and drapes it on my forehead.

"You need to get some rest while the baby's sleeping." She peeks in the little plastic tray beside my bed. "I wouldn't miss a chance like this if I were you, not when she's sleeping so nicely."

When the nurse leaves, I pull the washcloth over my eyes, keeping them open and blinking through the white cloth. Maybe when I take it away, everything in the room will be changed and I won't be alone anymore. Maybe if Mark had met me earlier, then he could have saved me from every bad thing. My parents would still be alive. Mark would be with me instead of Maddie. And he would've married me instead of leaving us all.

Maybe when I open my eyes, Mark will be sitting on the edge of the chair by my bed, holding a cup of water in case I get thirsty. And my parents will be in the corner, Mama sitting in the other chair and Daddy behind her, pulling down the window blinds so I can sleep. I say their names out loud, pretending I have the power to bring them back. But they don't appear.

Eventually I fall asleep, dreaming I'm at the Caswells' house. Mrs. Caswell, somehow looking like a scarecrow, screams at me on the porch. The wind tosses her long gray hair around and the words coming out of her mouth look like black bats. They flap up against the dark sky and then toward the barn. Mrs. Caswell pushes me down the porch steps until I stumble and fall.

"You stop touching me! Get your hands off me!" I yell at her, flinging her hand away. The anger in me is so strong that it comes out in flames, catching first on the grass and then on her. She grabs at her hair but it comes out like burning straw while the flames lick toward the barn the way a hungry dog goes after a piece of meat.

When I wake up, my heart thrashes in my chest. The washcloth is only damp and nobody is with me and the baby starts crying again. Trying not to panic, I rub her stomach, tracing circles with my fingers. Finally she whimpers and settles down, a tiny bubble of spit hanging on her lip.

While I was asleep, someone brought in dinner and left it on the table that swings over the bed. The pieces of potato are almost see-through and they don't taste like anything except air so I give up trying to eat them. The baby wakes up and—in a daze—I feed her a bottle until she falls back asleep.

A different nurse comes in later, one I haven't seen before. I don't know what time it is, only that the sun is streaming through the window and the streetlight has blinked off. Leigh said she and Travis would come by to see me, but now it's a new day and they still haven't shown up.

"How are we doing in here?" the nurse asks. "Getting some rest?" She touches the baby's stomach. "You did good with the blanket." Earlier a nurse had shown me how to wrap her up tight. She watched me do it and wouldn't leave until I did it right. Now the baby is sleeping wrapped up like that. Every once in a while her mouth remembers and makes a sucking shape and her lips go in on themselves disappointed.

"When did she eat last?" The nurse picks up a clipboard and frowns. "Have you been keeping the log?"

I shake my head.

"She isn't eating or you're not writing it down?" She has dark circles under her eyes and a sour, worn-out look even in the way she's standing, leaning mostly on one leg.

"She's eating just fine." I try to roll over on my side, but it hurts too much and I decide I'll have to stay this way forever, lying on my back and barely moving.

"So you're not doing the log then? Did somebody show you how?"

I shrug, halfway remembering some other nurse, one with red hair and pink lipstick pointing at the lines on the paper and showing me how a pen was tied to the clipboard with string. This nurse sighs and comes closer to the bed. I'm all alone and I hurt too much to hold the clipboard and the baby is even heavier than it is.

"It doesn't even matter," I tell her. "I'm not keeping the baby. She's not really mine."

"What do you mean, sweetie?" The nurse sighs again. "What's going on? Is there somebody I can call to help you?" She squeezes my foot under the blanket and puts the clipboard back on its hook.

"There's nobody to call. I don't have anybody."

"Now I'm sure that's not true. What about the baby's daddy? Or your family?"

"You don't know anything." I start to cry and everything hurts worse.

"We'll see what we can do," the nurse says, but she turns to leave and I can tell she doesn't mean it. "I'm so tired," she says to somebody in the hall.

CHAPTER 38

— *Tinley Greene* —

The next day, the nurse with red hair and pink lipstick comes back again. She tells me I need to figure out the baby's name before we can go home.

"I told her I wasn't keeping the baby."

"Oh my goodness, what do you mean? Honey, I'm not sure what you're talking about."

"The other nurse. The one who was in here yesterday."

"Sheila?"

"I don't think she said her name," I answer with a shrug. "But I told her this was all a big mistake."

"Sweetie, do you want me to get somebody in here to talk through your options? Go through what you're looking at here?" She bends down and straightens the blanket at the bottom of the bed.

"I don't need to know anything except how to make it like none of this ever happened."

"But you're her mother. That counts for something, doesn't it?"

I shake my head. "I don't know how."

"You'll figure it out. We all do. One way or another."

She doesn't mean what she says because she doesn't know anything about me, how bad things seem to happen when I'm around, how the people I love end up dying. "I just want to get out of here."

The nurse stuffs a package of pacifiers, a thermometer, and a pink plastic baby-sized bathtub in a bag. When she comes up close to the bed, she smells like peppermint. I decide she must be the kind of person nothing bad ever happens to.

"We're working on getting you released," she says. "Last I checked, they're finishing up the paperwork."

"But what about the baby? She can't come with me."

"Hmmmm. Well, if you're serious about all that, then I'll get somebody in here—a social worker and somebody from family services and administration."

"But I told her yesterday—"

The nurse shakes her head. "I don't have anything in the file. Sheila must not have written it down. Sweetie, like I said, if you're serious about it, there are requirements. A checklist. There's a procedure we have to follow."

"I'm too tired for all that." I imagine taking the baby to Leigh and Travis and saying you can have her. Here's the baby you wanted. But to make it right they'd have to do the paperwork at the hospital.

The nurse coughs like she can read my mind. "Well, I wouldn't make any big decisions when you're tired."

She doesn't understand what I'm saying. I want it all gone. I want to start over—to meet Mark another way and for us to be together now. No Maddie Spencer. No bridge. No baby. But what's she saying, all those people in here talking to me, pointing at stacks of forms and saying things like "Consider all your options" and "This is a decision you have to live with for the rest of your life"—thinking about all of that makes me more tired than anything else.

Out of nowhere the baby opens her eyes and makes a little sound. At first, it almost sounds like Calico meowing. It's not the kind of noise I ever imagined a baby would make. I rub her stomach like I've done before. Amazingly, it calms her down again and she closes her eyes, even though she still squirms around.

"Is she wet?"

"I don't think so. I changed her right before you came in." I point to the trashcan where I threw the diaper away.

The nurse unwraps the blanket. "I'll check. It's not that I don't believe you. It's just that sometimes they go again right away. Did somebody get you a case of diapers to take with you? We have a bunch of extra."

"They said I could take that pack over there. I won't need them though."

When she's satisfied the baby doesn't need to be changed, the nurse fixes the blanket and starts to hand the baby to me. I could say no, but it won't hurt to hold her one last time. Holding the back of her head like somebody showed me, I prop her up on my shoulder. Daddy would have liked to see me holding her this way. Everything else wouldn't matter—dropping out of school, what happened with Mark. None of that would matter if my father could see this baby. I know he would've liked to see us together.

The baby pushes her foot out of the bottom of the blanket and digs it into my chest like I'm a hill she's trying to climb. As little as she is, her legs are surprisingly strong. She keeps trying, grunting and pressing her tiny foot into me. She wants something and she tries to get it. Only two days old and that's how she is. The nurse reaches to take her back, but I shake my head. I move the baby off my shoulder and hold her on my lap, running my finger over her ear and the side of her face.

The nurse watches me. "I really think it's going to be okay," she says and I start to cry, tears trickling hot and sticky down my cheeks.

"You don't know that, not really."

"Well, I can't promise it. You're right about that. But I bet things are going to turn out better than you think."

"Why would you think that?"

"Sometimes you just get a feeling about people, I guess. And I get the feeling you're a better person than you think you are. Stronger, I mean. I don't know if I'm making any sense." She reaches for the baby. "Here, I need to check her ears and her temperature."

When I hand the baby over, my hand brushes hers. I lean back against the pillows, still crying, but starting to calm down. "You don't know how I lied to her father, how I lied to try to keep him."

"I don't know anything about that, sweetie." The nurse shakes her head and writes something on the baby's chart.

I could try to explain how it was true when I said it. I was pregnant. But I didn't know it, and that made what I did as good as lying. It takes too much out of me to explain, to try to make the nurse see how I made Mark do it. How I made it harder on him instead of easier. I tried to get him every way I knew how because I wanted him for myself. He belonged with me, not with Maddie Spencer.

"I never imagined that he would jump." I wait for the nurse to be surprised, but she doesn't seem to react.

"Lots of people who come in here have done worse than what you've done. You can be sure of that." She starts stacking up the paper water cups on the table.

"But he died." She has to see how bad it really is. "The baby's father killed himself. And when I met him, he was getting ready to marry somebody else."

The nurse bends down to put the water pitcher on the bottom of the cart. "The way I look at it, grace—whatever it is, whatever you call it, wherever it comes from—ought to be enough to cover it. No matter what. Or it's not good for much of anything."

As she goes over to straighten the blinds at the window, what she has said fills up the room like new air. I imagine her words as a pale pink cloud floating over the sticky tile floor, drifting around the bed and the chairs and the little plastic tray where the baby kicks her legs, all the way up to the long tubes of light in the ceiling. I can almost see the cloud moving, its taste sweet in my mouth, and maybe this is what kindness feels like.

"I need to think about her name." I say, realizing how right the words sound once they're out of my mouth..

The nurse raises her eyebrows. "You know you only name her if you're going to—"

"I know." I nod and meet her eyes, and she nods back.

This baby is mine. She belongs to me, not Leigh and Travis or the Caswells or anybody else. I don't need the nurse to remind me of what I was about to do. It's already behind me and growing smaller every minute, the way something looks when you've gone way past it. Before long, you can't even tell what it is anymore—it could be a pond or a pile of leaves or nothing except the heat shimmering in the air. "I understand. I promise I do."

"Okay. Just making sure." The nurse touches the blanket where it rests around the baby's middle.

"What's your name?" I ask.

"It's Rebecca." Her cheeks turn pink. "But you can take your time and think about—"

"Good, it's a pretty name. Her name can be Rebecca then."

She smiles and glances down at the baby, then back up at me. "Okay, we can do that. If you're sure about it. You should be sure though."

"I'm sure."

"Okay, then. What about a middle name?"

"I don't know about that. I just know Rebecca."

She smiles again and nods. "Maybe you'd want something like a family name for the middle name? That's what a lot of people do." She takes a piece of paper and a pen out of her pocket and hands them to me. There's a line for first, middle, and last name and rows of boxes to fill in, one box for each letter. After I write *Rebecca* on the line for the first name and *Greene* for the last name, I stare at the empty boxes where the middle name will go.

The longer I look at the bright white paper, the further back in time I go and the whiteness melts away until it's not paper anymore. It's a flower petal.

Early in the spring, my mother would gather up camellia blooms that had fallen off the bushes and carry them back to the trailer in her apron.

"What's your mother's name?" the nurse asks.

I don't explain that my mother is gone because it's like she can see inside my mind and she sees Mama too, the way she would lay the fallen-off camellias on wet paper towels across the kitchen counter. "Cora. Her name was Cora."

The pure white camellias usually turned brown around the edges right away. But not always. As I write *Cora* on the form in the space for middle name, I remember the bedside table I used to have in my room, where sometimes after school, I would find a white camellia floating in a little dish of water. Even when I got up close, the flower would look like it was made out of buttercream icing, like it could've come from the top of a wedding cake. That's how perfect it would look.

CHAPTER 39

— Sadie Caswell —

After Clive left, Libby and Warren didn't have any other people coming to visit, not until Thanksgiving when their daughter and her husband would come down. There was no telling where I would be by then, but I wouldn't hang around Libby's, not with all those people around—hugging everybody and talking all the time and sitting around the table holding hands when they said grace. It would just remind me of everything I didn't have.

Even though Libby told me I should think of the guest room as my own, I didn't do much more than put my clothes in the dresser and my shoes and coat in the closet. Every morning and night I carried a little travel bag to the bathroom in the hallway so my things didn't take up space on the counter.

It didn't seem like I'd been there long, but I guess if I'd looked at the calendar it was coming up on August. When I thought about all the work there was to be done back at home, getting up the corn and the beans and tomatoes, I knew I ought to head back. Pulling down the pressure cooker and washing all the mason jars for canning wasn't anything I wanted to be doing, but the next time I spoke to Clive, I offered to come home to help out. But he said the Honeycutts and the Kellers were helping him this year. He said he had more help than he needed and for me not to worry about it.

After I hung up the phone, I remembered how Mark used to help me snap the beans, how there would be leftover tiny strings on the porch floor like hairs. And later on when we would eat what we'd put up, he always put an extra dab of butter in his beans.

It wasn't like I meant to stay that long, but every time I thought about going back, there was some reason not to. Libby needed my help because she was having a big group from the church over for supper, or I had an eye doctor's appointment, something like that. It was easier to stay and the more time that went by, the easier it got. Clive and I talked on the telephone about once a week. Sunday nights he called after supper and told me how things were getting on, how the weather had been and who all had taken sick. He sounded worn out sometimes, but he said it was nothing more than the time of year with all there was to do. Libby once asked me about joining the pastor search committee at church, but when we found out the meetings were on Sunday evenings, I told her she'd better find somebody else since that was my time to talk with Clive.

When the weather was hot out, Libby stayed inside watching the television. I've never been one for television. It's nothing more than a bunch of made-up stories that don't seem real no matter how you look at them. On the stories she watched, the women wore make-up when they first woke up in bed. People stared at telephones until they started to ring and looked at doorways for a while after somebody walked out. They slapped each other when they were angry and called each other names not fit to repeat.

After her story, Libby watched a talk show run by a man with a thick mustache just like a caterpillar sitting on his lip. He always said they would be right back after the break, like we couldn't stand to be apart from him for more than a second. One day when the program came back on, the man said they were going to be talking about a serious issue. I didn't know how serious it could be if he was going to blab about it all over the television.

After the commercial, a girl maybe twenty years old came out onto the stage made to look like a living room. She sat down on the couch while everybody in the audience clapped for her. Her mother was with her and there was enough hairspray in that woman's hair to start a fire.

"Now let's talk about your highs and your lows," the man said, easing into a chair beside the couch. After the girl talked and cried some, the man said if somebody you know or love has times when they're full of energy and others times when they can barely get out of bed, you should take them to see a doctor.

"And avoid stressful situations," he said.

Libby stared real hard at the screen and then at me until I'd finally had enough.

"Everybody has good days and bad," I told her. "Maybe the bad hits some people harder than it does others, but that's not something you run up to see some doctor about."

Besides, the doctor had said Mark was fine. I didn't need to hear any more from that television show. It didn't have anything to do with me, and even if it did, none of it would help me now. I got up to get started on supper.

On my way out of the room, I pointed at the television. "That mess doesn't have a thing to do with me, Libby. Or Mark either."

"I never said it did, Sadie." Libby shook her head. When she looked back at the television her cheeks were bright red.

That night I went to bed before she and Warren did. I told them I was tired and it was the truth. Still, I couldn't get to sleep. I heard the television turn off and Libby's footsteps coming down the hall. She usually went straight back to their room at the end of the hall, but that night she stopped. She knocked on the door of my room and I didn't answer her. She would either come in or she wouldn't. It didn't make any difference to me. The door opened, not more than a sliver, and I closed my eyes like I was sleeping. *Say whatever it is you need to say. Tell me I did wrong or that I didn't. I don't know.*

She whispered "Sadie, are you awake?" and I kept my mouth shut. "I don't think you're asleep yet and even if you are, I guess it won't hurt a bit for me to say this. You and I both know we weren't raised to run up a doctor's bill for any old thing. And the truth is, there wasn't a thing you could've done to stop what happened to Mark. Not a single thing. That boy, bless his heart, he was going to do what he was going to do. It's not on anybody but him. That's the sad truth of it." Libby seemed to wait a minute, then turned to leave.

Down the hallway, the door of their room opened and closed and I held my pillow right up to my face and let everything out—screamed into it, cried into it, did whatever I could to get rid of the garbage inside me. Remembering how when Mark was in school his teacher had called up at the house asking me if we'd noticed Mark's moods—episodes, she called them. She acted like she'd never seen a growing boy before, and I told her we had better things to do than to worry about made-up problems. I bit the pillowcase so hard I thought my teeth would break.

But Libby didn't know anything. It wasn't my fault and it wasn't Mark's either, no matter what she said. It was Tinley Greene's. Anybody could tell what she was about, with those tight jeans and those hoop earrings with her hair all tangled in them. Even if she'd told the truth about being with Mark, everything that happened was her fault. She never should've come near him. She poisoned him when he was doing better.

What good would it do to explain all that mess to Libby? It was some kind of a miracle she hadn't heard about it already, especially with the way gossip usually flew around and her usually in the middle of it, whether it was in Greenville or Garnet or anywhere in between. The more I thought about it, I knew she must have heard. The only real miracle was that she'd kept her mouth shut about it to me.

Libby never would've understood why I sent Tinley away or why I kept it from Clive. Some days I didn't see it myself either. Even so, Libby didn't know what she was talking about. Mark was mine, not hers.

The next morning I told Libby it was time for me to be going. "I've stayed long enough." She was sitting at the kitchen table holding a cup of coffee and when I started talking, she set it down. My suitcase was packed and ready to go. "If you've got something to be doing today, Warren can take me up after he gets back."

She got up from the table, pulling her robe tighter. "Sadie, look here, if this is about that television program, you know I didn't mean anything by it. I only meant that sometimes you have to look at things head-on, the way he really was. They had a grief counselor on there one day and he was talking about—"

"Are you going to take me, or should I wait and ask Warren?"

Libby sighed. "Let me have another cup of coffee first." She reached up and started taking the curlers out of her hair and when she dropped one in the sink, she didn't seem to notice.

On the drive back up to Garnet, Libby knew better than to try talking to me. She kept her eyes on the road and her mouth shut. We made good time for a little bit, but then we had to stop for gas.

"Want anything from inside?" she asked me after she filled up the car. "Water? Some crackers or an apple? They have fruit these days—bruised sometimes, but not always."

"It's not been but an hour since breakfast," I told her, and I stayed in the car while she went inside.

Before we got to the North Carolina border, we hit bad traffic and slowed down almost to a stop. I pressed my foot against the floorboard like I could make us get there faster. I didn't have any real reason to be in a hurry. I didn't even know what I'd do once I was back. But Libby should've gotten off the road at the first exit after the slow-down. If she'd done that, then we could have gone the back way.

CHAPTER 40

— *Clive Caswell* —

With Sadie still gone, the women from the church kept bringing casseroles. It wasn't that I didn't appreciate them, but I missed Sadie's cooking. I lost a fair amount of weight and my back stiffened up, ached worse than it ever had. I might have gone to the doctor except I didn't have the time.

Besides, I decided not to put much stock in doctors once I remembered how we'd taken Mark to be checked out, back when he was younger. The doctor said he was fine, just a growing boy.

His teacher at school thought different, called the house to complain about what she described as Mark's mood swings, his trouble concentrating. I had to hand it to Sadie—she gave them a piece of her mind. The teacher and the school principal too. By the time she was finished, they were tripping over themselves to compliment Mark instead of criticizing him. Say what you will about Sadie, but she's a good wife and a good mother. What others might call a stiffness in her, I see as backbone. And she says what's on her mind because she thinks better of people than to lie.

The more women who came up to the house, the pans and dishes and baskets of food they dropped off, the more I thought of Sadie and wished she was back home where she belonged. Seeing her in Greenville might have helped, only the house seemed emptier than ever when I got back. The television was my only company once it was dark out.

When Sadie offered to come home to help put up the garden, I worried that it was because she felt like she should, not because she really wanted to. I figured before long she would make her way back without me asking—once she was good and ready.

Every night after I climbed into bed, I prayed for Sadie until I ran out of words. She had lost her way a little, but I knew her better than anybody did and I was sure she would turn out all right in the end. I'd known for a long time that a core of goodness runs through her, same as the veins of garnet around here.

CHAPTER 41

— *Sadie Caswell* —

After we passed the sign for Haird and the old mill, I told Libby to go through town so we wouldn't have to cross over the bridge. For once she did what I asked without saying a word about it.

On the way up to the house, most things we passed looked the way I remembered. It was August by then, and everywhere you looked there was a dried-out feeling. The rain gauges in people's yards were dusty and the river was low. I counted up the time I'd been gone and it must have been five months, give or take. Enough time for some things to change. Enough for a lot to stay the same too.

Kudzu had grown over some of the telephone poles and started to come up on the power lines. Past Dell's body shop, we made the turn onto Maranatha Road where the land still opened up, like there was more room to breathe, only this time pressure built up in my chest. I thought the closer I got to the house, the more different things would seem. It wasn't right that anything would be the same as when I'd left.

Closer to where we lived, the houses were set back from the road, and most of them had fences running across. I remembered a day when Mark balanced along the top railing of our fence with his arms spread out, looking down at his feet. His shoes were muddy from where he'd been running in the field and I could picture exactly how his smile was.

"You'll fall," I told him. "Watch out."

"Watch this, Mama," he'd said, holding one foot up in the air and bringing it down on the fence again so he wouldn't fall, like the ground was a hot, burning thing he didn't want to touch. A chainsaw was cutting in the distance, and close by squirrels skittered on the tree limbs and acorns fell. The wooden fence creaked under the weight of him and when he started to sway, I put out my hand like I could keep him from falling. But he righted himself and kept going.

"I like being high up. Hey, there's a bird's nest up there." Mark pointed to one of the oaks by the house. One of the yard cats hopped up behind him and he laughed, the kind of laugh where his whole face lit up. And when he got to one of the fence posts, he chewed on his lip and studied his feet. Then he stepped over it and landed on the other side, the same way that old yard cat would do, like he'd been sure about it the whole time.

"Watch out, you'll fall," I'd told him again.

"I won't," Mark said. "I'll just fly away."

———

The weeds along the driveway had been cleared out and the gravel was in good shape, not washed away like it sometimes got when the rain came heavy. Even though it wasn't fall yet, webworm nests were already starting to choke around some of the tree branches. First thing I did was look for Clive's truck, but I didn't see it and since it was Thursday, he was probably down at the stockyard. It seemed just as well.

Even though the flowers on the front porch had dried out, the concrete steps were swept off and the paint was in pretty good shape. I let Libby come in to get a glass of water, but as soon as I could, I sent her back to Greenville and I wandered around the house checking on things. Most of the downstairs looked the way it did when I left, except for Clive letting the mail pile up on the kitchen table. There was a dried-up stain or two on the green tablecloth, and I scraped off what I could with my fingernail.

Upstairs, the wood floors gave off that honey smell they always had in the summer. It was hot up there with no windows open. When I opened one to get some air, I could hear somebody's cows moaning down the road, a sound like heavy furniture being moved.

The door to Mark's bedroom was closed and when I went in, my footsteps left marks in the thin layer of dust. The room hadn't been touched since I'd left. All of Mark's things, the bird nests and the pinecones, the leaves and the rocks, and a few soda cans here and there, were stacked up on his shelves. The blue quilt hung off the side of his bed, crooked, the way he'd left it.

I had meant to move back in for good. Be a wife to Clive again. Hadn't I been in such a hurry to leave Libby's and get back? But as I left Mark's room, my throat almost closed up. I was slick with sweat, my dress stuck to my back. I wasn't ready to be in that house again with Mark's old room down the hall. I tried to talk myself into staying and couldn't do it.

I could have gone to see if one of the rental places was empty, but they seemed too close by. Then I remembered my Aunt Callie's old rock house, the way it could be so quiet up there. I hadn't been in years, not since we'd cleaned it out after she passed on. But she'd left it to me and Libby. I could have gone any time I wanted—maybe I ought to have gone there first thing instead of going to Libby's.

After I packed a few more clothes and things I needed from the house, I left Clive a note on the kitchen table. I told him I was going up to Wyeth's Mill for a few days, maybe a week or two, to see about Callie's old place. I signed it "Love, Sadie" because I did love him. I was still his wife.

The car started up fine and the drive didn't take too long, not more than twenty or thirty minutes. As soon as I turned off toward Wyeth's Mill, the trees were so thick, they blocked out the sun in most places—a good place for some kind of animal to hide. The air felt at least ten degrees cooler. Callie's old rock house was tucked back in the holler, and parts of the road were washed out. The car bounced all over the place no matter how slow I took it.

It didn't seem like anybody had been at the house in a while, but my key worked fine. It was a little place, just the front room and the back bedroom with the added-on bathroom and kitchen off to one side. The front room had a wood stove, an old brown couch, two light blue recliners, and a braided rug on top of the rock floor. After I cleaned up that room, I made my way to the others. The window in the bedroom opened after I worked on it for a few minutes. Through the screen, I heard the creek not too far away, the water moving over the rocks like I remembered. And the wet, black dirt smell was the same too. I'd forgotten it, but when I breathed in deep, I could almost believe I wasn't any more than eight or nine years old and Libby was holding up my hair to braid it, her fingers touching the back of my neck the way someone might play the piano.

First thing the next morning, I went around back, where I found a short stack of kindling and some larger pieces too, all of it covered with a blue tarp to keep out the rain. I carried a few pieces back inside to get the wood stove started.

The kitchen cabinets were full of mouse droppings so I cleaned them out with bleach. I'd brought some canned apples and beans up from the house, and I was heating up some of the apples on the wood stove when a black snake slithered under the back door—came in like he owned the place.

My heart beat fast and I stepped back, looking for something heavy or sharp. It didn't look like anything but an old water snake, but I couldn't be sure. As quick as I could, I grabbed the broom from the kitchen. The snake was moving into the bedroom by then and before it could get under the bed, I brought the broom down hard, again and again until it stopped moving. It was a shame having to do it, but that was the way Daddy had taught us. For a minute, I wondered if I should leave and go back home. But staying at Callie's old place by myself seemed better than going back— where Mark's things were just down the hall, where Clive took up all the room and we still wouldn't have anything to say to each other. As soon as I found the shovel, I buried that snake out back just past the pile of wood where I must have woken it up earlier. The dirt was soft and it didn't take me long.

CHAPTER 42

— *Sadie Caswell* —

I heated up some beans for supper and went to bed early. As tired as I was, I should have gone right to sleep but you can't make a body do that any more than you can keep milk from turning. The longer I lay there, the more I wondered how things could've been different for Mark. If Tinley hadn't come around, then Mark would have walked down the aisle to marry Maddie, taking his place beside her at the front of the church sure he'd found what he was looking for.

I put myself back at the logging yard the last time I saw him. Pushing him and trying to get him to fix something that was too far gone to fix. Before I finally went to sleep, I told myself that, out of all the minutes that make up a life, there's not one better or more important than the rest. I guessed if you could line them all up and weigh them, they would weigh about the same.

The time I held Mark when he woke up with a nightmare and his tears soaked through my nightgown.

All the nights I told Clive and Mark they needed to wash their hands for supper and they went over to the kitchen sink while I got biscuits out of the oven, Clive going over each of his fingers like you'd bathe a newborn baby and Mark slapping water all over the place and leaving streaks of dirt on the dishcloth.

Standing in the kitchen with him that last Sunday he and Maddie came up to the house after church. His hand streaked with blood. Wanting to make him better and not knowing how. When the only way to make things better would've been to make like none of it had ever happened at all. To turn time backwards on itself the way a dog tries to bite his own tail.

Over the next few days, I did what I could around the house. Some people like Libby act like cleaning a house is something they've got to be dragged to do, but I never minded straightening things up. Once I got the rooms in pretty good shape, I found an ax propped up beside the woodpile and chopped a few more pieces of wood until my arms got tired. When I stopped to catch my breath, I listened to the water slipping over the rocks and the birds calling to each other, getting ready to fly south for the winter. I couldn't do anything to stop the seasons from changing. Nobody could. Maybe it was the same with Mark. Nobody could have done anything to save him, not from himself. It was a hard thing to wrap my mind around, but deep down I knew it was the truth.

After I'd been at Callie's a couple of weeks, I had to go into town for more food. Even though I went first thing when the store opened, it was fairly crowded. Some of those people moved so slowly in the aisles you'd think there was going to be a test on what all the labels said. The older pastor from up at the church, Pastor Mason, was buying up sandwich meat and bread. Once he spotted me, I couldn't get past him without speaking. He touched my arm like we were long-lost kin.

"Sadie Caswell, I heard you were back up from Greenville."

"How'd you hear that?"

"Oh, I don't know." He laughed. "Word just gets out. We're just so glad you're back."

I put a package of sliced turkey in my cart and then took it back out again. "I won't be coming up to the church, though. I'm in Wyeth's Mill for a spell. Checking on some things up there."

He nodded like he knew that too. "Looks to me like Mr. Caswell has lost a good bit of weight here lately. He's doing all right?"

"He seems to be."

"Well, I've been praying for him. We all have. Both of you."

All the praying in the world wouldn't bring Mark back. I knew because I'd tried it myself. But I said thank you and went on to get what I needed.

On my way back to Callie's, I drove by the house on Maranatha Road to see how it looked. But a big truck behind me was going faster than it needed to, and I couldn't slow down without it running into my car. So I didn't really see much as I went by—couldn't even tell if Clive's truck was there or not. I would call him on Sunday anyway. Every time I talked to him, I waited for him to ask me to come back home. I asked if he needed me to do some cooking for him, how he was getting on, anything I could think of to make him ask me. But he always said he was fine and eating good and needed to get back outside. That's how he was. Clive didn't talk easy about anything but farming, and he never did ask for much.

Going by the house that day made me remember Tinley standing on my porch. The mind is funny that way sometimes, the way something will show up whether you like it or not, with no good reason. There wasn't any point in wondering about that girl. The Lord only knew if she was telling the truth about expecting—or about who the baby's father was. But if she was, then I wondered what the baby would have looked like— if she'd ended up having the baby instead of what I'd told her to do.

That's what wondering will do to you, give you questions that come up with other questions. Going over those things didn't do a bit of good. She probably did just as I'd said. And I knew that was the end of it. But there's a difference in knowing something and in being able to keep it out of your head.

I guessed if that baby had lived, she would have been a girl. I never considered the baby being a boy. I don't know why. Sometimes you get an idea about something and you can't convince yourself there could be another way.

I guessed she would have liked butterflies, especially the orange ones with black spots. For her birthdays she would have wanted yellow cake with lemon icing, the kind our mama used to make for me and Libby on our birthdays. Her eyes would have been green like Mark's and she would have liked great big books about fairytales, books so heavy she'd barely have been able to carry them around. Her favorite color would most likely have been pink, like most girls.

———

One day toward the end of August, I heard a knock at the front door. "Who is it?" I called out from the bedroom where I was getting dressed.

"Sadie, are you in there?"

"I'm here. Who's there? What is it?"

"Can I come in? It's Vinson Keller."

"I'm not dressed. I'll be out there in a minute."

"I—I really need to talk to you. There's something I need to tell you."

"I guess it can wait a minute." I pulled on an old house dress and shut the closet. I wasn't thinking about why he'd come all the way out to Callie's place to talk to me. I picked up the comb from on top of the dresser and started to run it through my hair.

Vinson called through the door again. "Sadie, it's about Clive."

The way he spoke, I knew then there was something to it. I tossed the comb down and ran to open the front door. "What about Clive?" I pulled Vinson into the house. "What is it that's happened to Clive?"

He said something about Clive falling outside and being confused, something about him being in the hospital and not being able to keep food down, but I couldn't hear much of what he said because I was getting my suitcase out of the closet, opening drawers and throwing things in as quickly as I could.

CHAPTER 43

— *Tinley Greene* —

Sometimes Rebecca opens her blue eyes really big. She looks like she's trying to see the whole world at once. Other times she opens her fingers like she wants something to hold onto, and I look around for her pacifier or a soft toy. When I hand her the pacifier, she throws it down and I try the cloth kite that crinkles when you fold it, but she grunts and pants because it's not the right thing. It's not what she wants. I look around for the next thing to try. I put my finger on her cheek saying wait a minute, sweetie, just one minute and she reaches for my finger. She grabs onto it, really grabs it, and it's what she wanted the whole time. Sometimes she pulls it up to her mouth and rubs her gums against my knuckle and other times she studies it, like she's trying to decide what it might be good for. And sometimes she just holds my finger tight and that seems to be enough. I wonder if maybe it means she forgives me for thinking I didn't want her. Or that I'm good enough to be her mother after all.

By the start of July, the camp is full. The boys are always slapping each other on the back and racing to see who is the fastest runner. The girls whisper and braid each other's hair. Some of them can run just as fast as the boys. Their sneakers slap against the ground and when they're finished, they bend over with their hands on their knees, laughing. If the girls spot me and Rebecca, they stop whatever they're doing—they drop their canoe paddles by the lake, leave their spaghetti and meatballs uneaten at the table—to rush up to me and ask if they can hold the baby. My chest swells with pride when they say how cute she is, what a good baby, how sweet-natured. Before long, I reach to take her back and she snuggles against my chest and I start to believe I can do this after all.

One afternoon, Travis clears his throat and says I can't stay in the cabin any longer because they need it for paying campers.

"But you pack up the baby's things and yours too and you can stay up with me and Leigh, at least for now," he says. "I'm sure it will be fine."

In their cabin, Leigh and Travis have an extra back room where they store oversized cans of food for the camp. Travis carries up the folding playpen where Rebecca sleeps and sets up a cot for me beside it. Most nights after dinner, I spread out a blanket on the floor for her and she kicks her legs over and over again. Leigh comes in and we both watch the baby's legs, laughing. When I scoop Rebecca up off the floor, she bites down on my finger and Leigh frowns.

"Did you wash your hands? You really should wash your hands before you pick her up. Every time." She reaches for Rebecca, making her mouth go round to see if the baby will do it back and puts her on her shoulder, patting her back. "You go ahead and I'll hold her for a minute."

Sometimes after the dishes are washed and the dining hall is swept clean, we sit out on the porch—Rebecca asleep on Leigh's lap or bouncing on her shoulder. Watching them, my hands twitch to get the baby back. But I stop myself from reaching over. Leigh is good with her. Maybe we're making our own kind of family.

At night after I'm in bed and Rebecca is asleep in the playpen, everything falls quiet and I can talk to Mark. I tell him how much I miss him, that I know we were going to be together. That I haven't forgotten. I tell him everything I can think of. Some mornings Leigh asks why I look so tired.

"It's the baby, I guess. Getting up in the night when I need to feed her."

"Your eyes are all red." She shakes her head. "You need to be careful. Especially with the baby. You can't be off in la-la land all the time."

Whenever Leigh is around, she watches what I do with Rebecca—the way I change her diaper and feed her, how I soothe her when she cries and where I lay her down to sleep. Leigh's scrutiny feels like a spotlight and I'm nervous underneath it, reminded of how my face used to go hot in school—even when I'd studied, even when I knew the subject backwards and forwards—as the teacher passed out the test. I have no way to judge if I'm a good mother. Nobody has taught me. I go around imagining that Mark or my parents will magically show up, and I can't help talking to them even though they aren't really here. Maybe all that affects my baby somehow. Maybe she would be better off without me. When Leigh leaves and I'm alone again with Rebecca, I lean down and whisper against her cheek. I'll try to do better, sweet girl. I won't let anything happen to you.

CHAPTER 44

— *Sadie Caswell* —

Those doctors didn't know what they were talking about, especially the young one with the droopy pants. He couldn't find his way out of a paper bag. They talked about all the tests they had to do, when anyone with a lick of sense would've known Clive had simply worked too hard. He was ten years older than me and most seventy-three-year old men wouldn't be able to do all that Clive did—plowing and caring for cattle and splitting wood and everything else. Clive had been doing all that for years and he would never think of stopping. What good did it do to run all those tests? All he needed was some time to take it easy.

The doctors didn't even agree with each other about what had happened to Clive. You could tell by the way the older one with the big ears clipped his see-through papers to the lighted board before the young one—Dr. Wilkins—was even finished talking, something about how he was born and raised in Garnet and his brother had been sheriff for years.

"And here I am, only a doctor. The black sheep, I guess," he said. "I'm only kidding, Mrs. Caswell." When I didn't laugh, he said, "We'll get you in to see your husband right away."

As we headed down the hallway, I tried to get them to tell me how long it would be until Clive would feel better.

"Well, Mrs. Caswell, we have some conflicting reports about what exactly is going on and why your husband collapsed like he did," Dr. Wilkins said. "Even at his age, we wouldn't expect some of the numbers we're seeing." He stopped walking to flip through his papers like he would find the answer there. "The next step is to determine what's going on with his blood work," he said without looking up.

The older doctor nodded. "We just don't know. But we're going to need to keep him here for the foreseeable future. There's a fair amount of concern about what we're seeing so far."

"Well, go ahead and show me where his room is at least." I pointed down the hall, anxious to get going.

When I went in to see Clive, the bed was tilted up and he was half lying down and half sitting up. He couldn't have been comfortable with the bed like that. The first thing I did was ask him if he wanted me to move it.

"It's fine where it is," he said, twisting around to where I stood at the top of the bed.

"Don't move around like that," I told him, worried he would hurt himself worse. "Just stay put."

"You can leave that alone, Sadie."

"I'm only checking to see if I can get it a better way. Maybe move it up a little to where you can sit."

Once I got the bed fixed, I came around to face Clive head on. His eyes were tinged with yellow and red, not the right color at all. And his skin didn't look good either. It seemed like I was looking at him through glasses with a film on them. And he looked older too, the way his skin hung off him where he used to be filled out. "How are you feeling?" I pulled the blanket up where it had fallen down.

"Can you see about them letting me out of here?" Clive asked. "There's no way I'm staying cooped up in here like this. But they said something about more tests." He talked like it hurt when he took a breath. But I told myself it might not be anything more than him getting older and the way he'd fallen. Something like that could shake anybody up. That's what I had to keep telling myself, seeing him there in that hospital room with all the white. There wasn't anything to that room but white and gray. I promised Clive we would get him home as soon as we could.

After I'd stayed for a little while, a nurse came in and said Clive needed to rest, so I went on to the house. The phone was ringing when I went in and I didn't want to answer it, but I did. It was Libby, wanting to know how Clive was. She said she would leave Greenville as soon as Warren got home.

"How did you even hear about any of this mess?" I asked.

"That new choir director up at Solid Rock is first cousins with our organist. And they've started the prayer chain going, so they called her first thing and she called me because she knew I was kin. What are the doctors saying?"

"They can't say much, not yet anyway." I sighed and shook my head. "I have to get going."

"Sadie, I'm coming up there just as soon as Warren gets home with the car. It took out on my way back from the mall. You'd like to have thought it would burn clear up, the way smoke was roaring out. But surely it's just about fixed and he'll be back with it in a little bit."

"You can stay where you are. There's no need for you to come up here." Libby kept on talking and I was too tired to listen to her, so I hung up the phone and unplugged it from the wall. Later on, I felt bad and plugged it back in. I called her back and told her not to come up right away, and she made me promise to tell her if I changed my mind even if it was in the middle of the night.

Over the next few days, I was up at the hospital most of the time. Even though I told Clive I was taking care of everything back at the house and he didn't need to worry himself over it, he still wanted to go over things.

"Some of the fences have fallen down in places, especially down by the driveway, and you might want to ask Vinson about that big oak behind the barn, on the east side. I think a limb needs to come down."

"I'll tell him. I'm making a list."

"He probably ought to get to bush hogging that one patch we haven't gotten to yet. We'd started it—"

"Clive, he's already done that."

"Well, he can't let the grass get so tall that it goes to seed."

"I'll tell him that too," I promised.

———

Vinson Keller said he would look after the fields Clive rented out, and I went over the ones by the house. You could see where they'd gotten up the corn and tomatoes and the pole beans. There were open mounds of dirt where the potatoes had been dug up and I found them in bushel baskets in the barn, lined up on the silky gray dirt.

There wasn't any need for me to see about the rental houses. We'd sold the one where Mark had stayed sometimes and Clive said he wasn't worried about renting out the gray one, not anytime soon. It was sitting there empty, but I had better things to do than to worry about cleaning it out.

After I'd checked on everything else, I went out to the hill on the south side just to see about it. It looked the same as it always did—nothing but some shrubs and a few walnut trees. And I didn't waste any time picturing how it would have looked any other way, with apple trees or any other kind.

Seeing Clive in the hospital bed made me feel guilty about how I'd left him—and especially about how I'd stayed away for so long. If I'd been at home, I would have been able to help Clive. Instead, I'd been hiding out like a child, making him worry.

The first chance I got, I told the doctors what had happened to Clive was probably all my fault.

"I'd left and he probably didn't want me to," I said. "He might've wanted me to come back. But I didn't."

Dr. Wilkins said that wasn't the way it worked. "You don't need to worry about that. Sometimes these things just happen," he said. "We're having to re-do some of his panels, but we'll get to the bottom of it."

I nodded, even though I wasn't sure I trusted him.

"His age more than likely has something to do with it. Let's see what's going on when we get those results back, okay?"

I agreed, but only because I had no choice.

———

One night the nurse told me I'd better go on home to get some rest. "I don't want Clive here by himself," I told her. "I'm fine where I am."

"But you were here last night too. Do you have other family I could call?" She waited with a pencil and pad of paper. "I can call them if you'd like. Might give you a break." You could tell from her breath that she smoked cigarettes.

There wasn't anybody to call. Clive's brother had been a lot older than him and gone for a while, his widow long-since remarried and no blood relation anyway. Nobody was left in Clive's family but a second cousin over in Tennessee who didn't even send us a Christmas card. Libby kept calling up at the house, but I never talked to her for long. And I didn't say anything about her to that nurse. Even though Libby and Warren and their daughter would do what they could to help, Clive had always thought of them as my family, not his. And Libby wouldn't know the first thing about how to take care of him.

"I'm all he's got," I said. That nurse didn't say a word back to me, but she let me stay as late as I wanted.

CHAPTER 45

— *Sadie Caswell* —

The Kellers and the Honeycutts and Pastor Mason came by the hospital and Clive talked to them, but you could tell he didn't feel like visiting. He was only being polite, the way he was brought up. He'd finally owned up and told the doctors that he was hurting, mostly in his stomach—not to where he couldn't stand it, but fairly bad sometimes. I'd never known him to say a thing like that.

One day before Dr. Wilkins left Clive's room, I asked him about it. "He shouldn't be hurting bad, should he? He's never been one to complain. Anybody would tell you that, anybody who knows him."

"I'll call in something that will make him feel better. At least for now while we're waiting on the test results to come back." He wrote it all down and left the room, that white coat of his whipping behind him.

When I asked the new nurse when Clive could get started on the new medicine, she promised to check on it. She was a pretty thing, pale like she wasn't out in the sun much, with some red in her hair.

"Do you need anything, Mrs. Caswell?"

"I can't think of anything else, as long as you check on the medicine."

"Well, my name's Rebecca. I'm not sure if I told you before. I've been so mixed-up because I switched over not too long ago from labor and delivery. But I'll be over here for a while now, probably a few months at least. Not saying you'll be here that long, but while you're here, you let me know if you need anything at all, okay?"

I thanked her, remembering how that other nurse had asked if she could call anybody. Clive didn't have any family left except me. And I tried to forget what I'd done, how I sent Tinley away and never breathed a word about it. If I hadn't done it—and if Tinley was telling the truth—then we might have had a grandchild. I counted up the months. She would have been born by then. If I hadn't acted like she wasn't worth anything, like she was something you'd throw away when you were cleaning house, she would have been close to a few months old.

But I couldn't tell Clive any of that. There are some things you can't face even if you come at them sideways.

One day toward the end of the week, Clive grabbed my arm, asking me if I'd seen it yet.

"Seen what?"

"Have you been out there? Is it October yet? That's the best time."

I shook my head. "It's September." I tried to ask what he was worried about, but his attention drifted off.

———

Later that week, when I came into his room, Clive must have been feeling good because he was sitting up in the bed. As soon as he saw me, he smoothed down his white hair.

"Anybody been by yet?" I lifted up his chart to see what the doctor had written down even though most of the time I couldn't read his handwriting.

"Pastor Mason came by earlier. He brought those tapes. Said I could listen to the sermons I was missing." He pointed to the stack of cassette tapes on the table.

"I can see about getting a player for them if you want. And before you start asking about it, the seeds came in, all except the limas."

"Good, that's good. But there's something else I want to ask you about." Clive started going over the bed sheet with his hand, the same way he would have run his fingers over a piece of sawed wood checking to see if it was smooth.

I figured he had something on his mind about the farm. Even in the hospital, he was always going on about what needed to get in the ground and when it ought to get there.

"It's about time we found out what happened to that girl." He looked at me, then leaned back against the pillow.

"What girl?" I reached behind me for the edge of the chair and sat down, holding the bag I'd brought with me. Thinking I knew what girl he was talking about, but I didn't know why he'd bring her up. Thinking I needed to take one breath, and then another, and then another one after that. "There isn't any girl you need to be worrying about."

"The one who was with Mark."

"Clive, Maddie Spencer can take care of herself. She's doing just fine without our help. Last I heard from Libby she's already halfway to the altar with that Pittler boy."

"Not Maddie." Clive shook his head. He stared at me like there wasn't anything more important than me understanding what he was saying. "The one who was with him the day he died. Her last name is Greene. That's what I heard."

I didn't ask how he'd heard that. "There's no need to worry about her," I said as firmly as I could. "She doesn't have anything to do with us." I looked down at my lap and started going through the bag I'd brought for him—clean socks and underwear, some candied ginger for his nausea. I kept looking down, trying to avoid the blue of his eyes and the way his ears were red at the bottom, the way they got when he was worked up about something.

"I've been going over it. All these days in bed and nothing else to do."

"Clive, what's the point of digging into all that? You're getting yourself worked up over nothing."

He sighed. "It seemed like we should let it be, that Mark would figure it out. But that wasn't right."

"Whatever it was, I guess it was too far gone."

"Later on I tried to help her—I took her some groceries. But the next time I went by, she wasn't there." Clive shook his head.

"What are you talking about? Where was she?"

He didn't answer me, just said again that we should try to find her.

"Finding her won't bring Mark back, Clive."

He looked at me like he could change my mind, and I thought about all the things he didn't know. He didn't know Tinley was expecting, or at least said she was. He didn't know I'd sent her away, and he wouldn't have understood. It wasn't something I could say out loud. There was no coming at it from the front or from the side. There was only forgetting. Pretending like it never happened.

Even though I tried not to think about what I'd done, how I'd told Tinley to get rid of the baby, the last few nights I had dreamed I was holding a baby around its neck, begging myself not to squeeze. The way I saw it, that girl Tinley killed Mark and I might have killed our grandchild.

"Clive, I'm going to leave if you don't stop talking like this. This is just a mess you're getting yourself in. All worked up over nothing."

"You think somebody from up at the church could tell us who she is, what's happened to her?"

I stood up and put the bag on the bed by his feet. "I'll be back tomorrow morning," I told him "Maybe you'll be calm then. More yourself." And I left, just like I said I would.

It was a long time ago, coming up on a year. That's what I told myself when I parked the car and went inside the house, the kitchen light left on above the sink and the dishcloth draped over the faucet to dry. I heated up some stew and sat down at the kitchen table to eat it.

As I ate, I wondered if things could have worked out differently. I put myself back on that porch with Tinley, watching her crying and talking about how much she loved Mark, and I imagined what would've happened if I'd taken her at her word. Maybe I'd have let her cry. *I know you must have loved him like you say you did.* Maybe I would've cried too. And when she told me about the baby, I guess I could have seen it for what it really was. Part of Mark going on when the rest of him couldn't.

Sitting at the table, I figured I hadn't seen Clive that way since he got sick—maybe even since Mark died. It wasn't just him sitting up in bed. It was the wanting that got to me, the way Clive wanted something for the first time in as long as I could remember. Once Mark was gone, it had seemed like there wasn't anything in the world worth wanting.

I shook my head and pushed myself up from the table. Sometimes all a wanting like that does is remind you of what you can't have. It was too late. Tinley probably did what I told her to do with the money and never came back. While I washed up the bowl and spoon, I told myself nobody would be able to help me find her. I didn't have anybody to ask anyway.

The next morning, the phone rang up at the house. It was one of the doctors, just like I thought. As different as they looked, I couldn't tell which one's voice it was and I skipped over when he said his name, impatient to find out what was going on with Clive.

"Mrs. Caswell, we'd like you to come down here to meet with us— this morning if you can."

"What is it? What's going on with him?"

"Well, you'll see when you get here that Mr. Caswell doesn't look or sound any different than he did when you were here yesterday."

I nodded, even though he couldn't see me. "So then what is it?"

"Well, we've gotten the results back from the various tests we've run, and that's what we'd like to talk to you about. We're going to get Dr. Clarkson from Mission on the phone in case you have questions for him too."

———

The way I saw it, those doctors spent three or four times longer talking to me than they needed to. All their talk about this and that test and what the studies were showing and Clive's age. Pointing to x-rays or scans or something, showing me numbers on a chart and mess like that. When all they had to do was say from the start that Clive had cancer, some kind with his pancreas. Those doctors wasted time talking about options when they ended up saying Clive didn't have any. That it had spread and they couldn't do anything for him. That they didn't know how much time he had left, but it wasn't much. You can tell somebody that in a few minutes, without all the papers and pointing.

CHAPTER 46

— *Tinley Greene* —

Whenever Lynette Barnes comes out to see us at the camp, she asks how Rebecca is eating and sleeping and what we need. She always brings things for us—formula and diapers and food from her garden. One time she asks if she can meet Travis and Leigh, and I jump up from the porch. "Let me go find them." *Let me show you my family.*

Leigh is out back unpinning blankets from the clothesline and folding them over her arm. I take a stack from her and she follows me around to the porch where Lynette waits. They nod at each other and Leigh asks if Lynette and I are related. Lynette says no so quickly that it hurts my feelings even though it's the truth.

Since Travis is off with his cousin somewhere, Lynette doesn't get to meet him. But I show her their wedding picture hanging up in the hallway and she says, "He's awfully handsome. You have to watch out for those."

"He looks like Mark Caswell, don't you think?" My voice sounds shaky, but I can't help it. I want her to tell me that I'm right. "Travis is a little older," I add, clearing my throat.

Lynette squints. "I guess they might favor one another a little."

———

In August, on my eighteenth birthday, Leigh makes a cake and, as soon as we've eaten some, she walks away holding the baby.

"I'm taking her down to the lake, okay?" A group of campers pass by on their way to the bus that will take them home. In the distance, Leigh shrinks smaller and smaller until I can't even see the baby I know is propped on her shoulder.

———

At Rebecca's three-month check-up in September, the doctor at the health department says I need to take her up to the hospital for a special kind of shot.

"There's a serious virus going around and it could get in a baby's lungs," he says. "With her being as small as she is, that makes—" he looks down at the paper he's holding—"That makes Rebecca high risk for something like that, okay?" He jingles the change in his pocket. "But they only have it up at the hospital in Garnet. They didn't cover us to get it here." He gives me a printout of directions to the hospital, even though everyone knows where it is.

In the hospital waiting room, the television is turned to a news channel. The sound is off so the words run across the bottom of the screen, and sometimes they don't keep up with the people's mouths. At first I set Rebecca's carrier on the chair beside mine. But then she starts kicking her legs and if she kicks hard enough, she could fall off the chair, so I move the carrier to the floor. I don't care what Leigh says. I'm careful with her.

People walk past the waiting room to the elevators, but I don't see anybody I know except for the pastor from the church. He's swinging a plastic bag and waves over to the desk where they hand out visitor badges. When he calls out "Caswell," the woman at the desk nods and puts down the badge he didn't take. I loop the carrier over my arm on the way to the desk. The elevator doors ding and the pastor steps in.

"Did he say Caswell?" I ask the woman at the desk. She starts to answer, but Rebecca lets out a cry and a nurse pushes open a swinging door and calls out "Greene." With my finger in Rebecca's mouth I promise her it's going to be okay, and I tell the woman at the desk never mind.

When the nurse stabs the needle in Rebecca's leg, she cries so hard her face turns purple and I feel like crying myself until I get her to calm down by bouncing her on my lap and stroking her cheek. "Do I have to pay something?" I ask the nurse on our way out. "I brought some money."

She shakes her head and her long gold earrings sway like feathers. "You gals are all set."

————

Every day in October I wonder what Mark and I were doing on that day the year before. Was he moving closer to me, whispering my name? Were we planting flowers? Was it the day I waited for him and he didn't come?

One day toward the end of the month, Rebecca opens her eyes and, all of a sudden, they have turned green. They were blue before and now they're green. It must have been happening and I didn't see it, not until today. They are the same light, milky green as Mark's eyes, a green I've never seen before except on him. I keep looking to be sure, and I know it's Mark watching over us. It must be some kind of sign.

CHAPTER 47

— *Sadie Caswell* —

After I met with the doctors, I went on back home instead of going to see Clive. I had a lot to do up at the house. The trashcans needed emptying, and I rinsed them out with bleach and set them out in the yard to dry. After that, I cleaned out the cabinets and refrigerator. When the wind died down, I burned the trash. I washed the bed linens and the towels and went through the mail and took checks to the post office to pay the bills. Vinson Keller called, and I told him what needed to be done outside and he promised to take care of it.

By the time I finished with everything, it was dark and I went to bed without eating supper. I was sleeping in the extra bedroom, where I'd slept before I went down to Libby's. It didn't seem right to go back to sleeping in Clive's room, not after I'd left the way I did. When I laid down that night, I was sore from being on my feet all day. I thought about how my arms and legs hurt and I didn't think about anything else. Not Clive or the doctors or the hospital. Not Tinley or her baby. Nothing except being tired.

———

As time went on, you could tell Clive was starting to hurt more. I guessed it was the cancer getting worse. Seeing him like that—weak and pitiful—was like seeing a completely different person.

I told the nurse, the one who smelled like cigarette smoke, that I was
going to start bringing food from home for him and they could stop
delivering it from the cafeteria. The food they had didn't even look real.
It looked like plastic food a child would play house with. The nurse said
we were paying for it and I told her that didn't matter.

Once they finally gave him a new medicine to help with the pain,
Clive looked better off. His face eased up and didn't look as tight as it
had before. But sometimes the medicine made him confused and he
forgot Mark was gone. He asked me when Mark was going to be home
from the lumberyard, and why he left his boots in the kitchen instead of
on the back porch. Or he talked about Mark like he was five years old,
about how he'd always bring stuff in from the yard—pieces of rock and
arrowheads in his pockets and stacks of bird nests on his shelves. The way
he'd climb up on the fences even when we told him not to. When we told
him he'd fall. When we didn't know that one day he would pick falling
over anything else.

On his good days, Clive remembered Mark—knew he was our son
and that he was gone. He missed Mark just like I did. The way anybody
would. It had been close to a year, but some things time can barely touch.
Even so, I was always glad to see Clive sitting up with his pillow propped
behind his back and his hair combed. Those days, he smiled when I came
in the room. He wanted to know how I was doing and how the house
was. He remembered the state of the garden when he last saw it—told
me the hornworms hadn't gotten to the tomatoes like they did last year—
things like that.

Even on the good days, Clive kept asking me if I had seen something,
if I had been somewhere up at the house, but I couldn't understand what
he was saying. I didn't know what he meant. He said something about
outside, and I figured whatever it was, Vinson Keller would see to it.

I patted his hand. "Clive, you need to get some rest."

After he calmed down, I settled myself back in the visitor's chair. On
those good days, I stayed as long as I could.

Early in October, the doctors said Clive should be moved to some kind of a hospice place. They said nothing could be done for him except help the pain.

"So how much time does he have?" I crossed my arms over my chest and held my breath.

"It's still hard to say." Dr. Wilkins shook his head. "It's a fairly aggressive cancer and we don't like to make predictions."

"Isn't that what you went to school for?"

"Mrs. Caswell, if I could give you some firm guidance, I would. But I can't. I'm sorry."

Later that day, Rebecca, the nurse with the red hair, told me they were doing what was best.

"They'll take real good care of him." She unzipped the duffel bag and put Clive's shirts in it. "I can fit some more things in here if you want to hand me what's in the bottom drawer." A lot of nurses came through, but she was the one who took the most time with me and Clive. Even if she was walking fast down the hall, she would stop if she saw me and ask how he was doing.

On our way out, Clive's legs weren't strong enough to walk, but he didn't like having to be pushed in the wheelchair. When he said he wanted to go home, I acted like I hadn't heard him because I didn't know what to say. Any promise I could make would end up hollow.

After we got to the hospice place, I fixed the bed with the blanket folded at the bottom, the way Clive liked, and he was able to rest some. Every night I prayed the doctors were wrong. Every day I went by to see him.

One day toward the end of October, I was sitting on the porch swing, wiping off gourds from the garden with a dishrag when a truck turned off the road and started down the driveway. It was a rusty old thing with a big trailer on the back. When the truck went around the curve and came up in front of the house the trailer lagged behind it, swaying like a child trying to catch up. I put the twisted gourd I was holding back in the basket and stood up, wiping my hands on the clean part of the rag. The truck pulled up in front of the house and I could see the shapes of trees in the trailer, covered with a tarp. When a man got out of the truck, I opened my mouth to tell him he must be lost.

"This the Caswell place?"

I came down the steps, nodding. "It is. But what's all this? I don't think—"

He reached back into the truck and pulled out a clipboard, flipped a page over the top and looked at the next page. When he looked up, he said, "Caswell, right? You know a Clive?"

"That's my husband. But he's not here."

"I'd heard something about that. Awfully sorry about it too. A thing like that, with what y'all have already been through." He wiped off his chin with the bandana from his back pocket and tilted his head toward the back of the truck. "But I wanted to bring the order once it came in, seeing as how it's already paid for."

"I'm sorry you came out here, but we didn't order anything. My husband plants from seed, always has. He wouldn't do something that's costing what I guess those do."

"Real tall feller? White hair, wears overalls, and keeps a navy blue one of these in his back pocket?" He held up his red bandana and I nodded. Still, a lot of the men Clive's age in Wynette County looked the same way.

"You must be Sadie then." He put the clipboard back in the truck and closed the door. He reached out his hand for me to shake and I stuck out mine, wondering the whole time what was going on. In all the years we'd been married, we never had a nursery delivery, not of bushes or trees or anything else.

"He placed the order back in May. I've got it all right here. Like I said, it's already paid for, if that's what you're worried about."

I tried to work out the timing in my mind. Clive had gone down to Greenville in May—and come back by himself. I went to the back of the truck and lifted up the tarp. I still couldn't see much, only some of the root balls. But an idea came to me and I couldn't let go of it. When I tried to swallow, something seemed caught in my throat.

"What are these? What did he order?"

Before he even got his answer out, I had started to cry.

"Are you all right? Is there something—"

I tried to gather myself and pointed at the truck bed. "I'm sorry. Can you just tell me what they are?"

And the man said exactly what I thought he would. "Apple trees, ma'am."

I couldn't say anything, just nodded.

"Your husband said you've got a good piece where it's full sun. And you'll need to watch the drainage because standing water will rot those roots for sure." He patted the tarp. "You've got Gala here. Everybody likes those. And some Ginger Gold too, those new ones. They don't even have those up at Ingles, not yet anyway. But boy, are they pretty to look at, and they've got a good bit of sweetness to them." He handed me some papers and a pen. "I've got this here for you to sign and I'll get these unloaded."

CHAPTER 48

— *Sadie Caswell* —

After I called Vinson Keller, he came by first thing the next morning with some boys he knew to get the trees in the ground. Since I would have been in the way, I stayed back at the house.

"Y'all come back down here when you're finished and I'll have some food ready," I told him.

Vinson raised his eyebrows. "You don't need to do that."

It would've been easier to stay by myself, to leave the money for them out on the porch and not have to talk to anybody. But they had come out so early in the morning, and I knew they must have had other jobs they could have been doing. The least I could do was offer them a bite to eat.

It was the middle of the afternoon when they came down the hill, all sweaty and dirty and every one of them wearing some sort of faded plaid flannel shirt with the sleeves rolled up. There must have been four or five boys with Vinson, laughing and slapping each other on the back, some of them with the laces of their work boots dragging on the ground. I guessed they were about Mark's age when he died. Even though some of them probably went to school with Mark, I didn't know their names.

By the time they got up to the house, I opened the back door and told them to come on inside, but Vinson said they would eat out in the yard. When they were almost finished, I took out the money and gave them each a brown paper bag of sliced pound cake to take home.

After they left, I started washing the dishes, wondering how the trees looked, how many rows there were and how they were spaced apart. Before long I couldn't wait anymore and I headed up there, leaving the sink still full of dirty dishes, my sweater tied around my waist. The fence had broken down in one place and that saved me from having to climb over it. Most of the oaks and poplars still had their leaves—bright yellow and dark red, and here and there some orange and green. Going through the old pasture there were weeds and chiggers almost everywhere I stepped, but I kept thinking about how those trees would look once I got to the hill on the south side.

I always thought people didn't change. If you're trying to change somebody's mind, you might as well save your breath for all the good it'll do you. People are who they are, and nothing that happens will make them any different. Especially people like Clive. I never would have thought Clive would change his mind about something on account of what I wanted, especially something outside. It wasn't how he was made. But when I went up the hill on the south side, when I saw for myself those trees planted in straight rows with the brown dirt turned up red around their roots, it seemed like just about anything could happen.

Lord only knows how long I was up there, walking back and forth between the trees. As I made my way back to the house, the air smelled like smoke from somebody burning leaves and it was chilly enough that I pulled my sweater on. I barely saw anything, nothing that I registered anyway, because I was still seeing the apple trees.

At the house, I grabbed the car keys and went up to see Clive. He was hurting a lot that day, lying flat out in the bed with something brown crusted on one side of his mouth. He didn't say much of anything, but the whole time I was up there, I sat on the cushioned chair beside the bed holding his hand and telling him thank you. It was hard to know if he understood what I was talking about, but I kept saying apple trees and I thought he smiled and nodded a time or two.

Before it got full-on dark, I went back out to the orchard again with a flashlight. It would be years before the trees started bearing fruit, and they were skinny, but most of them were already taller than I was. Walking up and down the rows with my barn jacket wrapped around me against the wind, it was easy to see how the trees would look come spring—all fuzzy and white and pink, like something an artist would want to paint. Over time, the branches would grow out wilder and the trees in one row would reach out toward the ones in the other. Sometime years down the road, it might be hard to work out where one started and the other ended.

Being out there did something to me, kind of opened me up. That's the best way I can think to tell it.

As soon as I woke up the next day, I knew what I should do. And I needed to hurry before Clive ran out of time.

CHAPTER 49

— *Sadie Caswell* —

I found Willa Dunn's address in the church directory and, on the way over there, I pictured how Clive would look showing that orchard to some little girl, to our grandchild. It didn't make a bit of sense, especially when I didn't know if Tinley was telling the truth about being pregnant, and if she was, whether she even had the baby. But I couldn't help myself any more than I could stop the moon showing up at night.

Willa came to the door in an old pink housecoat and slippers. As soon as she saw me, she grabbed my elbow and pulled me inside.

"Would you look at you?" she said. "How long has it been, Sadie Caswell? You get on in here."

"I'm sorry it's been so long, Willa. I've been away for a spell."

"I heard all about that, about you going down to Greenville to help out with your sister." She nodded and I didn't correct her. "Here, let me take your coat."

I shook my head. "I'm not staying long."

"Well, at least sit down."

She pointed at the couch and when I sat down, she eased into an old recliner across from me.

"Can I get you something to drink?" Willa leaned up with her hands on her knees, ready to get back up. "Some tea or coffee?" You could tell she didn't care one thing about me seeing her in that old pink housecoat.

At least pink was a good color for her. She kept her white hair down over her shoulders, not like most women our age who cut it short or wore it pinned up. I'd always thought it was silly, but sitting across from her that day, I had to admit it made her look younger.

"I don't need anything," I said. "Just need to talk to you about something."

Willa nodded and settled back in her chair like she was ready to hear some big story. The round clock on the wall behind her ticked, its thin red line scooting around the numbers, while I tried to work out what to say.

"I guess I never said anything to you about that day. The day Mark died," I said finally. It was as good a place to start as any.

"Sadie, you didn't need to say a word about it. Anybody would've done the same thing I did."

"But I ought to have thanked you for calling me when you did."

Willa brushed her hand through the air. "I'm sorry it happened, Sadie. That's all."

"Well, I do appreciate it." I stood up with my pocketbook, already tired of the conversation and wishing I was at home or by Clive's bed. "I shouldn't keep you."

"You're welcome to stay a while."

"I'd better get on," I said. It felt good to have thanked her, but I was disappointed in myself for not asking what I'd come there to ask. I didn't know how to work up to it.

"Well, come by another time and stay for dinner. Or at least a cup of coffee." Willa pulled herself up out of the chair and followed me to the front door. We stood by the wood stove and you could hear the logs shifting inside. The heat from it made me sweat inside my coat, but even so I've always liked the warmth a wood stove gives out.

"You let me know if there's anything I can do for you now that you're back in town—especially with Clive sick and all."

"I appreciate that, Willa. And we got your card in the mail too. Two cards, I guess. One after Mark died and one after Clive got sick."

"Wish I could do more."

I put my hand on the door, then gathered myself and turned back to Willa before I could lose my nerve. "There is one thing I need to ask you." "Anything, anything at all."

"I'm wondering if you know anything about the Greenes, about how I could find a girl named Tinley Greene." I guessed she wouldn't spread it all over town that I'd asked about Tinley. And even if she did, it wouldn't make a bit of difference.

Willa frowned and shook her head. "I'm afraid I don't know any Greenes."

"I didn't guess you would." My voice cracked and I coughed to cover it up, trying not to think about how Clive might be running out of time. "I don't think she went to church. I never saw her there anyway."

Willa looked at me hard. "I'm real sorry."

"Figured I'd ask anyway." I opened the door. Outside, the sky had turned white like it might snow.

"You take care, Sadie," Willa called out as I walked away. "And come back some time, I mean it."

———

The next day, I decided to own up to Clive about how I'd gone to see Mark at work before he died. Maybe I should've told him a long time ago, back when it happened. But I couldn't have done it then. I couldn't have said it to myself, that maybe I pushed Mark when I shouldn't have. It takes time to get out from under the weight of something like that— guilt or grief or both.

As soon as I got to his room and poured him some water, I got right to it. "Clive, you might as well know I went out to see Mark that day when he was out working. I tried to talk to him. You said I shouldn't, but I did."

He perked up at that, a brightness in his eyes. "You go see him," he said, grabbing my hand and pumping it up and down. "You'll work out what to do about it, whatever's got him upset."

I squeezed Clive's hand back. "I always left other people alone, but not Mark. And I didn't say the right thing—maybe I shouldn't have gone out to see him at work. Maybe I should've left earlier or stayed longer."

Clive shook his head. "You'll see. All you've got to do is go talk to him. He's always listened to his mama." His chest heaved up and down like he was having a hard time getting enough air.

"Do you need me to call the nurse in here?"

When he didn't answer, I touched his chest. "You calm down, you hear?"

"If he doesn't want to marry that girl, he ought to do the right thing and talk to her, that's all. It's not too late. You'll bring him around him to it, won't you?"

"I can't do that, Clive. Mark's gone." He tried to sit up in the bed and I tapped his chest. "You lay back down."

"But you need to go see him."

"Okay," I whispered, playing along. "I'll go talk to him. You calm down now."

"That's what you should do. Go see him," Clive said. He rested his head on the pillow, calmer than he'd been before.

"It's all right. It's going to be all right," I told him, like everything was settled. He grew quiet then. He thought whatever was broken could still be fixed, that I was going to do it.

CHAPTER 50

— *Tinley Greene* —

After the camp closes for the summer, the weather gets cold even before Thanksgiving. Leigh tells me not to worry about keeping the cabins cleaned up, and we stay indoors where it's warm. I could move back to my old cabin, but the baby needs to be somewhere warm. Leigh carries Rebecca around with her all over the house, and sometimes it seems like she leaves the room with her as soon as I walk in.

One day when it's almost Christmas, Leigh asks if she and Travis can keep the baby for the night. "That way you can sleep the whole night through." She's feeding Rebecca in her highchair. The baby flaps her arms and the spoon flies out of Leigh's hand. Green baby food splatters on the floor and I grab paper towels and bend down to clean it up.

"She's sleeping just fine now. But I appreciate the offer." I can't explain why I don't want it to happen—just one night and I'll be down the hall—but I don't. After the mess is cleaned up, I bundle up Rebecca in a pink snowsuit that Lynette brought. I'm hurrying out the door when Leigh shows up again. The wind is blowing, flinging sleet against the roof and windows.

"You're not driving out in this weather, are you?" She's stopped smoking since Rebecca and I started staying up at their cabin, and now she rubs her arm where I know there's a nicotine patch under her barn jacket.

"I'm going outside for a minute to get some fresh air. We'll stay on the porch." All of a sudden the room feels too hot and she's too close. All I want is a minute alone with Rebecca.

"Let me have her if you're going out in that."

I shake my head. "We'll only be a minute."

Outside on the porch, I gulp in air and tell myself I'm worrying over nothing, but I can feel things starting to fall apart, the way they always do one way or another. When I run my hand up and down Rebecca's back, she falls asleep, drooling on the hood wrapped around her face. We're only outside for a minute or two, but by the time I get back inside, the playpen is gone from our room.

Their bedroom door is closed, but I can hear Leigh and Travis inside arguing. Leigh says the baby needs two parents, not one, and especially not one who's only halfway there.

"Something could happen to her in a split second," she says. "One day Tinley will be sorry. I saw on the news the other day that social services took a little boy away from his mother because she hadn't fed him in two days."

My face feels hot and then cold again and I shake my head even though they can't see me through the closed door.

"Leigh, she feeds her just fine. You know that."

"You're not around them like I am. She's daydreaming half the time. Once the baby is old enough to walk, she'll have to pay more attention. It's an accident waiting to happen."

"But what's all this about tonight? What's gotten into you?"

The only sound is Leigh sniffing and then Travis tells her not to cry. I tiptoe down the hall to our room and close the door. Still holding the baby, I push four heavy cans up against it to keep it shut. I unzip the snowsuit and ease it off Rebecca's arms and legs, then change her diaper. The whole night I sit up in bed holding her so that she can sleep.

The next morning there's a knock at the door and I don't say anything, but Travis calls out and I push the cans aside with my foot and open the door because I have to get out to the kitchen for Rebecca's bottle. He follows me to the refrigerator and says he's sorry, but maybe it would be best if Rebecca and I find another place to live.

"I thought it would work out fine, but it's not. This is harder on Leigh than I thought it would be. She's wanted a baby for so long. I'm awful sorry, Tinley."

Rebecca starts to cry and I tell her I'm getting her bottle. My voice sounds like I'm choking, and I wipe my nose with my sleeve.

"Leigh, she's—she can't take this." Travis coughs. "Like I said, it's too hard on her. Not when she can't have one of her own."

Everything is falling apart—this family I thought I had, all of it. "Leigh can watch the baby all she wants during the day. I've always told her. She knows that." I find the bottle and Rebecca reaches for it with her tiny hands and now I'm crying full on. "But she can't try to take her away from me. I'm her mother."

"Look, we'll help you out with finding an apartment, get you started on the rent. Of course we'll do that."

"You don't have to." I shake my head. There's nobody left who wants me around. Everything is broken and gone. The coolness of Mama's hand when she felt my forehead and the way her tongue touched her lip when she was pinning a pattern. The way Daddy flipped open his pocket knife to peel an apple. How he would untangle my kite up at Poplar Springs, turning his back to shield us from the wind.

CHAPTER 51

— *Sadie Caswell* —

Come Sunday, I put on a good dress and went up to the church. Walking in there and seeing people turn their heads was like stepping into a cold river in the middle of winter. I didn't want to sit with anybody in particular so I found an empty seat in the corner of the back row and kept my eyes down. It wasn't long before somebody behind me reached up and touched my shoulder.

"Sadie, it's so good to see you back up here." I nodded without turning around, without even trying to figure out who the voice belonged to, who wore perfume like that. As soon as the singing started and we stood up, I saw the Honeycutts and the Kellers from down the road across the aisle. Darlene Honeycutt looked at me over the top of her hymnal and raised her fingers and I waved back. From then on, I made sure the service was between me and the Lord, the way it should be.

After church let out, I tried to get out of there as quick as I could. But I hadn't made it to my car yet when somebody called my name in the parking lot. I turned around to see Willa Dunn in a long gray wool coat with her hand on her car door. Her husband was already behind the wheel, messing with the radio.

"Sadie, I've been thinking—" Willa said and she closed the door and stepped closer—"about what you asked me the other day. I've been studying on it ever since. I think your best bet might be to check with Lynette Barnes."

"Lynette Barnes?"

"Yes, you know Lynette, don't you? Everybody knows Lynette. She sits on the right side about halfway up."

"I'm not really sure." I shook my head. "The name doesn't sound familiar."

"Well, you go look her up. She'll be in the church directory. She keeps up with everything about everybody around here." Willa nodded. "I'm not a betting woman, but if I was, I'd count on her knowing about that girl, as long as she's from around here."

As soon as I got home, I checked the church directory. Lynette Barnes' phone number was listed, but nobody answered and I couldn't think fast enough to say something to the machine that picked up. I spent the rest of the day visiting with Clive and making up his food for the next few days.

———

When I got out to Lynette Barnes' house first thing the next morning, it seemed familiar, but I wasn't sure why. It was a real nice brick house, one story but wide. The front door was painted bright red and you could tell somebody kept the pollen and dust off it in the spring and the snow swept away in the winter. I rang the doorbell and Lynette opened the door wearing brown pants, a long white button-down shirt, and a lighter brown cardigan. As soon as I saw her, I thought things were about to start, that I was getting close to finding Tinley.

"It's been a while," I said, not sure if I'd ever met her before. "Sadie Caswell."

"I guess it has." She kept her hand on the door like she might close it any minute.

"I haven't been around much on account of being down at my sister's."

"Of course it's a shame about Mark. Nothing worse than a parent losing a child." Lynette's face loosened up and I thought she might let me in. "And now Clive on top of it. How's he holding up?"

"He's pretty poorly some days, but not as bad others."

"They moved him to hospice care last I heard. Is that right?"

"They said they can't do much for him up at the hospital anymore."

Lynette frowned. "I'm sorry to hear that. People up at the church come to me asking because I keep up with everybody. Everybody's been wondering how long he has and how you've been holding up. Whether you want anything to do with them or not, people wonder."

"I figured. That's how people are. Even though I haven't been out much."

"I guess you've got it worked out by now, whether you want to stick to yourself or not."

"It's easier that way sometimes." I shrugged.

"Until you need something from somebody, I guess. I heard you'd been up to see Willa Dunn too."

"Well, the truth is I'm hoping to find out about Tinley Greene. Do you know her?"

Lynette stepped outside, closed the door behind her, and moved past me down the steps of the porch. After she bent down in the yard and pulled up a weed, she shook her head. "Can't keep up with half of what I need to and this stuff grows even in the winter." She held the weed in one hand and put the other on her hip. She looked around the yard and I waited for her on the porch shivering. The sky still seemed heavy with snow.

"Willa Dunn said you might be able to help me, that you might know where Tinley is."

She put her hand over her eyes. "Don't know what you're wanting with Tinley. That girl has had enough trouble as it is. What does she have to do with you?"

I guess I know about the trouble she's had. I guess I was part of it. "What kind of trouble do you mean exactly?"

Lynette shook some dirt from the weed she was holding. "You'd think everybody around here would know how her parents were killed."

"I didn't know." My ears filled with a rushing sound as I stared at

Lynette wanting her to spill every last bit of it. Who they were, how they died, when it happened. Whether it was before or after Tinley met Mark, before or after she came to see me. Lynette looked back at me, her gray hair cut short to just above the little gold bobs in her ears.

"What happened?" I asked her. "When was it?"

"When she wasn't but sixteen or seventeen. They went off the road in that bad storm last spring—not this past spring, but spring of last year."

I remembered hearing about the couple who died in the storm. But I never knew Tinley had anything to do with it. I tried to picture how she must have been then, all that hair hanging down her back, those big eyes of hers. "She's been through a lot, it sounds like. And at an awfully young age—her parents, then the rest of it too, with Mark." I waited to see how she would react.

Sure enough, Lynette nodded like she knew what I was talking about. "And between you and me I think there was some trouble with the Haughtrys too. I don't know what but I heard she left in a hurry."

"When was that? Where did she go?"

"Last fall is when I'm talking about." Lynette looked like she was thinking things over, then nodded. "Fran Haughtry was torn up about it at first. She came back from Atlanta and Tinley was gone. But she didn't go looking for her or anything. At least I don't think she did anyway."

I nodded and waited to see if Lynette had anything else to say.

Finally she sighed. "It was right around then that Lester saw Tinley and Mark together in Mark's truck. Somewhere around town. I'm not sure where."

There was nothing I could say to that. If Mark drove her around, then maybe he wasn't trying to get rid of her. All I could do was take it in.

Beside the porch, Lynette ran the back of her hand over the leaves of a bush. "Come spring I've got to get these trimmed back."

I nodded, looking over her yard. She had a strip of dirt in front where she could have jonquils in the spring and mums in the fall. I could just imagine how they would look. It struck me then—a memory of the mums I'd seen in front of the gray house. When had we ever planted flowers at a rental house—an empty one at that? I thought of Mark's truck when we got it back. Clive had rinsed it off in the yard—got all the dirt out of the back of it and threw away the empty plastic containers he found there. The kind you buy flowers in.

"Lynette, did he ever see Tinley around town with any boy other than Mark?"

"Not that I ever heard."

Even though what she'd said didn't prove anything, I guessed the pieces were falling into place. I remembered Clive saying he'd taken groceries to Tinley. He hadn't said where she was. I met Lynette's eyes. "Do you think, once she left the Haughtrys' place, Mark might have helped Tinley find a place to stay?"

"I suspect as much," Lynette said, nodding.

CHAPTER 52

— *Sadie Caswell* —

When I told Lynette I needed to find Tinley, she shrugged. "It's not my place to be giving out her personal information."

"Please—I only want to talk to her." She went around the side of the house and I followed her. She kicked a little rock with her foot until it went under the bushes. "Lynette, I can't do right by Tinley unless you help me find her."

Lynette kept walking, her open-back shoes kicking up dirt behind her, and I decided I might as well come out with it. "Was she really expecting? Did she have the baby?"

Lynette stopped. "I guess that's her business and not mine." I came up beside her and she threw the weed she'd been holding out toward the back yard. The back of that house looked a lot different from the front. Nothing much was planted back there, just a few old tomato plants and some marigolds, but mostly it was just a big pile of weeds and what looked like a compost pile.

"All I want to know is if she had the baby. Or if she—" I wanted to say "took care of it," but what I meant and how the words sounded were two different things. The only way to take care of it was to do the opposite of what I'd told Tinley to do—especially if it was our grandchild. Every time I thought about the realness of that baby and what I'd done, I started shaking. "Some people, I guess, in that situation might think the best thing would be to end it." I'd thought that way once, but I didn't know what I was saying. I couldn't look at Lynette so I kept my eyes on her backyard. Two old trash barrels were knocked on their side, one burned clear through, and some of the nylon straps on the metal lawn chair hung out of the bottom.

"It's a shame all the way around, and her being a good, hard worker and not knowing any better." Lynette walked back around the house to where I'd parked the car, like she was ready for me to leave. "I don't guess there's any way I can help you."

"I'm only wondering what she did. Did she have the baby?"

Lynette didn't answer me at first. She carved something out from under her fingernail and sighed. "You think a girl like her would kill her own baby?"

"I don't really know her. I didn't mean anything by it. But if she didn't—can you tell me where she's staying?"

"I've got a lot to do," Lynette said, nodding toward my car. "I guess I'll be seeing you now that you're back in town. Heard you were at church on Sunday, but I didn't see you, at least not where you always used to sit."

"Can you just tell me where she is? I'm not going to bother her. I only want—" I put my hand on the car door, trying not to cry. I hadn't noticed, but the sun had peeked through the clouds and the paint on the car was shining the way some gravel does, the pieces with mica in it. Lynette turned back toward the house and I tried to keep from falling down. I figured that was the end of it.

But she turned around with the sleeves of her sweater down over her hands. "You know, I've been thinking about the last time you were out here."

I tried to figure out what she was talking about, but I didn't know.

"You don't remember, do you? Years ago." She looked down at the ground. "I don't guess you'd been in town long. It had to have been right after you married Clive. Back when I lost the baby."

That red front door. The dark kitchen inside and the picture. The woman who almost tore herself up crying. I looked at her, blinked hard, and finally nodded.

"I was never that way with anybody else who came up here," she said. "But that day I needed to talk to somebody about it, about what had happened with Lou Ann."

"I only came on account of the church list," I told her, figuring that was the truth of it. "And I didn't know what to say or how to act or anything. Never have, really."

Lynette let out her breath. "I guess you did the best you could." I could see how she was remembering the way she'd cried in my arms that day so many years ago. She wiped her hands on her pants and squinted at the sun. "Maybe we won't get the snow they're calling for." Her voice sounded softer than before. "Sorry I couldn't be any help to you. But don't be a stranger, Sadie. You come on back anytime."

Before I left—before I gave up—I came up close to her. It was my one good chance. "If Tinley had that baby, then it's my grandchild," I said. Whispering, but the fierce kind of whisper. *You listen to me. You hear what I'm talking about. Please.*

———

The next morning I called up to the nurse's desk and asked them to let Clive know I would be by a little bit later. "I told him I'd be by in the morning, but it'll be the afternoon at least before I get there."

"I hope nothing's wrong," the nurse who answered the phone said, and I could tell she was chewing gum.

"Just something I need to take care of," I said, even though it was none of her business. "I'll come by when I can," I added, trying to sound nicer.

I wore my best navy blue dress, one I'd wear to church, and my good pearl earrings. I put my pocketbook on the passenger seat beside me and turned down the vents so the warm air wasn't blowing right in my face.

Rebecca Greene. That's what Lynette told me her name was. She had a middle name too. Lynette wasn't sure, but she thought it was Cora. Rebecca Cora Greene.

To get down to Haird, I drove by where the Watsons lived and past the church. When I got close to the bridge, I slowed down and thought about turning off the road to get there some other way. But it was quickest to drive across the bridge and that's what I did.

I went around the big curve where the Taylors kept their bee boxes, and past farms I didn't know and long stretches of nothing but trees. All the way down to where the old mill was, I made the turn onto Siler Road. The trees reached across the road toward the river. Like they knew there was something better on the other side.

CHAPTER 53

— *Tinley Greene* —

After we leave the camp, I consider venturing into Greenville, but instead find myself drawn back to Garnet. Despite all that's happened there, it's still home. Winding around the familiar roads, I can breathe better, like the air has more life in it. I remember how Leigh used to tease me when I said Garnet was full of ghosts, then shudder at how she and Travis made us leave, how twisted and bitter things ended up—another hope dashed.

As long as I stay in town and out of the countryside, Garnet almost feels like a new place—still familiar but with less to weigh us down. I find a tiny apartment for me and Rebecca in an area where there used to be warehouses. It's on a brand-new street that ends in a big circle. The rent isn't much and I pick up cleaning jobs in a new neighborhood nearby to cover it.

Sometimes Rebecca won't take her nap until I walk her in the stroller outside, hoping I won't run into anyone I used to know. One of those days, we're bundled up against the cold, and as I walk back and forth on the sidewalk waiting for her to go to sleep, I spot a man two houses up shoveling a path through the snow. It looks like he has thick, dark hair like Mark's. And when he stops leaning on the shovel and stands all the way up, he is almost as tall as Mark was.

I tell myself I deserve to have him, that we need someone like this man to become a real family. That if I'm with someone who reminds me of Mark, then I will stay close to him. I won't forget him.

I walk quickly—almost running—down the icy sidewalk, the baby jostled in the stroller—until I reach him. Then I can see the truth like some awful bare thing. Up close he doesn't look anything like Mark. The man raises his hand to wave, but I turn away as quickly as I came.

The next day, the snow has melted. Rebecca and I stop by the grocery store and on our way back out to the parking lot, a man up ahead holds the door open. I'm pushing the stroller and the two bags of groceries are looped over the handles. The man waits for us to get to the door. He's older than me—thin build and dark curly hair, a whole head of it.

"Thank you." I nod as we go past him.

Dark-meat chicken was on special and I had a coupon for canned peas, so for supper Rebecca will have mashed-up peas and chicken and some applesauce. I always make sure to cut the chicken into little pieces for her so she won't choke. Leigh used to tell me to be more careful. But she can't see the way I am now, how hard I'm trying.

As we walk past him, the man turns his head. In the parking lot, I fasten Rebecca in her car seat and start folding up the stroller. If Mark had let his hair grow a little longer, he might have had curls like that. I let the stroller slip and it clatters to the ground. The man jogs over to pick it up.

"Hey," he says. "Let me help here." He picks up the stroller from the pavement and starts folding it up. His eyes are brown and he's older and not as tall. But his long fingers are exactly the same as Mark's.

"Thank you." I bend down to put the bags of groceries in the back of the car. "Appreciate the help."

"No problem at all. The name's Landry, by the way." He holds out his hand for me to shake.

"I'm Tinley." I wipe my hand off on my jeans and reach for his. "And that's Rebecca in the car, my daughter. It's nice to meet you."

"Nice to meet you too," he says, checking my left hand. When I hold it up so he can see I don't have a wedding ring, he laughs—a real big laugh. Already I know he laughs a lot, just like Mark did.

CHAPTER 54

— *Sadie Caswell* —

Sometimes you get yourself worked up over nothing. Our mother always told me and Libby that the hen never cackles until the egg is laid. What she said went through my mind when I couldn't find Tinley. She wasn't where Lynette told me to go. I ought to have known she might not be there.

The camp was surrounded by scrawny pine trees and hardly any signs to tell you where to go. Finally I found what looked like the owner's house, a log house newer than the rest, beside what looked like the mess hall. After I knocked on the door, I brushed pine needles off the porch with my shoe. I didn't hear anybody moving in the house, and the curtains on the windows didn't move. I knocked again and waited.

When I started to get cold, I went back to the car and waited some more with the motor on and the heat going. Then I went back and knocked one more time, louder. Finally one of the curtains moved and the door opened.

"Sorry, I wasn't sure if that was the door or not. We don't have many people out in the winter. What can I do for you?" The woman had long curly hair. She shivered and crossed her arms over her chest. I told her what I'd come for, and she said Tinley and the baby had moved out. She lit a cigarette and I asked if she knew where Tinley's new place was. She shook her head and held up her cigarette. "I quit and then started back again."

"So you don't know where she's staying now? She didn't tell you?"

The woman shook her head again. "Sorry."

Going back up the dirt road, I tried to keep my spirits up. Maybe Lynette could find out where Tinley had gone. Maybe I could still find her before Clive ran out of time.

Before the week was out, I called up Lynette again.

"She isn't at that camp anymore. I went out there to check."

"I didn't know about that." She sighed.

"Where do you think she went?"

"There's no telling, Sadie. She could be out working or something."

"Doing what? Where?"

"Cleaning houses. She used to do that around here."

"If you hear from her, can you tell her I'm looking for her? Maybe give her my telephone number?"

She sighed again. "I don't know. I'd have to think on that."

"Well, from where I'm sitting, it wouldn't hurt for you to tell her I'm looking for her." *Please. We're running out of time.*

———

Later on when I was at the post office, I noticed a bulletin board where people posted about jobs and things like that. There was one for house cleaning, and I lifted up the paper on top so I could see the whole thing, but the phone number was faded from the sun.

One day up at the hospital, I started telling Clive all about it. He was sitting up in bed and you could tell he'd been washed and shaved. His hair was combed and his color looked fairly good, not as bad as it had been. He wore navy blue pajamas, buttoned all the way up. He looked better than he had in a long time, and there wasn't any bad smell in the room either.

"Clive, I've got something I need to talk to you about. When you asked about the girl who showed up at the bridge, Tinley—the thing is, I guess there was something going on between Mark and her."

"Her truck was there one time before Mark died." Clive nodded. "His truck was there too."

"All right. You didn't tell me that, but it doesn't matter now, Clive."

"She was still there later on. After Mark passed. I took her some groceries. I didn't know what else to do."

"I know you did. You told me. And that was the right thing, what you did."

"Then she was gone." Clive shook his head, frowning.

"That sounds about right. I went by and didn't see a thing out of place. But you did the right thing, Clive. You tried to help when you could. Not like what I did."

"What do you mean?" The plastic tube leading into his arm flapped when he patted his stomach. He left his hand there like he could press the pain back.

I paused, then tried to stand up straighter. "Tinley came up to the house one day. After the funeral, I mean. Saying she was having a baby. Talking about how it was Mark's."

Clive was looking at me hard and I had to let go of the rest too. I told him how I'd sent her away. Told her to get off the porch. To get the baby taken care of. That I never wanted to see her again.

But Clive skipped over all that as easy as a sweetgum takes root. "Where's the baby now? She had the baby, didn't she?"

"That's what I hear from Lynette. A baby girl—Rebecca Cora Greene. I'm trying to find her. Both of them."

He was starting to look tired but before he closed his eyes, Clive asked me what the baby was like.

That whole day surprised me, the way he felt so good and took it all in stride. It was like part of him knew it all along, the way sometimes you know deep down that something is bound to happen.

"I haven't met her—not yet," I told him. "But Lynette says she's a good baby. She doesn't have a thing wrong with her—healthy and a real good eater."

Clive closed his eyes and whispered, "You bring her with you next time, okay?"

I couldn't promise him that I would, but I said I would try.

———

The next time I caught up with Lynette, I gave her two letters, one for Tinley and one for her baby. I'd written them quickly, without thinking much about what to say except what was on my mind. Somebody isn't going to write much differently than they talk. And there wasn't much point in beating around the bush.

I put the baby's letter on a separate piece of paper even though I knew Tinley would have to read it for her. I guess I wanted this one chance to say something directly to her.

It was up to Tinley whether she read what I wrote or just threw it away. I didn't know what she might do, but it was all up to Tinley, every last bit of it.

CHAPTER 55

— *Tinley Greene* —

The first time Landry starts to kiss me, I grab his chin and press my lips harder against his and he opens his mouth, except it's Mark's mouth, not his. I'm lost in imagining he is someone else until Landry pulls back and asks me if I'm okay. I nod and pull him toward me again.

"Are you sure?" he whispers, his fingers warm on the back of my neck and we're kissing again, but it's Landry then. When I try to find Mark again, he's gone. He has left me again.

———

It's not long before Landry asks me to move in with him. Clutching Rebecca to my chest, I tell her that Landry will be our new family and he smiles and wraps us both in a hug.

The first Saturday night we're living with Landry, I tell him I don't want to go up to Solid Rock on Sunday. "Not tomorrow, not any Sunday."

He shrugs. "I usually go to the Methodist church." He comes closer to where I'm standing in the kitchen, getting the mixer down from the top cabinet. "Hey, are you going to make some mashed potatoes?" He pulls me up close and kisses my neck. "I'll bet you make the best mashed potatoes. I can tell."

"You leave me alone or I'll never get them made." I laugh and push him away, remembering how my mother made them, circling canned milk into the bowl as the mixer hummed.

———

Now we've been with Landry long enough to have settled in to one another. Sometimes I wonder if I should be with someone closer to my age, but Landry isn't that old. He's barely thirty. If somebody saw us getting in the car or going for a walk after supper, they would see a mother and father and baby girl. *Oh, what a lovely family.* That's what they would think. It doesn't matter if Landry isn't Mark, if I can only bring myself to kiss him by pretending he is someone else. I'm close to having a real family.

We live near the apartment where Rebecca and I moved after we left the camp. Landry owns one of the new houses—painted green and squeezed up next to the neighbors on both sides with a garage in front.

———

On Rebecca's first birthday in June, Landry suggests going out to eat and he says the steakhouse is the nicest place.

"You've been there, right? Diller's? The one with the yeast rolls?" I shake my head and he groans. "Oh no. You can't tell me you've never had those rolls with the honey butter. You'd better get in the car right now, my dear. I'll get Rebecca in the back."

And I see myself in the side mirror of the car as I climb in, looking like someone else, a woman who gets driven around in a nice car and who eats steak.

At the restaurant paper is draped over the tables, and Rebecca smacks at the edge until it makes a snapping sound. Landry draws letters for her, asking her to point to which one is the "A" and which one is the "B."

"She's not old enough. She can't do that yet."

"I know." Landry laughs. He's almost always laughing. Some mornings he starts out laughing about how he can't find his coffee cup and I realize who I'm becoming—the girl who finds it for him, who laughs with him when it was in the cabinet the whole time.

We eat steak with mushrooms and potatoes wrapped in foil to keep warm. My mind drifts off, imagining what Rebecca's first birthday would be like if it was Mark sitting here with us. I don't even notice when she spills her milk. It's only when Landry hops up to wipe the spill that I snap out of my trance. I have to stop doing this. I know I should let go of Mark's ghost and be grateful for what I have.

"Any dessert this evening?" The waitress stands with her hip out, almost touching Landry's arm. "You look like a man who'd love a hot fudge sundae, that's what I'm guessing."

Landry smiles and shakes his head. "None for me, but we've got a birthday girl here." He points to Rebecca, who is smashing a piece of bread on the table.

"This little one? Oh my goodness, is this her first birthday?" Landry and I both nod. "You know, it's nice y'all came out for something quiet like this. Some people have those big blow-out parties, you know? My niece had hers just last month and I'd be willing to bet you most of Wynette County was there, and half of Yates too. They had two picnic tables end-to-end with food. Popcorn and caramel apples and two kinds of cake." She shook her head. "People everywhere. Aunts and uncles and cousins. And all the grandparents fighting to get the best pictures, trying to get her to say *Memaw* or *Nanny* and her barely one year old. Well, y'all know how it is."

Landry touches the wet spot under his glass. "We can imagine, I guess. Yeah." He doesn't explain how his parents are up in Virginia, how they only speak once or twice a year, how he doesn't even remember what they started arguing about until it was too far gone. When I asked him about it the first time, he laughed. Sometimes I think he laughs because he doesn't know what else to do.

The waitress shrugs. "Well, let's see here about bringing this little one some cake. Has she had it before?"

"Not yet. I bet she'll like it. But she's not going to know what to do with it and it will get everywhere." I smile and smooth out my napkin.

"Honey, that's how it should be." She comes back with a slice of cake covered in white icing and a lit candle in the middle. Landry and I sing to Rebecca and the waitress, squatting down to watch what Rebecca will do, joins in. When we finish singing, Landry takes the candle out and gets a smudge of icing on his finger. He holds it out to Rebecca and she licks his finger and her eyes widen. She squirms when he takes his finger away and we all laugh before the waitress goes to help another table. Rebecca puts her hand flat on the cake, pressing on it. *You can have it, sweetie. You can have just about anything you want. Any good thing I can give you.*

CHAPTER 56

— Clive Caswell —

I guess she won't realize it at the time, but the way I imagine it, an afternoon with her grandmother will be one of her favorite memories. Even after she's grown up, even if she moves away from Garnet, our granddaughter will sometimes find herself back on the hill coming up on the rows of trees.

On this afternoon she is still a little girl. Her grandmother will tell her that sometimes apple trees take up to eight years to bear fruit, but these have only taken six. Our granddaughter will nod and reach up for Sadie's hand, already hungry.

The sky will be blue, this day in September when the first fruit is ready to be picked. They'll fill one bushel basket, and then another. The baskets will be as tall as the little girl and too heavy to carry once they're full. The first apple she tastes will be sweet, its skin still warm from the sun.

CHAPTER 57

— *Sadie Caswell* —

When I was getting ready for bed, the phone rang and I answered it in my nightgown, shivering and wishing I had something on my bare feet. Thinking they wouldn't call this late unless something had happened.

"Mrs. Caswell, It's Dr. Wilkins. I'm sorry to call so late."

"I'm here," I told him. I waited for him to say what he was calling about, but part of me knew what he would say before he said it. He must have talked for several minutes because my legs got tired from standing up. We had a little table in the upstairs hallway with the telephone on top and the phone book on a little shelf. That night I wished we had thought to put a chair there, some way to get a rest. I was so tired.

I told the doctor I'd be up there as soon as I got dressed. There wasn't any kind of a hurry though. The doctor said the arrangements could wait until the morning. There wasn't anything anybody could do for Clive anymore. He was gone.

I couldn't help but think about how Clive never got to see the apple trees. And worse than that, so bad it was like another dying to think about it, he never got to meet our granddaughter. But the way I saw it, Clive could be walking out in the fields right then, looking around for something that needed doing, pushing something in the ground or pulling up a weed the way he did. Carrying a little girl on his hip, one who favored some part of Mark if you got up close to her.

Over the next few days, I tried to keep my mind on times when things were good for Clive. I remembered the way he'd carry around those butterscotch candies in his pocket. He would hand them to Mark when he thought I wasn't looking. When I drove down the driveway and saw the barn in the distance, I could picture the way he and Mark would be out mending its walls. Clive would tell Mark, "you grab hold of this wood right here," and Mark's mouth would go down at the corners and he would try so hard to hold still that he wouldn't even blink. "That's it. That's real good," Clive would say, whether it was or wasn't.

After the funeral, Libby asked me about coming down to Greenville with her.

"Not again," I told her. "Not right now, I mean. Maybe some other time."

She frowned. "I could use your help with the bake sale. And you know I'm redoing the den. Those drapes look like something off of a cruise ship."

"I'm better off up here. I think so anyway. If I change my mind, I'll call you." I knew why Libby had asked. I didn't have any reason to stay. I had no family left in Garnet.

"By yourself? I'm not sure about that, Sadie." She crossed her arms and looked at me like she was trying to see if new wrinkles had popped up on my forehead overnight.

"I know she probably won't come. But she might. One day, I mean."

Libby tried to work out what I meant, her eyebrows all crinkled together. Then she nodded and kept her eyes closed for a second before she grabbed hold of my arm and squeezed. I knew then that Libby had heard about Tinley, but she had the sense to keep it to herself. She didn't say anything else, just pulled on her cardigan and buttoned it across the front.

The truth was, I didn't have any reason to stay. But Libby knew why I did, or part of it anyway, and she never said a word about how plumb crazy I was for thinking Tinley would come around. Before, I'd thought

I went looking for her because of Clive. But once he was gone, it was like what he wanted ended up settling on me instead, the way a bird will go from one branch to another.

CHAPTER 58

— *Tinley Greene* —

After her first birthday, Rebecca starts doing everything at once. She talks and walks and points at things, wanting to know what they are. She wants me to say the word for everything. *Up, down. Inside, outside. On, off. Hungry, full. Awake, asleep.*

She gets bigger every day and she watches me and tries to do what I do. It's going to be different from now on. I'm going to stop talking to people who aren't real. I'm not going to let my daughter see me whispering under my breath or forgetting where I am. Everything around me will shift into focus and the ghosts will disappear. I'll make them.

Lynette Barnes comes by one day when Landry is at work.

"I've got a little something for the baby's birthday here. I'm just sorry it's late. Howard had to have surgery on his foot and I've been carting him back and forth to the doctor's. But I was glad when you finally called to tell me where you'd gone."

"Thanks for coming out. Landry's at work, but you'll get to meet him next time, I guess. Look, you can see how big Rebecca has gotten."

"Let me see this girl here. I still can't get over how her eyes changed—such a pretty green. Unusual. And her hair has gotten so long." Lynette picks up one of her pigtails and Rebecca giggles. When she squirms away, the elastic band falls out, leaving her lopsided, a pigtail on one side and her hair loose on the other. Lynette laughs and tries to fix it, but Rebecca shakes her head no.

"Well, Tinley, you look like you've got some get-up-and-go. What's gotten into you?"

"I'm trying to be better, that's all. And you didn't have to bring her a present, but thank you. You've always been good to her."

"What do you mean trying to be better? Have you been keeping up with the wash and the cleaning around here? I saw that basket of shoes by the front door."

"That's because we got new carpet. So we won't get it dirty with our shoes."

"Looks like a new house to me."

"But I guess the carpet was getting dirty. Landry had a woman out here looking at it the other day and she said we might need to paint too."

"Why would you need to do a thing like that?"

"I don't know. Landry said he'd update me when he knew for sure." Update. That's what he'd said. Like a business paper you need to fix.

"Well, I've got some berries out in the car if you want them. They'll go bad otherwise. Let me watch her while you go get them." Rebecca is scribbling on the big piece of paper I've spread out on top of the carpet. When I bring the basket inside, the berries give off a warm sweetness. Rebecca looks up at Lynette from her coloring and pushes the hair out of her eyes, and I think about asking Lynette if she wants to come by more often. But before I come up with what to say, she's on her way out.

"I'd best be getting on. You take good care of yourself and that baby. She's getting so big. Before you know it, she won't be a baby anymore. You blink and they're in high school."

"I'm sure you're right about that." Rebecca toddles over and presses her face against my leg.

Lynette has her hand on the door when she asks if I heard about Clive Caswell dying. "You get the paper, don't you?" She frowns.

"No, we don't. I mean, Landry might read it, but I don't except for checking the coupons, not most days."

"But you'd heard about him, I'm guessing. Took sick real bad with cancer and now he's gone."

I remember him at the bridge, tall and quiet. At the visitation with red eyes telling people it was good of them to come like he really meant it. But not me. He didn't say that to me.

"You staying here for a while, Tinley? Is this where you figure on being the next time I come out?"

I nod and bend down to run my fingers through Rebecca's hair. "Of course. Where else would we be?"

After Lynette leaves I find an envelope in the basket. It's covered with strawberry juice, pink blooming across the white.

CHAPTER 59

— *Tinley Greene* —

Landry has a fancy wine opener that's weighted at the bottom so it won't tip over, even when he puts a bottle of wine on it and brings down the metal arm to take out the cork. Whenever he's asked if I want any, I've said I'm not interested, that everything is confusing enough without knocking it further sideways. And he laughs and says that's okay. But tonight I say yes, I want to try it, and Landry smiles and sets another glass on the counter.

The wine tastes like syrup and smoke all at once, and it's cool at first and then warm going down my throat. Landry talks and I listen without really hearing what he says and he pours more. After a while I put the glass down even though a few sips are left.

"Are you okay, Tinley?" Landry rubs the back of my neck. "You have to remember you're not used to it."

"It's okay. I've just had enough." My head feels heavy, wobbly almost, and I'm not sure if I can keep holding it up. Everything in the room—the fuzzy brown couch, the knit blanket in different shades of white and cream, the light blue carpet with its pattern of white chainlinks along the outside border—it all seems blurred around the edges.

Landry puts his glass down on the table and rubs my neck again, his fingers tangled in my hair. With my eyes almost closed, things smash together until they look completely different. The pillows on the couch

240

could be flowers if you look at them just right and the wall behind the couch could be a pond of dark blue water, like the one I used to wander around at the Haughtrys' place when I was a little girl.

The folded-up paper is in my pocket, and I touch it just once, knowing that before I fall asleep I'll tear it up. Slowly at first, a big rip across the middle, and then more quickly until it's in tiny pieces, half-moons and stars spinning through the air as they fall.

———

On my birthday in August, Landry gives Rebecca a new book about horses. It's wrapped in gold paper and a red curly ribbon that Rebecca twists around her finger like a ring. When she sees the book, she claps and looks up at Landry, and he presses down on the cover until the book makes a sound like a horse.

"I know it's not her birthday, but I saw it and I knew she would love it. I'm taking you shopping on Saturday." He lays his arm across my shoulder. "A special dress for my birthday girl. Then we'll go out to eat."

That night when I'm in bed with Landry, I pretend to float above our two moving bodies, watching. I'm not myself anymore. I'm someone else, someone who has everything she wants. I'm Maddie Spencer. My hair is gold on my shoulders and I have shiny fingernails and porcelain skin. When I see a boy I want, I put out my hand to touch him and he's mine. That's all it takes.

On Saturday, we leave Rebecca with the neighbor for a few hours. At the mall, Landry asks me how old I am now, a question he first raised at breakfast.

"I don't get why you won't tell me." He opens the door for me and I shiver against the cold air-conditioning. "I don't have any secrets from you, Tinley. Well, just one. But I'm telling you everything later on at dinner. Then you'll know all my secrets."

If I admit that I'm nineteen, Landry will probably grind his teeth and hiss in air through his mouth, the way he did last week when he saw a dead bird on the front steps.

"Twenty-five," I lie, thinking that's close enough to his age and still young enough to be believable.

"Well, you're the most beautiful twenty-five-year-old I know. Let's go find you a dress." He smiles and I smile back at him. This whole idea of going to the mall, of having money to spend on whatever I want, is as brand new as the clothes around us.

Landry waits in a chair while I try on clothes in the dressing room. There are mirrors everywhere and a woman who says to let her know if I need anything in a different size or color. Smiling, she writes my name on a chalkboard hanging on the door by a white ribbon.

When I come out to show Landry a black sleeveless dress, he claps. I turn around to show him the back and he says "That one's really nice. What do you think?"

"I like it." As I go back into the dressing room, I see myself in the mirrors and in that dress I could be anybody. I could be someone who owns a bookstore. An actress on television. A teacher.

We go into another store with a floor made out of smooth rocks and candles burning on little wooden tables. Landry sits down on a couch near the dressing room. The cushions are aqua, and the back part of the couch is pale pink like the inside of a sea shell with tiny red dots along the edges. The clothes hang on thick wooden hangers. Long soft shirts that swing around almost like dresses. Skirts knit like sweaters and jackets with jeweled buttons. I could be somebody in these clothes too. Somebody with a flower garden. An artist.

Landry nods and smiles when I pick out a light green dress with sleeves coming almost to my elbows and cream-colored crochet trim around the bottom. On the way home, I finger the trim, the little knots that almost look like roses, and I wonder if this was the dress he wanted me to pick. Then I remind myself that I could choose whatever dress I wanted. I can be whoever I want to be.

At supper Landry announces that he is being promoted at work. "Going all the way to district manager," he says. "Sooner than I expected."

"Wow, that's amazing." I've never really worked out what he does at his job. Something with insurance, but I didn't understand at the start and then it was too late to ask again. "You must be really good at your job."

"That's not all. The new position is in Kenosha, Wisconsin. Remember I told you the headquarters are in Chicago? Kenosha isn't too far from there. And I want you and Rebecca to come with me. I mean, we haven't talked about it, but I know you must want to see more than Garnet." Landry reaches for my hand and I let him hold it even though I wish I could have a minute—just a minute—to myself. "It's been a mess trying to think about getting the house ready to go on the market and working out the relocation package, but they're giving me six months to try and sell the house. You can get a better price that way than if the company has to buy it."

Six months. I have six months to work up the nerve to tell him I can't go. But Landry thinks I should, and this new person I am with him— maybe she's the kind of person who wants to live in a new place.

Every night as I fall asleep, I try to convince myself that I want to go, that leaving here wouldn't destroy some deep-down part of me.

CHAPTER 60

— *Sadie Caswell* —

Once I found the number for Patrick Maybin's office in the phonebook, I called and made an appointment. I hadn't been up there since Mark died, when we had to change all the papers. Back then I didn't pay much attention to what was going on. It was enough to keep the breath going in and out, enough to sit still in the leather chair in Mr. Maybin's office with the heat coming in through a vent on the floor. Half-asleep.

This time I was wide awake. The office had glass doors with the name of the firm, Corbett & Maybin, painted in gold letters. The lobby floor was covered with carpet the color of oatmeal. In the middle was a table stacked with magazines, and around the edge of the room, navy blue leather chairs. It seemed to me that leather ought to be brown or black, not a color like blue, but that's how they were.

Directly in front, a young woman sat behind a desk. Real pretty, with dark hair that curled right at her chin. She wasn't wearing a lot of makeup, not like a lot of women do, acting like they're some kind of an actress on a stage when all they're doing is going down to Ingles to buy a loaf of white bread. When I told her who I was, she told me I could have a seat and she would let him know I was there. She was real nice and made it seem like they'd been looking forward to my visit. I guess that's how she ended up with the job.

In a few minutes, Mr. Maybin came into the lobby and held out his hand to shake mine. He led me back to his office and I sat down in another one of those navy blue chairs. It was firmer than the ones in the lobby, like more people sat in the lobby ones and they'd loosened up over time the same way skin does.

When he sat down behind the desk and folded his hands into a little tent, the woman from out front came in to hand him a folder of papers. Mr. Maybin laid the folder down on the desk and opened it. "So Mrs. Caswell," he said, rubbing his eyebrow. "What can I help you with today?"

I told him how I wanted to do right by Libby, but I'd decided to leave the farmhouse and all the land on Maranatha Road for the rest of my family. For Tinley Greene and her little girl.

"So you'd like to add these two new beneficiaries to your will, is that right?"

"Yes, that's what I need you to do. But the way I want it, Tinley won't know anything about it until I'm dead and gone."

"I see. I don't think that will be a problem."

"Unless she gets into trouble and needs help before then. If you get word that Tinley is bad off and needs a place to stay, you'll let me know, won't you?"

"Yes, I can do that. I think I understand what you're saying. It will be a secret for now."

"That's right. But like I said, if in the meantime you hear she needs help and I'm still around, you tell me right then. Are you writing this down?"

Mr. Maybin cleared his throat and took a notepad from one of the desk drawers. He clicked the pen and started to write on the yellow lined paper like it was an ordinary thing to do, something he did every day. The same way I'd make up a grocery list.

When I got home, I called Libby and told her what I'd done. Before she had a chance to say much of anything back, I told her that I was sorry for treating her the way I had and that I loved her. She started crying and I could barely make out what she was saying on top of the noise. Ever since we were little, she always made everything bigger than it needed to be.

CHAPTER 61

— *Tinley Greene* —

Whenever Landry talks about leaving for Wisconsin, I tell him that I'll miss Garnet. Maybe I'd like to visit another part of the country sometime—just not live there.

"You won't have to worry about running into people," he reminds me. "The Haughtrys or the Caswells, none of that. You can finally put it all behind you."

But when I imagine putting this place behind me, I have nightmares about it being destroyed or disappearing. I imagine the kudzu growing until it chokes all the farms and houses and swallows the bridge, dipping down in the river so that the water soaks into the vines as they keep swelling and moving. If you could see Garnet from all the way in Kenosha, maybe it would look green all over, like a strange planet where the cool wind reaches the hill at Poplar Springs and nowhere else.

If I want to be with Landry, then it shouldn't matter where he takes me. I would've gone anywhere with Mark. But he never asked.

———

Right before Christmas, Landry starts talking about us getting married. He doesn't come right out and propose, but he starts dropping little hints. He asks me if Rebecca would like to have a father, and when I say "stepfather," he smiles and says, "Of course, that's what I meant. I'm sorry."

"You don't have to apologize. I just think stepfather might be better."
I shrug, reminding myself this is what I've been waiting for. It's what I want.

"Of course." He nods. "You're exactly right."

That's how Landry is. There is nothing rough about him. He is smooth and easy—vanilla and cotton and fresh-cut grass. The few times he frowns, all I have to do is touch the side of his mouth and it goes up again and he laughs like I've done some sort of trick. Otherwise he's always smiling. He's the same way with Rebecca. He tells her she looks pretty in her new dress. He makes up stories for her about frogs turning into unicorns and princesses who can do tricks on their horses.

If I marry Landry, I know how it will be. We'll take walks after supper, holding hands and listening to the cicadas buzzing, and we'll see other people in their houses as we go past. And maybe one day I'll finally stop wishing for what they have because I'll have enough with Landry. I'll be satisfied with what I have.

At night sometimes I watch Landry sleeping and I wonder when he'll ask me. He'll get down on one knee and take a beautiful diamond ring out of his pocket and my stomach will start to hurt, but I'll think about all those happy, satisfied people in their houses and about all the bad things that would never happen with him and how good he'll be to Rebecca. So I will say yes.

The next week when he asks me, it's exactly how I've imagined it. The Christmas lights blink behind him and the living room smells like cinnamon and pine needles. The electric heat sounds like wind blowing through the vent. Landry grins as he takes the ring out of his pocket, and it's like it has already happened once before and we're doing it over again. And there's nothing I can do to stop it, at least nothing I can bring myself to do.

CHAPTER 62

— *Tinley Greene* —

After we get through the holidays and the weather warms up, Landry starts asking if I want to set a wedding date.

"Now that we've sold the house and we're finally on our way, we need to figure it out." He nods toward the stack of moving boxes. "What about September? The weather will be nice then and once we've moved and settled in, it'll be easier. We'll know our way around, where all the good spots are. We could do it the first Saturday in September." He flips through his calendar that looks like a spiral notebook. "That could work. What do you think?"

My nails dig into my hands and I take a deep breath. But all I can get out is, "I don't know."

"We don't have to do September."

I follow him to the laundry room. After we've moved the clothes from the washing machine to the dryer, Landry goes to get Rebecca up from her nap. The dryer buzzes under my hand and I wonder if I could say it to his back—something, anything to make him understand that this isn't what I want. I'm not ready to say forever.

———

When Lynette Barnes comes to visit again, she leans down to give Rebecca a hug. "Do you still like stuffed animals?" Rebecca nods and giggles and Lynette gives her a stuffed polar bear.

"White," Rebecca says, pointing.

"She's such a smart girl."

"You're so nice to bring her presents. You really don't have to."

"People up at the church have been asking about you, Tinley. You ought to come up there sometime before you leave town."

"We're okay where we are."

"And when's this wedding?"

"After we move, I guess."

"Aren't you awfully young? If I were you, I wouldn't jump into anything."

"Landry's a nice man. If you met him, you'd see what I'm talking about."

"I'm sure he's nice. But you—well, you've got to figure some things out for yourself, I guess. Here's some corn from the freezer. I had extra. You can heat it up and have it before you leave. Don't you have a lot of packing to do?"

"I haven't really been able to do it. I know I should, but it's too hard to think about actually leaving."

After Lynette is gone, I hold the stuffed bear she brought for Rebecca, remembering the notes she left for us the last time she was here. Ever since I read them, something in me has woken up. I'll be drying Rebecca off after her bath, or picking up her toys, and Sadie Caswell will pop into my head. Sometimes I can't sit still for thinking about her. I pace around Landry's house overcome with the idea that she went to the trouble to find us. When I think of Sadie wanting to meet Rebecca, I find myself practically bouncing on my toes.

Still, I know it doesn't make sense to be too eager. Look at how she treated me, how she sent me away. I shouldn't want anything to do with Sadie Caswell.

———

Toward the end of March when the boxes are mostly packed, there's an ice storm, past when spring should be here, and I tell Landry that it's a bad sign.

"I don't believe in signs," he says. "Don't you know that about me?" And I click through in my head all the things I do know about him. His favorite song and how much he weighs and what his handwriting looks like. How he likes the burnt edges of grilled chicken and takes vitamin C when it's cold season and the way he washes himself in the shower. Things I never knew about Mark. We're in the car and the trees are silver with ice along the sides of the road. Landry asks what I mean, about the storm being a bad sign.

"What are you thinking about, Tinley? What is it?"

I glance at Rebecca in the back seat, strapped into her car seat with an alphabet book on her lap. She touches the page with her fingertip and I remember the way, when she was a baby, she used to grab my finger. As she grows up, I want to teach her to grab onto the right things. And to let the others go.

When I turn back toward Landry, tears well up in my eyes and break down my face as I imagine how he might react when I tell him, the hurt and surprise turning his face slack. No matter how hard it is, I have to do it. I have to make myself. Because Rebecca needs a mother who can be herself and know what she wants, someone who can do the right things even when they're hard—especially when they're hard.

That night when I tell Landry I can't move away with him, can't marry him, can't be with him anymore, he asks if I'm doing what's best for me and Rebecca.

"I don't know," I say. But I'm only saying it to be nice. Now that I've made this decision, I do know it's what's best, that, as nice as he is, I don't need Landry the way I once thought I did, that Rebecca and I can be our own family—that we have been all along. I just haven't seen it clearly until now.

"I'm caught off-guard here," Landry says, biting his lip.

I shake my head. "I know. Me too. I thought this was what I wanted, but it's not."

He asks me what changed. "I thought we were happy," he says. "I thought I made you happy. Is something different?"

"I don't know how to explain it," I tell him. Nothing is different. Or everything is.

CHAPTER 63

— *Tinley Greene* —

The ice melts and Rebecca and I find a new place to live, a tiny house outside the city limits between Garnet and Wyeth's Mill. The way it's tucked into the woods below the road you'd think the house is hiding, but it's not. It's painted bright blue, nothing hidden about it, the kind of haint blue my mother used to say kept bad spirits away. I've seen it on porch ceilings before but never on a whole house—not until now when Rebecca and I live in this house protected on all sides.

———

One day in June, I go to clean Julia Price's house. Rebecca looks at the shelf where Mrs. Price's porcelain horses are lined up in a row, like they're on a stage being judged for their manes and tails, the way they're thick and full and rich brown like chocolate.

"I touch, I touch," she says and you can see how much she wants to reach up and touch one of the horses, just like you'd pet a real one, right on his warm neck.

"You can't touch them, sweetie, they'll break."

"No break." Rebecca shakes her head. She reaches toward one of the horses, a light brown one that looks weaker than the rest, like it's smaller even though it's really the same size, it's just that its color has faded. I take her hand to keep her from touching it. If she breaks one, Mrs. Price will make me pay for it and I need the money for rent. And someday soon I'll go back to school, so I need to save up money for that too.

"When you're older, maybe you can touch it then." I try to get my daughter to sit down, but she wants to stand by the shelves. "Okay, as long as you don't touch. Just look. Eyes only, okay?" She touches her eyelids with her fingers and nods.

After I finish the vacuuming and the bathrooms and start the laundry, Rebecca is standing where I left her looking at the horses with her hands by her sides. For the most part she stays still except sometimes she bounces on her feet. That's how much she wants to move, to reach up and grab a horse and maybe make it run around the room on the air, but she doesn't because I told her not to. That's the kind of girl she is. Two years old and she already wants to do the right thing, even when another part of her wants to run or make something else run.

On the way back to our little blue house, we pass a school bus stopped at a bus stop. Kids rush down the steps laughing and talking.

"Where they going?" she asks, turning almost backwards as we drive past.

"They've been at school and they're going home now, back to their houses. That's a school bus."

She's still looking out of the car window. "I go to school?"

"Yes, you'll go to school later on." I stop at a red light and whisper, "Me too."

"Becca goes to school later," she says.

"Becca?" I turn around to face her, something nagging at the back of my mind. "What happened to Rebecca?"

"Becca go to school later," she says with a big smile showing all her teeth, like she's sure, like she can see herself with a backpack looped over her shoulders waiting for the bus with this new nickname of hers, the one she's given herself.

That night I pull her up on my lap and she squirms to get down, squealing and laughing when I don't let her go. She is growing up so quickly that the weight of her on my lap is different than it was just yesterday. But her hair still smells like baby shampoo and I take a deep breath, remembering the promise I made on her first birthday—to give her every good thing I could.

"I'll give you every good thing I can," I whisper into the side of her head. "My sweet girl. My sweet Becca," I try out the nickname and realize it fits.

Once she's in bed, I pull out the notes from Sadie, which I ended up keeping after all, tucked under my mattress.

Dear Tinley,

I guess I wouldn't blame you if you never want to see or talk to me again, not after the way I treated you. Especially since you needed my help and from what I hear, you didn't have anybody. I didn't know that at the time, but it probably wouldn't have made any difference. I couldn't look at you without seeing Mark down in the gorge when he ought to have been at home with me sitting at the table eating something he liked, or driving through town in his truck with the window down and his elbow hanging outside like he always did when it was good weather. I don't know how I could've helped what I was seeing, but I'm real sorry that's how it worked out. I couldn't make it any different then. Most of all I'm sorry I haven't gotten to meet your daughter. I bet she's a real nice girl.

Clive is bad off and I don't know how much time he has left. We're kin whether you like it or not and she'd probably like to know her grandparents if you'd let her.

I flip the page, a lump in my throat, nodding as I realize what was nagging at me earlier.

Dear Becca,

I've heard from Lynette what a good girl you are. I'm guessing you know what's what and you don't take any mess from anybody. And I bet there's a sweetness to you too. That's the best way to be, I guess.

Strong, but bending when you need to.

Your grandfather, Clive, and I would like to meet you one day and I hope it can be sometime real soon.

I trace my finger over Sadie's spidery handwriting, wondering what made her say "Becca."

———

A few days later, I leave her with our closest neighbor, whose daughter, Samantha, just turned five. Becca watches everything she does, the way Samantha puts her hand on her hip and points her pink glittery sandal before she tries to do a cartwheel, how she brings her ponytail around to her mouth and chews on her hair. Becca listens carefully, almost solemnly, when Samantha says her grandmother gives her chewy candy with Christmas trees in the middle, even in the summer.

———

To get where I'm going, I don't need to go past the Haughtrys' house, where everything bad started, or the gray house, where Mark and I started. But I drive by them anyway, checking from the road to see if they look the way I remember. I promise myself no magic will happen, good or bad, and it turns out that I'm right.

At Poplar Springs, the creek below the path still makes the same sipping sound it used to, winding its way through the whole county, the same water that's in the river, that goes all the way to the ocean maybe, across the whole state. Maybe it's bigger and louder in places, dancing over rocks as big as cars. And in other places, like this one, it barely moves, trickling along the soft dirt.

The briars are thick in places and I push through them, careful to duck so they don't scratch my face. I remember how Mark touched my face when he got up close to me, saying he wanted me. The memory, I realize now, doesn't carry the sting it once did.

At the little bench by the pond, I brush the leaves off before I sit down. The water is so dark that I can't see any fish, but they must be there, swimming below the surface, blinking their eyes and opening their mouths for food I don't have. And I already remember the rest, what I've kept pushing down, what I thought I could convince myself he never really said. *Maddie is the first thing I think about when I wake up every morning. It's an awful thing to say—that you were some kind of a mistake.*

The longer I sit there, the further away some things seem. For a long time, what happened to me has seemed too big to hold and now it seems right to let it go. I used to think that I—the real me—started when Mark came to save me, and that I somehow ended when he died. That if I didn't have someone like him around to save me then I was nothing. But now I know that's not true.

And even though my parents are gone, and this is the biggest loss of all, it is part of who I am. It will get easier over time. In some small way it already has, especially as I realize how proud they would be now—to see that, after being lost for a while on what seemed like a twisted road, I've found my way to this place where I know myself. I can almost feel Daddy's hand on my shoulder.

The water in the pond looks like wrinkled skin, and I imagine Mr. Haughtry's face in one of the creases near the edge. It slides away until it dissolves into the dirt bank. Another one stands for the hurt that tears through my chest when I picture Mama and Daddy being swallowed up by the river. Before long it slides away like the other one did. Water bugs jump on the surface and the fish still move dark and slow underneath. I pick out another tiny wave of water and wait until it—the one called mistake—disappears too.

When I get up from the bench, I touch the notes in my pocket, remembering the word *Becca* in Sadie Caswell's handwriting, the way she called her that before anybody else did. The way my mother used to say there are little signs everywhere.

At the top of the hill, I'm lighter, like I've put down something heavy. And even though I'm not even trying to remember, now I can see Daddy the way I've tried to before. We're up here at Poplar Springs. It's a Sunday afternoon, a perfect day for flying kites. The sun is shining—not too bright—and the wind blows just enough. This is a day when my kite will soar up and I'll run across the hill to keep up with it, not worrying about where I step.

Daddy unrolls the string and hands it to me, holding up my kite. As I take it from him, I forget what comes next. "I don't know if I can do it," I tell him. The orange and black flashes like a monarch butterfly.

"What do you mean, you don't know if you can do it?" He shakes his head, smiling, and Mama waves from down the hill, her dress flapping in the wind.

"What if I've forgotten how?"

"There isn't much to it," he says. He rolls out his own kite, yellow with red and black diamonds.

"What if I forget what to do with my hands?"

My father lays his hands on top of mine. "There really isn't much to it," he says again. "You put your hand on that spot and keep it there. Now just hold onto the string." He laughs. "Hold on and let it fly."

I place my hand where he shows me. Let it fly. It doesn't have to be any harder than that.

———

The long driveway cuts through the fields like a part through hair. When I park beside the white farmhouse, the front door is propped open and Sadie Caswell is sweeping off the front porch. I get out of the truck and she stops sweeping and leans on the broom, watching me. Her gray hair is pulled back into a bun and she holds tightly to the broom with both hands, staring at me without blinking. It's almost like she is worried I'll disappear if she looks away. She waits for me to come to her, not saying anything and not moving. I could get back in the truck and forget I ever came. Becca doesn't ever need to know about it.

Sadie stands still like she wants to leave it up to me, hoping I'll somehow make my way to where she is. We don't need her help, and that's not why I've come. Not this time. Every good thing. That's what I promised Becca. Every good thing.

For a second, the last bit of resentment clings on, holding me back. I can't reach Sadie, not until I remember what my father said, until I remind myself of what I want Becca to learn—what to hold onto, what to let fly. My feet start moving, and I say her name out loud. Once more I say it, this time louder, and as I near the porch, I imagine the wind carrying the shape and color of it to where she waits.

CHAPTER 64

— *Sadie Caswell* —

I had a lot to do if I was going to be ready in time. Wash the floor of the porch. Oil the chains on the porch swing. Plant flowers in the pots by the front door. Inside, I needed to mop the floors and go over the furniture with a dust rag and straighten up most everywhere. When I was done with all that, I called Willa and Lynette to see if they needed anything at the store. Willa said she could use some face cream and I told her I'd pick some up.

At the shopping mall, I had to wait for a big crowd of teenagers to come out before I could get in. They saw me and not a one of them made any move to hold the door.

First thing, I went to Belks and got Lynette's face cream and myself a new dress, the first one I'd had since Mark passed. It was the color of fresh cream and made out of a real nice material with a little weight to it—not one of those things that's so thin you could shoot a straw through it.

Even though I didn't know for sure how big Becca was, I picked up a dress in the children's department, a white one with purple flowers, which Lynette said was her favorite color.

After that, I went by the toy store and the bookstore. Last time I talked to Lynette, she said Becca carries around books hoping somebody will read to her. And she likes dancing and tumbling. "Watch this," I figure she says, holding her arms straight up in the air when she's ready to start. Lynette says her eyes are green. Same as Mark's.

At the grocery store, I got some lemonade and some cheese, that expensive kind with the black wrapper. They had chocolate bars on special, and I got one with caramel and one plain. Everything was ready and I called up Libby to tell me how to work the television, in case there was a program on that Becca wanted to watch.

When they finally got to the house, Tinley said she'd be back soon and I told her to take her time. She bent down to tie Becca's shoelaces.

"Remember, you're going to play here for a little while, Becca. Mama will be back this afternoon."

"She'll take you back home after we visit for a little bit, just me and you." My voice came out hoarse and I cleared my throat.

That little girl took a big, deep breath, gave Tinley a hug around the neck, and came up to me like it was nothing. Her brown hair was falling out of her braids. She had on navy blue pants printed with tiny red cherries and a little white cardigan buttoned over a red t-shirt and red shoes with a buckle, shoes like I'd never seen before.

Mostly Becca looked around with those green eyes of hers. When I told her we could go around and see whatever she wanted, she took hold of my hand. I didn't expect her to do something like that—reach for my hand—but that's what she did. A lot of children go around with sticky fingers all the time, but Becca's were clean. You could tell her mama was raising her right.

We went through the den where she hopped up on Clive's old lumpy chair and sat with her legs pulled up under her. "Becca, do you want to sit down for a minute? You want me to sit over there?" I pointed to the couch. She shook her head and jumped off the chair and headed for the hallway. I held out my hand and she grabbed hold of it again.

In the kitchen I offered her lemonade or a chocolate bar or some strawberries, but she shook her head and we kept going. She didn't want to stay still. Going up the stairs, Becca did a little jump between each one.

Before they came, I had cleaned out Mark's room. There wasn't any use in keeping it like it was, not with him gone. It was a good thing I hadn't touched it right when he died. The way I was then, I'd have tried to freeze everything in there like it was under a sheet of ice, like it needed to stay looking the same forever. Or I would've set it all on fire, not wanting to see it, not being able to. One or the other. As it was, I cleaned it up good, got all the dust and dirt wiped up and the sheets and quilts washed. When I started going through his dresser and the closet, I kept seeing Mark in his plaid shirt, the one worn clear through on the elbows, and remembering the way he let out a little grunt when he kicked off his work boots. It was hard, but the kind of hard you can get through. I threw away his underwear and socks, but the rest of his clothes I washed and packed up for the Bargain Box. Somebody who needed them could get some good wear out of them.

That day when I was cleaning up, I saved the shelves for last. I picked up every piece of what Mark had found, the things he'd thought were worth saving, and I pictured the way he used to walk around the yard, looking down and knowing he would find something to pick up. Some of it I ended up keeping—some leaves that had dried up nice, a blue and white feather, a few hollowed-out eggs with a little color left on them, and two of the pinecones. Those pinecones looked perfect, top to bottom, like nothing had ever touched them, nothing except Mark with his long, careful fingers. The rest of it I saw for what it was—crunched up and dirty—so I threw it away. When I was finished, I arranged the things worth saving—the leaves and the feather, the eggs and the pinecones—on the shelves. Once they weren't surrounded by clutter, they looked nice up there. It was like the middle place between too much and not enough, the place Mark looked for and couldn't ever find. But maybe he had finally gotten there.

I never went by his grave. He wasn't there anyway, no more than he was sitting at the kitchen table dipping his finger first in the butter bowl and then in the sugar. The way I figured it, he was down at the river, with his cap on backwards, the water cool against his legs, letting out his line, smooth and long.

When I took Becca in his room, I didn't tell her whose it was. That was up to Tinley to explain sometime later on. But I let her look around and those pinecones were her favorite, just like I knew they would be.

"No break," she said, pointing at them and shaking her head.

"You can hold one if you want to."

She put out her hands, one right next to the other, the same way you'd put out your hands on Communion Sunday, and I gave her one of the pinecones. She brought it right up next to her face and peeked in one of the dark spaces. Then she poked her finger in it and laughed, looking up at me. It had been a while since I'd heard anyone laugh like that. After Becca handed the pinecone back, she watched me put it on the shelf.

In the bedroom where I slept, I showed her the sewing machine and an old picture of Clive I kept in a silver frame. He was leaning back against the wooden fence, looking down at the dirt and patches of grass instead of at the camera. But it wasn't that he was looking in the wrong place. He looked like he was doing the right thing, studying about what needed to get planted or what needed pulling up. That was just Clive.

"See there, that was your grandpa."

Becca plopped a piece of hair in her mouth and stared. After I set the picture down, an idea came to me out of nowhere—something I hadn't thought about in a long time.

I took her down the hall to the room Clive and I used to share. The old pillowcase was still in the top dresser drawer, the white cotton almost as soft as silk might have been. When I sat down on the bed to unwrap it, Becca climbed up too. Her hair smelled like baby shampoo and she settled in my lap like she'd been doing it her whole life. I put the garnet in her hand, nodding as she ran her fingers over it.

"You can see how dark it is," I told her. "You'd think there was no color in it, not until the light hits it right."

AUTHOR'S NOTE

— *The Story Behind the Story* —

Although Garnet is not a real town in western North Carolina, it bears some similarity to Hendersonville, where I was born and raised, and nearby places where I've visited grandparents and other relatives: the town of East Flat Rock, and closer to the South Carolina border, the communities of Zirconia and Tuxedo along Green River. I don't know of a road in the area named Maranatha, but the name, which roughly means *the Lord, or hope, is coming*, seems to fit the character of the place.

Our house in Hendersonville was on Kanuga Road. Follow the road in one direction and you soon reach a charming downtown filled with antique shops and host to North Carolina's Apple Festival. Or take it the other way to arrive at summer camps with rock walls and long dirt driveways, not very different from Emerald Cove.

Growing up, our dad took me and my sister to the annual Henderson County Gem and Mineral Show, where we learned about the area's history of gem mining—especially rubies and emeralds—and the more modest garnet, which seems right for Sadie and Clive.

Years later, this story began with the image of a girl, sheltered from the rain in a dark shed, waiting for her parents to return. When my sister and I were in high school, we waited for our mother to return home from Winston-Salem where she was undergoing treatment for leukemia. And like Tinley, what we hoped for didn't happen—our mother died.

Now that I'm a mother, I'm often struck by the fierce desire to shield our son from harm and unhappiness, especially knowing how arbitrary life can be. Sadie first appeared to me as an older woman who sees that her adult son is headed for disaster, but she is powerless to stop it. I love Sadie because of her limitations and her conviction that she is bound to make mistakes, whether it's by speaking up or staying silent. There might be a little something of her in all of us. Or maybe it's just introverts. Or maybe it's just me.

In any event, I knew these two women would have good reason to be angry at each other, but that in the end they would need to make their way to one another.

The bridge in the story is inspired by—although different from—the Peter Guice Memorial Bridge. At two hundred and twenty-five feet high, it is the highest bridge in North Carolina, spanning the Green River Gorge, where there might be countless gems buried underground. According to family gossip, my parents on one of their first dates toured the site while the bridge was being built. Now, when I drive across the bridge with my husband and our son, that is one of the stories I like to imagine. The other is a story about two strong, Southern women who find a way to bridge the gap between them.

DISCUSSION QUESTIONS

———

1. Do you feel more connected to either Sadie or Tinley? If so, why? Did your feelings change as the story progressed?

2. If you could ask a question to a character in the book, what would you ask? How do you imagine the character might respond?

3. In some parts of the story, Sadie worries about gossip around town. What role does gossip ultimately play? Did this surprise you?

4. Although Garnet is a fictional place, does it remind you of anywhere you've lived or visited? How does the setting impact the story?

5. Sadie and Clive have a long-lasting but complicated relationship with much left unsaid. How would you characterize their marriage?

6. How do Sadie and Tinley fulfill, or fail to fulfill, society's expectations of motherhood?

7. If you were in Sadie's shoes, what would you have done when Tinley showed up claiming she was pregnant with Mark's baby?

8. Do you think Tinley did the right thing by ending her relationship with Landry?

9. Tinley's mother used to tell her there were signs everywhere. How does Tinley's belief in signs shape her actions? Do you believe in signs?

10. The characters in the book face significant adversity. The word "maranatha," loosely translated from Aramaic, means *the Lord, or hope, is coming*. In what ways is the story ultimately optimistic?

ABOUT THE AUTHOR

Heather Bell Adams is from Hendersonville, North Carolina, and now lives in Raleigh with her husband and son. Winner of the 2016 James Still Fiction Prize, her short fiction appears in the *Thomas Wolfe Review*, *Clapboard House*, *Pembroke Magazine*, *Broad River Review*, and elsewhere. This is her first novel.

CPSIA information can be obtained
at www.ICGtesting.com
Printed in the USA
LVOW13s0750010817
543388LV00004B/4/P